Well before ~~I reached the door~~, I could smell the blood. The aroma was thick and cloying and metallic—so strong that I knew a great deal of blood must have been let. When I paused in the bedroom doorway, I was stunned to see just how much it was.

The bedclothes and mattress were soaked with red. On the floor next to the bed was a crying pool created by a steady drip from above. It hadn't yet coagulated, hadn't begun to turn fetid and awful-smelling. Small consolation, since imagining what had happened to cause what I saw was nauseating enough.

Forthcoming from Worldwide Mystery by
WILLIAM RELLING JR.

SWEET POISON

DEADLY VINTAGE

WILLIAM RELLING JR.

WORLDWIDE.®

TORONTO • NEW YORK • LONDON
AMSTERDAM • PARIS • SYDNEY • HAMBURG
STOCKHOLM • ATHENS • TOKYO • MILAN
MADRID • WARSAW • BUDAPEST • AUCKLAND

*For Nick Romano, to whom I owe debts
I can never fully repay. I hope this is at least a start.*

DEADLY VINTAGE

A Worldwide Mystery/December 1999

This edition is reprinted by arrangement with Walker and Company.

ISBN 0-373-26330-9

The town of San Tomas in the Santa Ynez Valley of Santa Barbara
County, exists solely in the author's imagination.

All characters in this book are fictitious, and any resemblance to
actual persons, living or dead, is purely coincidental.

Visit us at www.worldwidemystery.com

Printed in U.S.A.

This is the excellent foppery of the world, that, when we are sick in fortune—often the surfeit of our own behavior—we make guilty of our disasters the sun, the moon, and the stars; as if we were villains by necessity, fools by heavenly compulsion, knaves, thieves, and teachers by spherical predominance, drunkards, liars, and adulterers by an enforced obedience of planetary influence.

—William Shakespeare,
King Lear
Act I, Scene 2

Wine is thicker than blood.
—Mike Gallo

ONE

Oswald Cole wasn't the last person I'd expect to drop in on me in the middle of the day. It's true that people in our business—Ozzie's and mine—work flexible hours. For much of the year, when we're not involved in some key step in the process of making and selling our wares, say, during harvesting or blending or bottling time, it's easy for us to come and go as we please. Having plenty of free moments during certain seasons is one of the perks that goes with the job.

But Ozzie and I weren't on what you'd call good terms, nor had we been for a while. Consequently, his visit was no small surprise. As I said, Ozzie Cole might not have been the last person to pay me an unexpected call, but he would have been among the half dozen or so finalists.

It was a Monday afternoon, and I was in the fermentation room, taking a sample of the chardonnay my dad and I had vatted the previous September, seven months before. I try to spend as little time down there as possible, since the room tends to be chilly and damp, which plays hell with my bum knee. I'd just drained an ounce or so of juice into a glass and closed the spigot on the tank that held the fermenting liquid when I heard a voice calling from the top of the steps that led down to the room.

"Jackie? Jackie, you down there?"

"Who is it?" I called back, frowning as I held up the glass in the electric glow of a shaded overhead bulb.

It wasn't the wine that was making me frown. Its color was just fine—a nice, wheat-straw hue. I was frowning because the only people who call me "Jackie" anymore are the ones who've known me since I was a kid. But this wasn't a voice I recognized right away.

"Ozzie Cole."

I turned toward the steps to watch him as he came down. He looked much the same as he always did: short and somewhat dumpy; dark brown eyes magnified owlishly behind thick, horn-rimmed glasses; unkempt mop of curly black hair; an equally unkempt fringe of beard. He was wearing baggy corduroys, Birkenstocks, and a short-sleeved sweatshirt with the O.C. Vineyards label printed above the words LIFE'S TOO SHORT TO DRINK BAD WINE. He came toward me, clutching the rolled top of a brown paper bag in his right hand. Whatever was in the bag was bulky and made of glass. I could hear it clinking and clunking.

The bewilderment I felt at seeing him was evident on my face. "Bet you weren't thinking I'd ever be one to drop in on you out of the blue like this, huh?" he said without apparent humor. He wasn't wrong. It was more than that we were rivals in the same business. It had to do with my opinion that Ozzie was, deep down, a prick.

He gestured to the glass in my hand. "What'cha got there?"

"Our new chard."

He raised an eyebrow inquisitively, then held out his free hand. "May I?"

I passed the glass to him. He held it up to the light for a moment, lowered it, swirled the glass, sniffed the juice carefully, and tilted the glass to his lips. He swished the liquid between his cheeks for a time, then spat it onto the floor. "Not bad," he said blandly as he handed back the glass.

I moved to a sink and dumped out what was left. While I was rinsing out the glass, I said over my shoulder, "What did you want to see me about? This isn't a social call, is it?"

I turned back to him, drying the glass with a paper towel. "I wish it was," he said.

"So? Let's hear it."

Ozzie scowled. He wasn't the handsomest man in the world when he looked happy, and the scowl made him downright ugly. "You got someplace private where we can talk?" There was a clear note of urgency in his voice.

"My office?"

"Lead the way," he said.

MY DAD AND I keep the "offices" of Donne Vineyards, Inc. in the main house that's also our living quarters. It's a fairly large structure: a single story, ranch-style home with three bedrooms and two dens—one for each of us. Dad supervised the construction of the house himself. In his previous life, before he became a winemaker more than two decades ago, he was an architect in Santa Barbara. A successful one, too, which was how he'd been able to afford the seventy-five acres just outside the town of San Tomas in the north end of the Santa Ynez Valley, where he and I live and grow grapes and make wine.

Our fermentation tanks are in the cellar of one of four outbuildings clustered in a U around the main house. I led Ozzie across the gravel lot to the house, stepping up onto the porch to hold the front door open for him. He preceded me through the living room and down a short hallway into the second den—my office. Without waiting to be offered a seat, he plopped himself in the leather armchair on the visitor's side of my desk. He set the paper bag he was carrying on the desk in front of him and looked over his shoulder at me. "You got any clean glasses?"

The wall behind my desk is comprised of built-in pine shelves I installed myself a couple of years ago. The shelves are occupied by stacks of memoranda and correspondence, framed photographs, awards from various county fairs and food festivals, several sample bottles of wine produced by my dad and me. I'd turned a couple of the shelves into a sort of breakfront by mounting some hinged cabinet doors. I went behind the desk, opened the cabinet, and pulled out a couple of large Orrefors wineglasses.

When I turned around, Ozzie was opening his bag. He pulled out two bottles of wine, then tossed the bag aside carelessly, onto the floor. I noticed that the bottles had been opened at least once—their foil caps were missing, and the corks of each protruded an inch or so above the mouths. As I sat down in my chair on the opposite side of the desk, Ozzie reached into the pocket of his corduroys and pulled out a Swiss Army knife. He opened the corkscrew attachment, took up one of the bottles he'd brought, and deftly withdrew the cork. After setting the first bottle back on the desk, he performed the same operation on the second one. He pointed his chin toward the first bottle. "Pour yourself a taste."

I reached across the desk for the bottle. Before pouring the wine into a glass, I examined the label. It was O.C. Vineyards's famous—or, rather, infamous—1990 Pinot Noir Special Reserve. I knew the wine, of course.

I even owned a case of the stuff. Not that I'd ever admit that to Ozzie.

I tipped a small amount into one of the glasses and set the bottle aside. I held the glass up to study the clear ruby color, then swirled the wine and sniffed it. It smelled delicious, with a lovely nose of peppermint and raspberries. I took a sip. It was just as I remembered from the sample I'd had a few months before when Ozzie had released it: round and full of fruit, with an earthy undertaste of tobacco to the finish. A damn good wine, as close as any Californian could get to imitating a fine Côtes de Nuits, in my estimation, anyway. Lay it down for six or seven years and you might really have something.

According to its label, the other bottle Ozzie had brought with him was more of the same, another O.C. '90 Pinot Special Reserve. I gave him a quizzical look as he passed me the second bottle. "Use a clean glass," he said.

I did as he instructed. The second wine's color was like the first's, but that's where the similarity ended. Wine number two was sour and thin, nearly vinegar. I made a face. "Ugh. If you're lucky, maybe you could use this for salad dressing."

The muscles were working in Ozzie's jaw. His eyes narrowed. "So it's your opinion that the first bottle's better than the second one?"

"What's this supposed to be, a test of my taste buds? You know, Ozzie, regardless of your personal feelings about what my dad and I make, I really do know how to tell the difference between good wine and bad wine."

He put on his scowl once more. Jabbing an accusatory finger toward the second bottle, he said flatly, "That's not mine."

"What do you mean, it's not yours?"

"That...swill." He jabbed his finger again. "I didn't make that."

I shook my head. "I don't get it."

"That first wine you tried," he said, pointing to the bottle, "*that's* mine. That other stuff is counterfeit."

"It's what?"

"Counterfeit. Somebody filled a bunch of bottles with this shit, then they took my label and my cork and stuck 'em on."

I didn't bother disguising my skepticism. "What in heaven's name would ever give you the idea that—"

He cut me off. "I'm not kidding, Jackie. Here." He got up from his seat to set the two bottles directly in front of me, side by side. "Look at both bottles," he said. "Look *close.*"

I resisted an urge to roll my eyes. Humor him, I said to myself resignedly. I studied the front and back labels of each bottle. They were identical: same logo, same type design, same information. I sniffed the mouth of each bottle, mostly for show, then looked at Ozzie. "As far as I can tell, these are exactly alike."

Somehow he managed to look smug and pissed off at the same time. "Pretty goddamn clever of them, don't you think? To copy my label just right?"

"Jesus, do you think maybe you could get a little more paranoid about this—"

"I'm *not* being paranoid," he said shrilly.

I picked up bottle number two. "Then tell me how come you're so positive this is counterfeit and not just gone bad. That kind of thing does happen. Even you are capable of producing a lousy bottle of wine once in a while."

He shook his head stubbornly. "Somebody's ripping me off."

"Who?"

"I don't know."

"Then how do you know that's what's happening?"

He filled his cheeks with air that he blew out in an explosive burst, then pointed at bottle number two and said, "I bought that the day before yesterday down near San Diego. I happened to be down there on business, and I stopped off at this store in La Jolla I'd never been to before. The Mission Bay Wine Company."

"I've heard of it," I said.

He was scowling again. "I introduced myself to the owner, this young guy, I forget his name. Jerry something or other. 'I'm Ozzie Cole of O.C. Vineyards.' 'Hey,' the guy says, 'I'm really glad to meet you. Maybe you can tell me how can I get some more of your '90 Pinot Reserve?' I look at the guy, and my mouth's hanging open. 'Some more?' I say. 'What do you mean, some more?' "

"Hang on," I interrupted. "You're losing me again. This guy Jerry isn't one of your regular retailers?"

He looked at me contemptuously. "Didn't you hear me say I'd never been to this Mission Bay Wine Company before?"

"Sorry. Go on with your story."

"Anyway, there I am with this guy, and he tells me that a couple of days ago he got in three cases of my wine, and now he's down to his last few bottles. He's been selling it to special customers only, ones he knows'd seen the review in the *Wine Spectator* and Parker's review and all, but they haven't been able to find the wine anyplace else. Then he goes into his office and comes back with this bottle. I'm shocked. 'Where the hell did you get this?' I asked him. 'One of my distributors,' he says. 'Which one?' I asked him, and he tells me the name of some fly-by-night liquor salesman I never heard of.''

"Did you check the guy out? The salesman, I mean?''

I was starting to get used to his scowl. "I didn't have time. I had to get home." He nodded toward the bottle. "I brought that back with me. I don't know why I did it, maybe it was just a hunch or something, but I decided to open it up and check it out. I'm telling you, Jackie, that isn't my wine. It's pinot grapes, but that's the only thing it's got in common with what I make. Everything else—the blend, the bottle aging, everything—is all wrong.''

I was scratching my head thoughtfully. "Let me see if I understand what you're saying to me. Your sales policy's the same as it used to be? You still deal with your retailers directly? No middlemen?''

Ozzie nodded.

"And some wineshop in La Jolla—somebody who *isn't* one of your regular dealers—managed to get hold of some of your stock, only they didn't get it from you. Am I doing all right so far?''

He nodded again.

"So however this Jerry guy got his hands on your product, he'd didn't get it through the usual channels.''

"Right.''

"But not only did he get hold of the wine in some wrongful way, it's also bogus. I only have your word on that, but I'll assume you've got no reason to lie. No offense. I'm just trying to get a clear picture." I paused. "Am I leaving anything out?''

He shook his head. "That pretty much sums it up.''

I picked up bottle number two and turned it over in my hands. "Then I'd say you've got three questions that need answering. Actually, the first one is easy to figure. 'Why?'"

"Somebody's trying to rip me off. Why else?" Ozzie grunted impatiently.

I nodded, agreeing. "'How' is a little trickier and might take some time and effort to figure out. Obviously, the toughest question to answer is 'Who?'"

"Obviously."

I set the bottle down. "I've got another question of my own. Why'd you come to me?"

He looked surprised. "You're a private detective, aren't you? And before that, wasn't this what you used to do for a living? Go after counterfeiters, I mean—?"

I held up a hand to stifle him. "Whoa, whoa. You want *me* to check this out for you?"

"Why the hell else would I have come here?"

It was my turn to scowl. "Let's get a few things straight, all right? First of all, if you're thinking I'm still a private detective, that's a misconception on your part. I dropped out a few years ago. And before then, I didn't chase counterfeiters—"

He cut in. "I thought you used to work for the Treasury Department."

"I did. But you're thinking of the Secret Service, and that's not who I was with. In any case, I don't have the slightest urge to get back into law enforcement. Besides…" I picked up the bottle again. "Why should I do you any favors? I don't especially like you. Why should I give a shit if somebody's ripping you off?"

He couldn't have looked more stunned if I'd hit him with a mallet. He turned away for a moment, trying to process what I'd said. When he looked back, he was wearing an expression I'd never seen on his face before: apologetic, hurt, supplicating.

"What if it's not just me who's being ripped off?" he asked. "What if it's a gang that's ripping off a whole bunch of people? Including you and your dad?"

I waited a beat before answering him. "You want my honest opinion? I think you should ride over to the county sheriff's office, ask for one of the detectives there, and tell him the same story you told me."

Ozzie snorted. "Cops. They wouldn't know good wine from donkey piss."

I shrugged. "That's my advice. Take it or leave it."

TWO

THAT EVENING I had dinner with Donne Vineyards's accountant, Margaret McKenney. Maggie's worked for us for the past three years. My dad hired her around the time my mother died, a little over a year before he himself had the stroke that induced me to abandon the private detective career I'd begun eighteen months earlier, following my retirement from the U.S. Treasury's Bureau of Alcohol, Tobacco and Firearms. After his stroke it seemed a good idea for me to go into the family business, something Dad had been after me to do for a long time anyway.

Besides being our accountant, Maggie is also my proverbial on-again, off-again "significant other." We'd been on again since February, when for her thirty-fifth birthday I'd surprised her by taking her to San Francisco for the weekend. She'd mentioned one time that she thought San Francisco was the most romantic city in the world. I'd gotten us a suite at the St. Francis. When I put my mind to it, I can be very charming.

Maggie is some years younger than me, and much pleasanter to look at. She is a true Irish colleen: copper-colored hair; creamy, freckled skin; high cheekbones; sharp green eyes. The only flaw in her looks—and I use the word *flaw* advisedly—is her nose. It has a raised bump at the bridge from having been broken by one of her brothers, with whom she'd been playing football when they were kids. When Dad talks about her—which is often—he's fond of saying that he hired her solely because she strikingly resembles Maureen O'Hara in *The Quiet Man*. He's teasing, since the real reason he hired her is because she's terrific with balance sheets and taxes and such. But he's teasing only a little.

Maggie and I met at Tito's, a Mexican restaurant on Highway 246, the Santa Ynez Valley's main east-west drag. The restaurant was my selection. She'd issued the invitation the day before and had asked me where I'd like to go. Since I wasn't in the mood to worry about what wine went with what course, Mexican seemed a good choice.

Upon being seated, we ordered bottles of Dos Equis to go with our chips and salsa, based on my conviction that anybody who drinks anything other than beer or tequila with a Mexican meal should be cited by the Ethnic Food Police. The beer and chips had been delivered and our dinner orders taken when I told Maggie about Ozzie Cole's visit. She recognized his name, though she'd never met him. "He's one of the famous Coles, isn't he?" she asked.

I raised an eyebrow. "'The *famous* Coles'?"

"Wouldn't you say they're famous?"

"I don't know if that's the word I'd use."

"You know what I mean," she said. She scooped a generous portion of salsa on to the last chip left in the basket, popped it into her mouth, and munched contentedly.

I couldn't help smiling. "Ozzie's one of those famous Coles, all right. The proverbial black sheep."

Maggie's expression questioned me. I asked her, "What do you know about the Cole family?"

She shook her head. "Only that they're rich and that they own a lot of land around here."

"That pretty much covers it," I said.

"C'mon, that can't be all there is."

I motioned to our busboy. As he approached I lifted the empty basket from the middle of the table. "*Mas* chips, *por favor.*" He bowed, took the basket from me, and walked away.

"Well?" said Maggie.

I sipped my beer. "First off, there's the father—or the patriarch, I should say. Perry Cole, Senior. He founded Cole Vineyards around 1964 or '65. Smart man, Perry. He was one of the first to recognize how the climate in these parts is, in a lot of ways, like Bourgogne's."

"Why's that so smart?"

I shook my head. "I can't believe you've spent as much time with my dad and me as you have, and you still have to ask a question like that. Either I must be a total failure as a teacher or it's hopeless to try to give you a cultural education."

The busboy returned with a full basket of chips. He set it down in front of Maggie, then went off again. She picked up a chip and munched it sarcastically, chewing with her mouth open. "I hate it when you act like a snob," she said while she smacked.

I looked heavenward. She taunted me by noisily licking the salt from her fingers, one by one. "You're hopeless," I sighed.

She responded with a very unladylike burp. "So tell me about the Coles."

I sighed once more for effect, then said, "The reason Perry's so smart is because he figured out what would be just the right kind of grapes to grow around here. In Napa and Sonoma, they grow a lot of Bordeaux grapes—cabernet sauvignon, merlot, cabernet franc, and so on. The cabs and Bordeaux blends from up north have gotten pretty good over the last fifteen years or so, almost as good as what you can make in France because the weather's much more predictable and consistent in California, and the guys who put the wines together are getting better and better all the time at doing it.''

I paused to see if she was still with me. "Go on," she said, "I'm listening."

"Napa's a bit more like the Bordeaux region," I said, "but here in the valley, the climate and the soil are a little more like Bourgogne. Burgundy."

She looked indignant. "I know what 'Bourgogne' is."

"I'm only trying to be helpful. Anyway, Perry was one of the first people to notice this. He figured the best grapes to plant in Santa Ynez would be Burgundy grapes—chardonnay, gamay, and so on. We grow Bordeaux grapes down here, too, just as lots of people up in Napa grow chardonnay. But in general, Burgundy grapes seems to thrive a little better down here than they do up there. Once Perry figured that out, he was on his way to making a lot of money. According to my dad, he had a pretty healthy chunk of change to start with. He used it to buy the initial three hundred acres of land where he built his winery and planted his grapes. Some inheritance money he brought with him from back east.''

"Whatever," she said, starting to look restless.

I grinned. "Cut to the chase, right?"

"If you don't mind."

The waiter reappeared with our entrees—a *burrito verde* for me and *arroz con pollo* for Maggie. "Perry retired from the winemaking business eight or nine years ago. This after he'd established Cole Vineyards as the Santa Ynez equivalent of what Gallo Brothers is to the north, and he'd gained control of two-fifths of some of the best grape-growing land in the county. When he retired, he passed the business on to his three sons: Ozzie, Grant, and Perry, Junior.''

''Ozzie's the oldest?''

I shook my head. ''The youngest. Also the most difficult to get along with. Although June and Grant aren't especially delightful people to know, either.''

'' 'June'?''

''Short for Junior. The oldest son. June is his nickname.''

She nodded. ''I'm with you.''

''They ran the business as a trio for about a year, and then they had a falling out—June and Grant on one side, Ozzie on the other. Ozzie spent time in France studying winemaking, and he was convinced that there was enough limestone in the soil to grow decent pinot noir grapes that they could use to produce a higher quality wine than they'd been making. June and Grant thought things were just fine the way they were. One thing led to another, and before you knew it, they were at each other's throats. They ended up splitting the business into thirds—the land, the equipment, everything. Ozzie took his share and started O.C. Vineyards.''

''O.C,'' she said. ''Ozzie Cole.''

I nodded. ''Ozzie hasn't had anything to with June or Grant in years. He despises both of them, and they despise him right back. That's why it galls 'em that Ozzie's become so successful.''

''What do you mean?''

''For the past four or five years O.C. Vineyards has been making some of the best wine in the Santa Ynez Valley. Not counting the Donne family, of course.''

She paused between bites. "That goes without saying."

I grinned again, showing gratitude. "Ozzie Cole may be a miserable human being, but he manufactures damn good wine, you've got to give him that. He's got the awards and reviews to prove it. One of the bigger problems his brothers have with him is that their reputation isn't nearly so peachy. When I say they're the Gallos of the south, I mean all the good and bad that implies. They sell a lot of mostly cheap product, and they make money, but that's as far as it goes. They tend to take a lot of shit from serious critics for being so commercially oriented, though I imagine they laugh off most of it all the way to the bank. It still has to burn their asses, though, that Ozzie turned out to be right all along. Not only does he make money, he's a wine critics' darling, too."

Maggie forked a piece of chicken, lifted it to her mouth, paused, then looked at me thoughtfully. "Is their father still alive?"'

"In a manner of speaking."

"What's that supposed to mean?"

"Perry's pretty sick, from what I understand. Alzheimer's, or some damn thing. That's another bone of contention between the Cole brothers. About a year and a half ago, June and Grant had the old man institutionalized. Ozzie fought his brothers tooth and nail. Perry didn't want to go, and he was vehement about letting his sons know it. In the end, though, there wasn't anything he or Ozzie could do. The only choice Ozzie had was to let the old man move in with him. He didn't want that, either, so off went Perry to a nursing home."

Maggie made a face. "Your basic dysfunctional family."

"You could say that."

There was a lull while our waiter returned to clear our plates and take our orders for *sopapillas* and coffee. After he'd gone, I looked across the table at Maggie. She was wearing a studious frown. "What's the matter?" I asked.

"I was just thinking." She reflected for a moment, then asked, "Just how badly do the Cole brothers hate each other?"

"None of 'em's ever attempted murder, as far as I know. But I'd be surprised if they're still exchanging Christmas cards."

Her frown deepened. "Do you think Ozzie's brothers might be the ones doing the counterfeiting?"

She reacted to my look of disbelief. "You just said they hated each other. What if they're trying to drive him out of business?"

I shook my head.

"Why not?"

"Because whoever's behind it—assuming it's not just some hallucination of Ozzie's—has to be in it to make a quick killing. There's no other reason to pull this kind of scam. It's the only thing that makes any sense."

"Then maybe you *should* check into it for him, Jack. If somebody's counterfeiting Ozzie Cole's wine, doesn't it follow that they might be ripping off some of the other winemakers around here, too?"

Our waiter reappeared, setting cups of coffee and plates of deep-fried, ice-cream-covered tortillas before us. "Just eat your dessert, sweetheart," I said to Maggie in as patronizing a tone of voice as I could muster. "I'd appreciate it if you didn't try to play detective."

It was the wrong thing to say, and the wrong attitude

to cop, but I was wearying of the subject of the Cole family. Big mistake. She chilled me with an emerald-eyed glare, and I could tell by the look she was prepared to not utter a word to me for the remainder of the meal.

THREE

MAGGIE AND I were back on speaking terms by the time dessert was finished. Apologizing to her was something that came more easily the longer I knew her.

After I paid the check, I walked her to her car. She invited me to her place to watch *Murder My Sweet*—Dick Powell as Philip Marlowe—on cable. It was tough to turn her down, and not just because Powell was my favorite Marlowe, Humphrey Bogart notwithstanding. It was only when she read the look of pain on my face that she knew I wasn't making it up when I said I had to get back so I could be up at dawn to drive my dad to Santa Barbara to make a 9:00 a.m. doctor's appointment. We kissed good night and headed off in opposite directions, she in her Celica and me in my Jeep Cherokee. All the way home I tried to disregard the throbbing in my groin.

I arrived a little after ten. As I pulled into the driveway, I was surprised to see that most of the lights were still on in the house. My dad has been an early-to-bed, early-to-rise kind of guy his whole life, and as I got out of the Cherokee, I could feel anxiety beginning to gnaw at the lining of my stomach. I lied to myself that it was only my dinner talking back to me.

I was relieved to find that everything was okay, Dad having stayed up a little past his usual bedtime, too engrossed in the Ross Thomas novel he'd been plowing through for the past few days to fall asleep. He was sitting at the kitchen table, dressed in pajamas and bathrobe and slippers, sipping a glass of milk laced with brandy. The bottle of Courvoisier was on the table in front of him. His quad cane stood beside his chair.

Our kitchen lay at the back of the house, and as I entered from the hallway, Dad raised his glass of milk with his good hand, greeting me. "Feel like a nightcap?" he asked.

"Sounds good to me." Crossing to a cabinet above the kitchen sink, I pulled out a brandy snifter. I took a seat at the table and poured a couple of fingers of Courvoisier into the glass. I set the bottle down and rolled the bowl of the glass back and forth between my palms, warming the stuff.

"How was dinner?" Dad asked.

"Fine."

"And Maggie? How's she doing?" His tone was purposefully nonchalant. Sometimes he thinks he's sly.

I smiled. There wasn't much my old man would like better than to hear the news that I'd proposed marriage to his favorite accountant, and that she'd accepted the offer. "She's fine, too," I said just as nonchalantly.

"What did you talk about?"

"Not much. The usual chitchat."

He raised his glass and sipped. The milk left a little mustache above his upper lip. He let out a satisfied "Ahhh" and lowered his glass. He looked over at me, still being sly. "You didn't happen to discuss Ozzie Cole, did you?"

When my mouth dropped open, Dad began to chuckle. "You'll never learn," he said, grinning crookedly, able to use the muscles on only one side of his face. "No matter how old you get, your old man's always going to be at least one step ahead of you."

"How in the hell did you know about that?"

He motioned for the Courvoisier, and I poured a little into his glass. "I got a phone call an hour or so ago," he said. "From Zeke Carlin."

I frowned, puzzled. It wasn't because I didn't know the name. Carlin was an ex-boxer who'd been employed for the past ten years by Perry Cole as a kind of Man Friday *cum* nursemaid. Over the last decade, Carlin seemed to be nearly always at Perry's side. When the old man was institutionalized, Carlin had gone with him. Perry's money paid for Carlin's bungalow at the nursing home, next door to his own. Anyone who was acquainted with Carlin knew that he was as loyal to Perry as a Saint Bernard.

I looked at my dad. "How come he wanted to talk to you?"

"He didn't."

My frown deepened. "You want to run that by me again?"

"He didn't want to talk to me. He wanted to talk to you."

"Me?"

Dad nodded. "About Ozzie."

I rolled my eyes. "Oh shit . . . "

Dad asked, "Why didn't you tell me Ozzie came by to see you today?"

"Because it wasn't important. He wanted me to do something for him. I told him no."

"What did he want you to do?"

I sipped my brandy, set it down, and glanced at my wristwatch. "Isn't it past your bedtime?"

"Quit stalling," Dad grunted, challenging me. "You gonna tell me what's going on or aren't you?"

I come by my own streak of stubbornness genetically. As my grandma Donne used to be fond of saying, in a

Scots burr so thick you could slice it, "The apple dinna ever fall far from the tree." I knew that Dad wouldn't budge until he'd heard the whole story.

IT WAS NEARLY eleven by the time I'd finished recounting my meeting with Ozzie. I also repeated Maggie McKenney's opinion that I should check into Ozzie's problem. When I'd concluded, Dad said bluntly, "I think Maggie's right."

His reaction surprised me. "You do?"

He nodded. "What if it's *not* an isolated incident? What if O.C.'s not the only winery that's being ripped off? What if they're doing it to us, too?"

I shook my head. "Look, Dad. In the first place, I'm a long way from being convinced that what Ozzie Cole thinks is happening is what's really happening. One of the primary things they teach you when you're learning to be a criminal investigator is that the simplest solution to a problem is also the likeliest one. That's why you always check out the obvious possibilities first. Nine times out of ten, the most likely suspect in a crime turns out to be the one who really did it."

He was eyeing me doubtfully. "What that means," I went on, "is that what's probably happened is somebody got hold of Ozzie's product—most likely by simply stealing it—and now they're trying to black-market the stuff. It also means that what I tasted today isn't counterfeit. It was just some of Ozzie's own wine that'd gone bad."

Dad was frowning stubbornly. "But what if it was counterfeit?"

"It's not. Trust me."

"How can you be so sure?"

I spread my hands. "You tell me. How difficult is it to counterfeit a bottle of wine?"

His frown deepened.

"I'll answer the question for you," I said. "First off, you have to stock up on a supply of the exact same bottles. Granted, it's probably not that hard to do, but it'd take time. Then you've got to find a way to copy the labels. The mechanical process isn't that tough to duplicate, for a professional, but that's also going to take time because you've got to find a lithographer or a printer or somebody who's either too dumb to realize what you're up to or is crooked enough himself to want to help you out in exchange for a fee. Then you've got to find a way to duplicate the corks and the caps, and *then* you've got to fill the bottles with your imitation wine, seal 'em up, and get your packaging together. If nothing else, it's an incredibly painstaking, time-consuming procedure."

He wasn't satisfied. "It does happen, though."

I nodded. "I'm not saying it doesn't. Every few years, there's a scandal in France or Italy where somebody gets caught counterfeiting wine. I'm aware of that."

He glared at me defiantly. "Well?"

"How many episodes of wine counterfeiting have occurred in the United States in the past twenty years?" I asked.

Another defiant frown. "I can think of a couple."

"So can I, but they're few and far between. The reason it hasn't happened here to the extent that it has in Europe is because there isn't the money-making potential here that there is there."

I paused thoughtfully. "Let's say, for the sake of argument, somebody's fixed up a bogus case of Petrus.

They've made it out of a case of some Bordeaux swill, faked the labels, the caps, crates, everything. Then let's say they've even found a sucker, somebody they've managed to convince it's a legitimate case of great wine. You with me so far?''

Dad nodded.

"Okay. A case of Petrus, assuming you had one to sell, what do you figure you'd get for that nowadays?''

"A lot.''

"Six, seven hundred dollars a case? For a new release?''

He shrugged. "More or less.''

"But we're talking about a bogus case of wine that'd cost maybe a hundred bucks to manufacture, if that. You sell it for a grand, that's a nice margin of profit. And let's say the counterfeiter's made up a whole bunch of cases for a whole bunch of clients.''

He made a face. "So what you're saying is that there are a lot of wines over there that are expensive enough, so it's worth it to try and counterfeit 'em. Right?''

"Exactly.''

Dad pursed his lips. "There's something you're not considering. Aren't we making a lot more wines nowadays over here that are just as pricey as anything from Europe?''

It was my turn to frown again, because what he was suggesting hadn't occurred to me. I could tell by his expression that he could read what was going on behind my eyes. "There're any number of California wines that've gotten pretty expensive,'' he added. "Opus One, Heitz's Martha's Vineyard, just to name two.''

My forehead was furrowing.

Dad asked, "How much is Ozzie Cole getting right now for a case of that Special Reserve he's peddling?''

"I paid four hundred for mine."

"Four-fifty," he corrected.

I shrugged, conceding the point.

He nodded smugly. "Do the math, Jack."

He had me, though I wasn't ready to give in just yet. "So there's money to be made by ripping off Ozzie Cole," I said. "So what? That still doesn't mean it's being done. Nor does it mean that somebody's doing it to us or anybody else. Hell, the most expensive stuff we sell only goes for half that."

"You're just being stubborn. You're mad because I shot down your profit margin argument."

"Yeah, right." I got up from the table, taking the bottle of brandy and my glass with me. I put the brandy away and went to the sink to rinse out my glass.

Dad watched me the entire time. "You still haven't asked me what Zeke Carlin wanted to talk to you about," he said over his shoulder.

I was drying my snifter with a dish towel. "I'm not interested in what Zeke Carlin wants to talk to me about."

"He said Perry wants you to come out to the nursing home for a visit. Tomorrow afternoon, around three. We'll be back from Santa Barbara way before then."

I grunted, acknowledging that I'd heard what he said. I put the brandy snifter back in the cabinet I'd gotten it from, then draped the dish towel over the sink faucet. I turned around. Dad was looking at me. Waiting.

"I'm going to bed," I said.

IT FIGURED I'D HAVE insomnia that night. As I lay in my bed, hands folded behind my head, staring up at nothing in particular, I could hear Dad shuffling down the hallway from the kitchen, heading for his room. For a man whose left side was all but useless, he got around pretty well. A testament to the strength of his will.

Presently the house was dark. On the night table beside my bed is a digital clock. Luminous green numbers spent the next couple of hours defying me to fall asleep. I kept telling myself, over and over, how much I didn't want to get involved in Ozzie Cole's business. Over and over and over. Until at last I rolled onto my side, turning away from the clock, pulling the bedcovers up over my head. "Fuck you, Ozzie," I muttered into my pillow. Then I fell asleep.

FOUR

MY CLOCK RADIO went off at 6:00 a.m., which was a good hour too early as far as I was concerned. By the time I'd rolled out of bed, showered, and dressed, Dad was in the kitchen, ready to go. I helped him into my Cherokee, and by six forty-five we were tooling west, heading for the junction of Highway 101. There are shorter ways to get to Santa Barbara from where we live, but they involve driving along some steep and winding mountain roads. The Jeep could tolerate it, but my father was considerably less willing. It was worth the extra time that going the long way tacked onto the drive if it meant making him a little more comfortable.

The marine layer was unseasonably thick that morning, a low fog bank heavy enough to claw its way as far inland as Los Alamos. The poor visibility slowed us down a little more, and we didn't arrive in downtown Santa Barbara until nearly eight. I brought the Jeep to a halt a few storefronts down from the café on State Street where we would be meeting our breakfast date.

I helped Dad out of the Jeep, and we walked to the café. Stepping inside, we spotted my uncle Gerry sitting in a booth, holding places for us. Gerry was dressed for work, in a navy-blue Brooks Brothers suit, a crisp, white, Oxford-cloth shirt, and a dark blue silk tie with an old-school pattern. As we sat down, he greeted us with a broad smile and a cheery "Good morning." He motioned to a waitress to bring coffee for Dad and me. We ordered breakfast—corned beef hash and scrambled

eggs for Gerry, two eggs over medium and wheat toast
for Dad, a stack of blueberry hotcakes for me. We made
small talk while we sipped our coffee and waited for
our meals.

Gerald Donne is one of the better financial lawyers
in southern California. Among his clients is Donne
Vineyards, Inc. He is also a partner in the business. He
and Dad were born and raised in Tulare, in the San
Joaquin Valley. That they chose to base themselves in
Santa Barbara—when Dad was still in the architecture
game—was a shrewd move, particularly on my uncle's
part. While the town isn't exactly a financial nerve center, it does serve as a vacation home to a number of
men and women who operate big companies all over
the world. Many of those people keep Uncle Gerry on
retainer because they like having quick access to a good
attorney, even if they don't happen to be in New York
or Zurich or Tokyo at the moment. If my uncle has to
get somewhere else in the world in a hurry, it's only a
thirty-minute hop from the Santa Barbara airport to Los
Angeles International. Flights from S.B. to L.A. on one
airline or another leave pretty much every half hour of
the business day, so Uncle Gerry can be anywhere he
wants just about as fast as any other serious player in
his field.

It's a perverse sort of pleasure for me to spend time
with my dad and my uncle. They're not quite two years
apart in age, Gerry being the older, but their personal-
ities could hardly be less similar. Gerry is the pragmatic
one—politically conservative, more clear-thinking and
methodical than anyone I know. Dad is the creative
one—his politics are diametrically opposed to Gerry's
and he's as generous and good-hearted a man as you'll

ever meet, but he's loose as a goose sometimes when it comes to making business decisions.

When they were starting the winery, Dad was the visionary and Uncle Gerry the one who executed the vision. They've made for a helluva team over the years. Why I like being with them is because they can be damned entertaining once you get them onto a subject on which they oppose one another—politics, sports, law, religion, you name it. Two mulish, hotheaded Scotsmen going at each other hammer and claw. It's fun to watch, though if you've got an opinion of your own to express it can be tough to get a word in edgewise.

It wasn't long before I found myself on the sidelines of a heated discussion of the President's latest decision to monkey with yet another of the country's trade agreements when our breakfast arrived. Dad took advantage of the lull to say, "Why don't you ask your uncle what he thinks about this Ozzie Cole business?"

Gerry looked at me. "What Ozzie Cole business?"

"It's nothing," I said. "Ozzie dropped by the house yesterday and asked me to do something for him. I told him no."

My uncle looked surprised. "Ozzie Cole dropped by to see you? There's something that doesn't happen every day."

"Tell me about it."

"Ozzie thinks his wine's being counterfeited," said my dad. "He wants Jack to look into it."

Uncle Gerry raised an eyebrow. "Somebody's counterfeiting O.C. wine?"

"That's what Ozzie says," answered Dad.

I shook my head, trying to dismiss the subject. "Ozzie Cole is full of shit," I said, then gave my uncle a shorthand version of the meeting the afternoon before. Uncle Gerry listened carefully, his eyes widening as I spoke, his interest piqued. "There really isn't anything to it," I concluded. "Ozzie's just got a bug up his ass. He's made up his mind somebody's out to get him."

Uncle Gerry stroked his chin thoughtfully and said, "Hmmm."

"What's 'hmmm' mean?" asked Dad.

"It means 'hmmm,'" said Gerry. "I imagine it's just a coincidence, but this is the second piece of major gossip I've heard about the Cole family in the last twelve hours."

Dad raised an eyebrow and said, "Oh?"

Uncle Gerry nodded. "I had dinner at Birnham Wood last night with Terry Elliott, who dished me some serious dirt about June and Grant."

My father and I exchanged looks of curiosity. Elliott was one of Gerry's clients, a middle-aged, executive VP with a Houston-based oil company. He owned a summer home in Montecito, just east of Santa Barbara. The home was a mile or so from Birnham Wood, a chichi, upscale country club to which several of Gerry's clients—including Terry Elliott—belonged. Elliott was also a serious collector of fine wines, the owner of a cellar conservatively estimated by the *Wine Spectator* to be worth somewhere in the low six figures. He knew the ins and outs of the wine business better than a lot of people who made their living at it.

"What did he say?" I asked, *he* being Terry Elliott.

"He just got back from Europe," said Gerry. "Every year he goes over on a little shopping excursion. He was in Alsace, and he dropped in on one of the vineyard owners he knows. The guy mentioned to him that there were rumors about a merger in the works between the

Coles and Trimbach, somebody like that, but that it fell through when it came to light that the Coles didn't have quite the assets it was assumed they had."

Dad was taken aback. "Are you trying to tell us that June and Grant are having money troubles?"

Gerry shrugged. "All I know is what Terry Elliott said." He turned to me. "You know, Jack, it might not be a bad idea for you to poke around in this a little."

I frowned. "Not you, too…"

"Hear me out, all right? I agree that Ozzie is probably full of shit about this counterfeiting business. But I also agree with Ray that there's a possibility he isn't. If he's not, then this could be the tip of a very nasty iceberg. Ozzie may not be the only one being scammed. But, in any case, what if in the process of looking into this you uncover information about Ozzie's brothers being in the soup, financially speaking? Tell me that news wouldn't have serious repercussions throughout the whole industry."

"Gerry's right," said Dad. "A lot of people could be affected by something like that, including us. It'd be worth our while to know exactly what kind of financial shape the Cole brothers are really in. Especially if we find it out before everybody else does."

I regarded him skeptically. "Since when do you and Uncle Gerry agree on anything?"

"There's always a first time," Dad said.

MY FATHER HAD BEEN going to the same general practitioner, Dr. Harold McLemore, for nearly three decades. Even after we moved to San Tomas, Dad remained a loyal patient. Dr. McLemore's office was on Anacapa Street, three blocks from the café. By the time we were through with breakfast, the sun had come out and burned off much of the early morning fog. The air was clean and bracing, and Dad decided it would be good for us to walk, even though it was exactly nine o'clock when we said good-bye to Uncle Gerry and we'd be late for the appointment. We needn't have worried. We got to the doctor's office at ten past nine, then sat in the waiting room for fifteen minutes before Dad was ushered into Dr. McLemore's inner sanctum.

Dad's appointment was for a checkup, which he received every four months since his stroke. While he was with the doctor, I went back to retrieve the Cherokee and drive it to the medical building's parking lot. I got to the Jeep just as a zealous-looking meter maid was circling it like a vulture, waiting for the meter to click off its last few minutes. As I pulled away I wagged a finger at her and grinned triumphantly. There are few forms of life I can think of that are lower than meter maids. It invariably cheers me if I can prevent one of them from meeting her ticket quota for the day.

I was back in the waiting room, paging through a month-old copy of *Sports Illustrated,* when Dad emerged, smiling, forty-five minutes after he'd gone in. The doctor had given him a clean bill of health.

We arrived home a few minutes before eleven. Our sole full-time employee, Jesus Fonseca, was at work in the aging cellar. A thirty-three-year-old, native-born Mexican who had become a naturalized American citizen two years ago, Jesus had arrived for work punctually at 9:00 a.m., even though he knew Dad and I would be gone most of the morning. He was the kind of person who would be upset because *he* knew he was being slack, regardless of whether anyone else knew it. That was one of the reasons we'd kept him working for us for the past fourteen years, since virtually the day he was coyoted across the border by a van of college students from UCSB.

After changing into work clothes, I spent the next hour and a half helping Jesus inventory the dates on several hundred bottles of wine. At twelve-thirty the two of us went into the house and joined my father for lunch. After lunch, Jesus and I went back to the aging room. I stayed there until two-thirty, at which time I went back into the house, washed up, changed my clothes once again, then came out and got into the Cherokee. By a quarter to three, I was traveling south on Highway 154 on my way to see Perry Cole.

FIVE

PERRY RESIDED AT the Costa del Sol Retirement Village and Convalescent Home outside Los Olivos. All I knew about the facility, aside from its location, was that it was not an inexpensive place to live. The institution lay on twenty-one acres of chaparral land just beyond the town's eastern border. It was comprised of some three dozen or so bungalows for individual residents who still possessed a high degree of independence; an equal number of duplexes; a small, acute-care hospital; a non-denominational chapel; an administration building. You entered the property via a wide driveway marked by a low wall of fake adobe with the words COSTA DEL SOL carved into the wall's sun-baked pseudomud. The driveway led to a parking lot that faced the ad building, which, like every other structure on the campus, had been designed to approximate somebody's idea of early nineteenth-century California architecture. Whoever did the designing had been deluding himself. The institution's structures had the same degree of authenticity to their inspirations as the Pirates of the Caribbean ride at Disneyland had to Montego Bay.

I pulled the Cherokee into a parking slot beside a silver, year-old Mazda half-ton pickup truck. Painted on the door panels was the O.C. Vineyards logo. As I got out of my Jeep I asked myself what Ozzie Cole was doing here, then guessed that he and Perry, and perhaps even Zeke Carlin, were going to overwhelm me with the force of their numbers, if they had to, to get me to check into Ozzie's problem. Then I decided it might be better not to anticipate anything and just roll with it for the time being.

The front doors of the administration building opened into a lobby that was decorated, as I expected, in nuevo hacienda style. Across the lobby from the front doors was a desk marked INFORMATION. Behind the desk sat a plump, plain-faced, forty-something chicana. She was dressed in a cleaned and pressed, white-blouse-and-dark-skirt combination, dark hosiery, and sensible shoes. Her name—Connie—was on a badge pinned to her blouse. As I approached the desk, she smiled. She wore too much makeup, but her smile was friendly enough, so I smiled back. Then I asked her how I might find Perry Cole.

She turned away to play with a computer keyboard on her desk, rapidly punching up a series of letters. Lines flashed across the computer's video monitor. Without looking up from the monitor, she said, "Mr. Cole is in Bungalow Twelve."

"How do I find that?" I asked politely.

She turned away from the computer and opened a drawer in the desk. From the drawer she pulled out a map of the institution and a yellow highlighter pen. She used the pen to draw a squiggly line on the map, then handed the map to me. "We're here," she said, pointing to a spot. "You go out the front doors and make a right and just stay on the walkway. You can't miss it."

I thanked her, and she smiled again.

The path she'd indicated on the map wound through the institution's grounds, which were landscaped with desert flora. Along the path I encountered severally casually attired oldsters taking their afternoon constitutionals. Only one of them was in a wheelchair, being pushed by an orderly. The oldsters and I greeted each other courteously. They seemed to be enjoying themselves, which led me to conclude that whatever kind of place Costa del Sol might be, it wasn't a snake pit.

Presently I came to the first of the private bungalows that lined either side of the walkway. The bungalows looked fairly small from the outside, about as big as a three-car garage. As I moved along the path, I noticed that the numbers on the doors were going up. I congratulated myself for heading in the right direction.

At last I found Bungalow Twelve. It lay to my left, on the opposite side of the walk and a little ahead of Bungalow Thirteen. A gravel pathway led to the threshold of Perry Cole's cottage.

As I approached the front door, I could hear loud, angry voices coming from the other side. Men's voices, though beyond that I could distinguish nothing, least of all what they were saying. I was reaching up to knock when the door was jerked open from the inside. On his way out of the cottage was Ozzie Cole, his face blotchy with rage. He came within a hair of bumping into me, catching himself at the last instant. He looked up at me, his eyes flashing, then registered who it was standing before him. He showed me his familiar scowl. "What the hell are you doing here?"

A husky, rasping whisper responded from somewhere behind him. "Your pa axed me to call him, Mistah Ozzie."

Ozzie looked at me, his expression shifting to one that seemed to be requesting confirmation. "You heard what the man said," I told him.

Ozzie scowled once more, then pushed past me. I watched over my shoulder as he stormed off in the direction I'd just come from. The raspy whisper croaked to me from the doorway of the cottage, "Sorry 'bout that, Mistah Jack. Mistah Ozzie come by to talk wiff Mistah Perry, and Mistah Perry din't take it so good what Mistah Ozzie had to say."

I turned. Standing in the doorway was a trim, middle-aged black man who was five or six inches shorter than my six feet three. He was dressed comfortably, in a Fila sweat suit and Nike cross-training shoes. His skin was the color of unsweetened chocolate, his eyes the color of loam. His nose was spread across his face, having been pulped one too many times. His hairline was somewhat receded; what hair was left was cropped close to his skull and peppered with gray. He looked as if he hadn't put on an ounce of weight since his last middleweight bout, fifteen years ago, the one that ended when a blow to his throat had crushed his larynx and damn near killed him. He was shaking his head apologetically.

"Don't worry about it, Zeke," I said. "I'm used to Mister Ozzie's manners. If he acted any other way, I wouldn't know how to deal with it."

Zeke Carlin showed me a sad smile, then stepped aside to usher me into the bungalow and push the door shut behind me.

There was more space inside than I'd guessed there would be, judging from the exterior. At the far end of the living room, a pair of swinging doors led to a small kitchenette. To the right, just past the front door, lay the opening to a hallway that I assumed led to the bedroom and bath in the rear. My hopes that the interior decoration of the bungalows would exhibit a little individuality were dashed, however. Like the rest of Costa del Sol, it was more of the same El Camino Real influence at work.

Carlin motioned me to a sofa against the wall to my

left. The sofa stood beneath an oil painting of a Mexican fiesta—a half-dozen señoritas in brightly colored dresses, whirling to the music of mariachis, catching the eyes of the vaqueros who stood outside the circle of *bailadoras*. The painting was signed by Remington, and it didn't look like a fake. I was trying to make up my mind as to whether the painting belonged to the bungalow's resident or to the institution when Carlin asked me if I mightn't like something to drink. I'd just begun to say that I would when a voice called from the back of the cottage, "Zeke, goddammit, is that Ozzie? Is he still here? Tell him to get his ass out!"

Carlin looked at me with an expression of weariness and pain. We turned to the sound of shuffling footsteps, approaching from the back of the bungalow, moving down the hallway toward the living room. An instant later, there appeared in the opening to the hallway a thin, stoop-shouldered creature who was using a black cane to help propel himself along.

I hadn't seen Perry Cole in a half-dozen years, and I had to clench my jaw in order not to exhibit how the degree to which he'd changed startled me. Like his son Ozzie, Perry—as I remembered him—was short and thick-bodied, though unlike Ozzie, he'd been stocky rather than dumpy, with massive arms and shoulders and an upper body like a wine barrel. The man who stood before me now had aged badly. He was gaunt, nearly emaciated, his head perched atop a long, scrawny neck that sprouted like a reed from his sunken chest. He'd lost most of the curly black hair he'd had when I was a kid; all that was left were a few snow-white wisps. The pale flesh of his face and skull was mottled with grayish spots, as if he'd been spattered with paint. His eyes had turned from brown to tan, and he squinted at me through coke-bottle lenses mounted in wire frames. He was dressed in a pajama shirt and dark trousers, the too-big clothes hanging from his scarecrow frame. The hand that held the cane was a gnarled claw. His feet were shod in slippers whose leather was worn and cracked and peeling. He looked like nothing so much as an ugly, overgrown, buzzard whose feathers had been plucked.

Perry paused when he reached the living room. He peered at me, then showed me a scowl he must have taught his son. He waggled his cane. "That's not Ozzie," he cackled to no one in particular. "Who the hell is that?"

Carlin stepped over to the old man, took him by the arm, and guided him to a club chair near the sofa. "You know who that is, Mistah Perry," said the black man. "Thass Jack Donne."

Perry allowed himself to be seated. He leaned forward to study me through the thick glasses. "Ray Donne's boy? The ballplayer?"

I judged that it wouldn't do much good to remind him that my baseball career had ended twenty years before, when I was still in college and had shredded my right knee in the middle of a game. "That's me," I said cheerfully. "How've you been, Perry?"

His reply was a wheezy cough. "Not bad for half-dead."

Carlin said to the old man, "I was jus' gonna fetch Mistah Jack somethin' cold to drink. Maybe you'd like somethin', too?"

Perry dismissed him by fluttering a pink claw in his direction. Without another word, Carlin moved off toward the kitchenette. I could hear him in there, opening and closing a cabinet, then opening and closing the refrigerator. I said to Perry, "Zeke called my dad last night and told him you wanted to see me about something."

The old man had been looking in the direction of the kitchenette. His head pivoted on the scrawny neck until he was facing me. He looked at me blankly, without recognition. "How'd you get in here?" he demanded testily. "Who the hell are you, anyway?"

Before I could respond, Carlin had emerged from the kitchenette carrying a glass of iced tea. "I already tol' you, Mistah Perry. Thass Jack Donne."

There wasn't the remotest hint of castigation in Carlin's voice, but the old man reacted like a child who'd been scolded. He lowered his eyes, looking down at his feet. When he looked up again at Carlin, his cheeks were stained with tears. "I forgot, didn't I?" he said. His head sagged to his chest, and he began to sob.

Carlin moved up quickly to hand me the glass of iced tea, then crouched beside the old man's chair. "It's okay, Mistah Perry," he cooed, resting a hand on Perry's knee. "Mistah Jack here, he ain't bothered you don' remember him." Carlin turned to me. "Are you, Mistah Jack?"

Until that instant I hadn't realized how far off-center I'd been knocked by Perry's appearance. It took me about a second too long to answer. "No, no, of course not. It's okay."

Perry brought his head up to look at me. Behind the thick glasses, his pale eyes were rimmed with red. He wore the most pathetic expression I'd ever seen on the face of anyone over the age of six. "I didn't mean it," he snuffled. "I didn't mean to forget."

Carlin patted the old man's knee. "I think maybe it's time we took us a nap. Okay?"

Perry looked at Carlin and nodded forlornly. Carlin helped Perry to his feet, holding the old man by an elbow to guide him toward the hallway. Carlin turned to look at me over his shoulder. "I be right back. This won't take long." I nodded, then watched them disappear down the hallway.

I sat alone for ten minutes, sipping my iced tea and trying vainly not to think about the myriad ways in which people deal with the bleak awareness that they're approaching the conclusion of their lives. I was recalling something I'd heard said one time by Truman Capote, of all people, who I've always felt was much more insightful than nearly anybody gave him credit for. He believed that death was at the center of human existence, and for the most part I agree with that notion. As I sat on the sofa in Perry Cole's bungalow, I was attempting to reconcile the scene I'd just witnessed with Capote's philosophy and my own cynical certainty that I'd never known anybody who didn't handle badly the realization that his—or her—demise was imminent. If you think about it, whose end *isn't* imminent? It's like another of my favorite philosophers sang one time: If you're not busy being born, you're busy dying.

Eventually Carlin returned, wearing the same pained expression he'd had on when Perry'd first come into the room. He fell into the club chair, seeming to sink into it more heavily than you'd expect someone of his size to do. He rubbed his eyes with a thumb and forefinger, then sighed. It was the sound of a man brought to the brink of exhaustion by emotional anguish. Until that moment I hadn't understood how much Perry Cole and Zeke Carlin meant to one another. The realization made me feel more miserable than I'd already been feeling.

I said gently, "I didn't know he was this bad."

Carlin nodded. "These last few months he be gettin' worse 'n' worse, all the time. Sometimes he don' even remember me, and I been wiff him nearly ever' day for almos' ten years. He see me an' he say somethin' like, 'Who let this nigger in my house?' I cain't get mad at him, though, 'cause he don' really know what he be sayin'…"

He paused, turning to gaze wistfully in the direction of Perry's bedroom. "Some days is worse'n others. Thass what I try 'n' tell Mistah Ozzie when he come by this afternoon. He jus' happen to catch his daddy on a bad day is all…"

He turned back to me. "Thass what that fight was about, when you come in. Mistah Perry's doctor thinks he should move on into the hospital, 'cause they got a ward over there for folks when they Alzheimer's gets too bad for 'em to be walkin' around by theirselves. Mistah Ozzie, he agrees wiff the doctor. Mistah Perry, though, he don' wanna go to no hospital. I try an' tell Mistah Ozzie I be glad to move outta my own place 'cross the way and move in here wiff his daddy. Be wiff him twenty-four hours a day, if I hav'ta. Mistah Ozzie, though, he jus' as stubborn as Mistah Perry." Carlin sighed again. "They two of a kind, all right. Two of a kind."

"What Perry wanted to see me about didn't have anything to do with his going into the hospital, did it?"

Carlin shook his head.

"Then how come he wanted to see me?"

"'Cause Mistah Ozzie tol' Mistah Perry about he was talkin' to you. Mistah Ozzie, he make it a point to visit his daddy ever' day, rain or shine. When he come out yesta'day, he tol' Mistah Perry he axed you to find out if there ain't somebody counterfeitin' his wine, an' how you tol' him to go tell the po-lice, an' that you din't want nothin' to do with it. Las' night Mistah Perry say for me to call an' see if you won't come here, so's he can ax you personal if you won't help Mistah Ozzie.''

I considered briefly. "Are you sure that's what Perry wants?"

Carlin nodded. "Sooner or later he'll remember. He'll ax me did I talk to you, an' then he'll ax me what did you say. He say if he has to, he'll pay you hisself. You won't have to deal wiff Mistah Ozzie at all, if you don' like.''

"What about that fight they just had?"

"It don't matter," said Carlin. "They fight all the time. But when it come to somethin' impo'tant like this, Mistah Perry, he don't take nobody's side but Mistah Ozzie's. Ever."

I considered again, then said, "Tell Perry not to worry about my fee. I'll get it from Ozzie. It's his problem, so he should be the one to have to pay."

For the first time since I'd arrived, the burden on Zeke Carlin's shoulders seemed to lift, however slightly. His wide lips split into a grateful smile. "Mistah Perry'll 'preciate you takin' care o' this, Mistah Jack."

"Tell him it's my pleasure," I said.

WHEN I GOT HOME, I went directly to my office, phoned Ozzie and informed him that I'd changed my mind. I'd drop by that evening with a formal contract for him to sign. He'd be paying what used to be my usual rate— $250 a day, plus expenses. When he started to bitch about the money, I reminded him that my services were something he could write off his corporate taxes as a legitimate business expense. I told him to have a check ready for a thousand dollars as a retainer when I brought over the contract. He was entitled to daily reports, if he wanted them, and I guaranteed an itemized bill when I was through with my investigation. He asked me when I planned to get started, and I answered, ''Tomorrow morning.'' He didn't bother to ask why he'd happened to bump into me at his father's bungalow, and I didn't volunteer an explanation. If and when he wanted to know, I'd tell him.

That night, toward the end of dinner with my father, I realized that I was studying Dad unconsciously, comparing him to Perry Cole. Though Dad and Perry were only a couple of years apart in age, Perry was a dying old man, and my father—in spite of his stroke—was still a vital, functioning human being. The difference between them, I concluded, was the difference between somebody who isn't afraid to fight and somebody who simply gives up. Dad noticed how intently I was considering him, and he asked me what was on my mind. When I told him, he ordered me to finish my dinner and quit worrying about him. I knew by the tone of his voice that I had no choice but to do what he said.

SIX

THE FIRST THING on which I spent Ozzie's money the following morning was a round-trip train ticket from Santa Barbara to Del Mar. It was one of three options I considered as a means of getting to La Jolla, home of the Mission Bay Wine Company. I could have flown to San Diego from Santa Maria, which is somewhat closer to San Tomas than Santa Barbara and has an airport about the same size, but that seemed a needless expense for the day trip I was intending. Especially when I factored in the extra time it would take getting in and out of airports, and I realized that that mode of transportation wouldn't get me to my destination too much faster than the other two. I could also have taken my Cherokee, but that meant facing the grim prospect of passing through the L.A. megalopolis on my way south. It was a chore which doubtless would have exhausted me beyond irritability—assuming that I managed to survive two hundred miles' worth of having my rear bumper chewed on by manic truck drivers piloting twenty tons of steel and rubber, and dodging self-absorbed, dim-witted lane jumpers who ignored both their turn-signal switches and their rearview mirrors. Taking the train seemed the best choice.

I drove to Santa Barbara, arriving at the Amtrak depot at 7:30 a.m. After leaving my Jeep in the commuter parking lot, I purchased a first-class ticket, thereby assuring myself of plenty of leg room for the duration of the five-hour trip. I boarded the train and found an open seat near the front of the car. The *San Diegan* pulled out on time, at precisely 8:00 a.m. I'd brought a paperback copy of a James Michener tome published in the 1970s, which I assumed would be sufficiently diversionary material. By the time the train pulled into the Del Mar station at ten minutes to one, I'd acquired more knowledge about the history of the state of Colorado than I'd likely ever need. I was, however, markedly more relaxed than I'd have been if I'd made the drive myself.

A short line of taxis waited near the end of a driveway that led up a steep hill into the town of Del Mar. I headed for the first cab in line and nodded a greeting to the driver, a transplanted Middle Easterner who was leaning against a fender and perusing the *Daily Racing Form*. He was probably hoping for a fare who'd want a lift to the track, less than a mile from the depot. There one could watch the ponies running elsewhere on closed-circuit TV. I disappointed him by asking for a ride to La Jolla.

The trip took about twenty minutes, the fare costing me a dollar per minute, including tip. I had the cabbie drop me off in front of the La Valencia Hotel on Prospect Street, La Jolla's main shopping-and-tourist-trap strip that stood on a bluff above the cove after which the town was named.

As the cab pulled away, I took a moment to gaze past the point above which the hotel stood, toward the ocean. It was a gorgeous afternoon, the air temperature a little brisk but the view absolutely stunning. The water of the cove, as it edged toward the horizon, turned progressively darker shades of blue. Sunlight glinted off the surface so brightly that it was near-blinding. The sight reminded me of why La Jolla was one of my favorite places, not just in California, but anywhere. Too bad it would never be anything other than a nice place to visit. To afford to live there comfortably, I'd need to start earning about three times what I now earned.

The Mission Bay Wine Company was one of several shops on the east side of Girard Street, half a block up from Prospect. I pushed open the door of the shop, causing a tiny bell somewhere above me to tinkle. Closing the door, I stood for a time looking around. The place was small, barely a thousand square feet in area, but the floor was shined and the wine bottles were dusted and it was crammed from floor to ceiling with product. I picked up a bottle of Cos d'Estournel, one of an assortment of recently released Bordeaux that were part of a display near the front door. It pleased me to discover that whoever ran the Mission Bay Wine Company knew not to gouge the customers too much. I took it as a hopeful sign that I'd get reasonable responses to reasonable questions.

I returned the wine to its display, then made my way to the checkout counter at the back of the shop. Behind the counter lounged a man who looked to be somewhere in his mid thirties. He was dressed comfortably and casually—baggy Levi's, Reebok sneakers, a faded Izod shirt. His face was round and full and somewhat florid. He had a blond mustache that was a shade or two lighter than his shaggy hair, which could have stood a trim. He was leaning near a cash register, hunched over the counter, turning the pages of a Hugh Johnson guidebook. His posture accentuated a slight paunch that pressed against the edge of the countertop. As I approached, he looked up from what he was reading and showed me a friendly smile. "Help you?" he asked.

I held out a hand. "I'm Jack Donne from Donne

Vineyards, up in Santa Ynez. I happened to be in the area, and I thought I'd drop in and say hi."

His smile broadened to a hundred-watt grin. "Jerry Wiedemeyer," he said, pumping my hand. "Nice to meet you, Jack. I carry a lot of your wine. I even drink it myself. If I can't recommend it to my customers, I don't stock it."

I returned the smile. "You're the owner?"

"That's me."

"Nice shop," I said frankly. "You've got some impressive stuff. Besides Donne, I mean."

His grin reappeared. "My regular customers tend to be pretty shrewd. They don't mind spending money, but they're big on getting what they pay for."

"You get much tourist trade?"

"Some. I usually have enough Bartles & James on hand to keep them happy."

I chuckled to let him know I got the joke, then said, "I was just talking to one of my fellow winemakers the other day. He mentioned that he'd met you."

"Who was that?"

"Ozzie Cole."

"Oh yeah," Wiedemeyer grunted. "Him." It was not a reply fraught with the tang of pleasant memory. For the first time he regarded me with an attitude that was anything but cordial. "He's not a buddy of yours, is he?"

"Not particularly. His business is just down the road from mine, and we bump into each other now and then."

Wiedemeyer rapped a knuckle on the counter. "Between you and me, I thought he was kind of a jerk."

"'Asshole' is the word you're looking for," I said.

He smiled, looking relieved. "I couldn't believe it.

The guy comes in and introduces himself, and everything is hunky-dory till I ask him, nice as pie, how I can get some more of his wine. Then he decides to throw a shit fit and starts making a major scene. 'How'd you get hold of my stuff ! How'd you rip me off, you son of a bitch!' Like that."

"That's Ozzie."

Wiedemeyer was shaking his head. "Man, I'd heard stories about what a turd he could be to deal with. You know, about how he fucked over a bunch of customers after those monster reviews for his Pinot Reserve came out?"

I knew what Wiedemeyer was talking about. Last fall, both the *Wine Spectator* and *Wine Advocate* had given O.C.'s Special Reserve remarkable—and totally unexpected—raves, a 98 from Robert Parker and a 97 from the *Spectator*. After the reviews came out, Ozzie immediately jacked up the price of the wine by a factor of 50 percent. He also decided it would be okay to short dozens of his regular customers, many of them private individuals who had handshake orders with him that went back years and who usually paid a comparatively cheap, pre-review, per-case price. The wine he held back he subsequently sold at full retail, directly from his winery, to anybody who took the trouble to knock on his door. Between the publicity engendered by the reviews, and the quality of the product, Ozzie made buckets of money he wouldn't have made if he'd dealt with his regular customers on the square, as they expected him to. He sold a lot of wine, but in the process he sullied an already spotty reputation for the manner in which he conducted business. Everyone who knew about it said the same thing, that it was too bad Ozzie made such great wine because if you wanted the damn stuff, you either danced to his tune or you did without.

Wiedemeyer was shaking his head again. "I tried to tell him all I did was say okay to this salesman who dropped in out of the blue one day and offered me a deal. Two hundred and fifty bucks a case. How could I say no?"

"I wouldn't have turned it down, either."

"I had absolutely no trouble selling it. Hell, it was all gone three days after he delivered the cases. I was lucky to save a couple of bottles for myself."

"This salesman," I said. "You say he just dropped in on you out of the blue?"

Wiedemeyer nodded. "He wasn't one of my regular guys. He told me he was working for a distributor that was just starting up. He said the reason they were cutting a deal on the O.C. was because they wanted to make friends with us retailers and build up their business."

"You remember the guy's name?" I asked.

He scratched his head, trying to recall. "Orson or Orton, something like that. Only more Spanish-sounding..." He paused thoughtfully, then said, "Hang on. I got his card right here."

He turned to the cash register and punched the No Sale button. The register drawer slid open. He reached into the drawer and pulled out a sheaf of business cards held together by a large clip. He undid the clip, and as he thumbed through the cards looking for the one he wanted, I asked, "This guy delivered the cases personally?"

Wiedemeyer nodded without looking up from the cards. "Uh-huh."

"How long ago was that?"

"Maybe a week. Last Tuesday or Wednesday."

"Has he been back to see you since then?"

Wiedemeyer shook his head, still looking through the cards. Then he paused, brightening. "Here we go."

He handed me the card, on which was printed: "Teodoro Ortiz. Southern Territory Sales Representative. Golden State Distribution Company, Inc. Wholesalers of Fine Wines and Spirits, Imported and Domestic." There was no address, but there was a telephone number with a 310 area code. Somewhere on the west side of Los Angeles County.

Wiedemeyer must have noticed the dark cloud that passed over my face as I read the card. "You know this guy?" he asked.

I nodded grimly. "I know him all right. I know him very well."

I SPENT ANOTHER fifteen minutes making small talk with the proprietor of the Mission Bay Wine Company, then concluded our conversation with an invitation to him to join my father and me for lunch should he ever find himself in San Tomas. Upon leaving, I crossed the street to a café I'd noticed on my way in. I allowed myself to be seated at an outdoor table. Ordinarily I might have spent more time admiring my waitress's scrubbed, healthy, cute-as-a-button good looks and her bright smile and lithe, firm body that was not disguised by the long-skirted, loose-fitting cotton dress she wore. Instead, after placing my order for a club sandwich and iced coffee, I was thinking—not fondly—about Teddie Ortiz.

The last case I'd worked on, while I was still with ATF, was a gun-running scam that involved a gang operating out of El Paso, Texas. The gang was led by a pair of brothers named Davis. The Davis brothers were Missouri-born, and they presented themselves as a couple of redneck, peckerwood, good ol' boys. They were, in fact, shrewd, first-rate con artists. They'd managed to dupe a drug lord from Juarez into believing they could supply him with several cases of hot, brand-new Chinese-made AK-47s—the hardware to be employed by the drug lord to eliminate some problems he was having with a few competitors—in exchange for an amount of cash equivalent to the monthly payroll of a major league baseball team.

I was attached to the Field Office in Los Angeles when the Bureau got tipped off about the transaction. Because we didn't want to use any local agents on the chance that they might be too well known, I was sent to Texas, where I infiltrated the Davises' gang by passing myself off as a California-based money launderer. I discovered that the guns were nonexistent around the same time that *another* con man who'd gotten wind of the impending deal showed up on the Davises' doorstep. He was posing as a corrupt Mexican *federale* and hoping to cut himself in for a piece of the action by playing both ends against the middle. As it happened, the con man and I had crossed paths before and were aware of each other's true identities. Unfortunately for me, he was able to blow my cover before I could blow his. By exposing me, he managed to ingratiate himself with the Davis brothers, and for my trouble I took a .22-caliber slug in the same knee I'd wrecked in college.

The con man's name was Teddie Ortiz.

As I ate my lunch, I told myself it was possible that I'd made a mistake. The Teodoro Ortiz who'd sold a dozen cases of O.C. Pinot Noir Special Reserve to Jerry Wiedemeyer wasn't necessarily the same Teddie Ortiz with whom I'd been acquainted years before. It was possible, but I doubted it. If somebody were running a wine counterfeiting scam, then finding Teddie Ortiz—or someone like him—in the middle of it wouldn't be much of a shock.

That was why seeing his name on a business card was causing me to reconsider my opinion that Ozzie Cole was deluding himself. That I also might have to apologize to Ozzie for misjudging him generated nearly as great a feeling of unhappiness in me as the prospect of encountering Teddie Ortiz again.

I didn't dare approach him directly. That is, I didn't dare go so much as to mollify him; I didn't call him. I planned on renting a vehicle and shopping for a change of clothes first. I'd made a few phone calls. I wasn't any of his business. Besides, wondering, as I was to waylay him. When the away few hours in great meaning that I presumed was a rather dull vocation.

The telephone was on a nightstand next to the queen-sized bed. I squatted, sat down on the side of the bed and then stared beside the phone while instructions on how to make local and long-distance calls. I picked up the receiver and punched a series of numbers that connected me with my home in San Tomas. After several rings there was a sharp click, followed by my own voice. "Hi, this is Jack Donne. My father and I aren't available to take your call at the moment, but if you'd like to leave us a message, wait for the tone and speak as long as you please." I listened for the beep, then said, "Dad, it's me. I'm in L.A.'s the Searchlight picked up, and I've decided to spend the night down here and check it out." I recited the number of the hotel and my room's extension, then added, "Right now I plan on

SEVEN

AFTER FINISHING MY sandwich and coffee, I returned to the La Valencia Hotel and booked a room for the night. I was ushered upstairs by a bellman who looked askance when I informed him that not only didn't I have a car, I didn't have any luggage, either. The five dollars I tipped him didn't do much to mollify him. I didn't tell him I planned on renting a vehicle and shopping for a change of clothes after I'd made a few phone calls. It wasn't any of his business. Besides, pondering what I was up to would help him while away the hours he spent pursuing what I presumed was a rather dull vocation.

The telephone was on a nightstand next to the queen-sized bed I'd requested. I sat down on the side of the bed and read a card beside the phone with instructions on how to make local and long-distance calls. I picked up the receiver and punched a series of numbers that connected me with my home in San Tomas. After several rings, there was a sharp click, followed by my own voice. "Hi, this is Jack Donne. My father and I aren't available to take your call at the moment, but if you'd like to leave us a message, wait for the tone and speak as long as you please." I listened for the beep, then said, "Dad, it's me. I'm in La Jolla. Something's turned up, and I've decided to spend the night down here and check it out." I recited the number of the hotel and my room's extension, then added, "Right now I plan on being home no later than tomorrow night, but if that changes I'll be sure to call you.''

Depressing the button, I punched a new series of numbers that I'd memorized from Teodoro Ortiz's business card. After the second ring, another answering machine clicked on. "You've reached the office of Golden State Distribution. No one's here to take your call at the moment, but if you'll leave your name, a number where you can be reached, and a brief reason for your call, somebody will get back to you as soon as they can.''

I hung up before the recorder could beep at me. The voice was a man's, but it wasn't anyone I recalled having heard before. I was neither pleased nor disappointed. That they had a working number didn't necessarily mean Golden State Distribution was a legitimate business, particularly when their calls were answered by a machine.

I punched a third series of numbers, and a bored-sounding female voice informed me that I'd reached the Los Angeles Field Office of the Bureau of Alcohol, Tobacco and Firearms. I gave her my name and asked to be put through to Assistant Special Agent in Charge Alan Feinberg.

While I was on hold, I opened the drawer of the nightstand and found a couple of San Diego telephone directories. I lifted out the Yellow Pages, and as I was setting the book next to me on the bed, a male voice that managed to sound cheerful and run-down at the same time uttered in a thick Bronx accent, "Jack Donne, how the fuck are you? Jesus, I haven't talked to you in a coon's age. How's things in the vino trade, boychik?''

I smiled, remembering my ex-partner who, shortly

after my retirement, had decided to get off the street and start making his way up the company ladder. I could picture him at his desk in the grimy, windowless cubbyhole that served as his office: leaning back in his chair, feet propped atop untidy stacks of memoranda and reports; his short-sleeved shirt stained at the armpits; a gaudy, too-wide, unfashionably patterned necktie loosened around his collar. Right now he'd be cradling the phone between his shoulder and ear while sipping from a cup of coffee that was as tasty as radiator fluid.

After catching Alan up on what my dad and I had been doing for the past several months, I said, "I need some information on a former playmate of ours."

"Who?"

"Teddie Ortiz."

There was a brief silence. "You're not thinking about maybe settling an old grudge, are you?"

"It's nothing like that," I said. "I'm temporarily back in the private eye business, and I want to find out if Teddie's alive or dead. If he's alive, then I'd like to know whether he's doing time somewhere or is on the loose."

"That's easy enough," said Alan. "Let me have an hour or so, and I'll see what I can find out. You at home, or what?"

I gave him the number of my room and pledged to stick around until he called back. I hung up, then took the Yellow Pages with me to an imitation-walnut table that stood near the room's only window. I sat down, opened the directory to "Wines-Retail," and studied the places listed there. I was hoping to be able to judge by the listings whether or not they tended to cater to an upscale clientele.

Three places looked promising. I got up from the

table and went to the dresser against the wall opposite the foot of the bed. In the dresser's top drawer I found a pen and a sheaf of stationery with the hotel's letterhead. I was returning to the table when the phone rang. I crossed to the bed, sat down, and picked up the receiver.

It was Alan Feinberg. "I got some information, boychik. You ready?"

"Shoot."

"Not long after he ratted you out in Texas, Teddie Ortiz got popped for a parole violation. He ended up going back to Terminal Island to serve out a stretch for income tax evasion. He only had a couple of years left on his sentence. He was released last December, free and clear."

"Any idea where he might be?" I asked.

"Hell, he could be anywhere. You want I should try and track him down?"

"Not just yet. If it turns out he's involved in what I'm working on, I'd rather not tip him off that somebody's interested in him."

Alan asked, "Is what you're working on anything the Bureau should know about?"

"It's possible," I said.

"How possible?"

"It depends. I'm not sure myself what's going on exactly, but believe me, I have no qualms about dumping it in your lap the instant I find out."

"Guns?" Alan asked.

"Booze."

He let out a disappointed sigh. Alan was like a lot of ATF guys who found cases involving firearms inherently more exciting than ones involving alcohol or tobacco. "Okay. I guess I just have to trust your judgment. Let me know if you need anything."

We said good-bye and I hung up. Then I took my stationery and pen back to the table and copied down the names, addresses, and phone numbers of the three wine retailers I'd chosen.

On my way out of the hotel I stopped at the front desk and asked the concierge for the location of the nearest car rental agency, then asked where I could find the closest bookstore that would sell me a *Thomas Guide Street Directory* for San Diego County. It turned out that the car rental agency and the bookstore were on the same street, less than a block apart. I went to the bookstore first, then off to rent the roomiest automobile the agency had available. It was an almost-new Ford Taurus whose interior smelled of stale cigar smoke and whose exterior was the color of baby excrement. Reminding myself of how often it is that beggars can't be choosers, I signed a contract that entrusted the Taurus to my care for twenty-four hours. Then I showed the rental agent my *Thomas Guide* and the sheet of hotel stationery on which I'd written the addresses of the wineshops I hoped to visit. It took the two of us ten minutes to map out an itinerary for me, and by 3:00 p.m. I was on I-5 heading for downtown San Diego.

BY SEVEN O'CLOCK that evening I was back in La Jolla, having made my final stop at a department store in the University Towne Centre, a shopping mall near the San Diego campus of the University of California, hence its name. At the department store I purchased a new Polo shirt, slacks, socks, and underwear. I debated whether I should also buy an overnight bag to pack everything in, but then decided my suspicious bellman could just keep on being suspicious—a somewhat nicer way of thinking he could go fuck himself.

My afternoon had been fruitful. Of the three shops I went to—one in the Embarcadero, one at the Old Town Galleria, and one in Mission Valley—the latter two had been visited by Teodoro Ortiz. He'd made the proprietors the same deal he'd offered Jerry Wiedemeyer. Neither had any of Ozzie's wine left, but they were able to provide me with a description of the man who'd sold it to them. Upon hearing the descriptions, I was all but certain that the salesman was that same Teddie Ortiz I'd once known but hardly loved.

By the time I was heading back to La Jolla, I'd devised a course of action. I felt safe in making the assumption that Teddie was working his way either up or down the southern California coast, going from retailer to retailer and offering a cut-rate deal on O.C. Special Reserve, which—so far—seemed to be all he was peddling. If my luck was holding, he'd started down here in San Diego and would about now be making the rounds in L.A. or Orange County. A few more phone calls tomorrow would, I hoped, put me on his trail.

I pulled up to the La Valencia and left the Taurus with the parking valet. On my way upstairs I stopped at the front desk to check for messages. I wasn't really expecting any, so I was surprised when the night concierge, who'd come on duty while I was out, gave me a slip of pink paper on which had been scrawled: "Raymond Donne. 6:45 p.m. Call back ASAP. Urgent."

I held the paper up to the concierge. "Did you take this yourself?"

He peered at the message for a moment, then nodded. "About twenty-five minutes ago."

"Was it my father who spoke to you?" I asked. "Or

was it somebody who wanted to tell me something about my father?''

He peered at the message again. "This is who called," he said, pointing at Dad's name. "Raymond Donne."

I exhaled a deep breath I was unaware I'd been holding in. "Did he say what was so urgent?"

The concierge shook his head. "Sorry."

I jogged to the elevator. Minutes later I was in my room, standing beside the nightstand and punching up my home number. The phone was answered in the middle of the second ring. "Dad?" I said. "It's me. I just got your message."

The brief pause he took before responding caused fingers of ice to tickle my spine. "What's the matter?" I said.

"It's Perry Cole."

"What about him?"

Another pause, then, "He's been murdered."

I stiffened. *"Murdered?"*

"They found his body a couple of hours ago," Dad said. "In his bungalow. Some detective called here looking for you. Somebody named Fitch. A lieutenant."

"Why did he want to talk to me?"

"He wouldn't say. All he'd tell me was that he'd be up at Costa del Sol for another few hours at least. I told him you were out of town till tomorrow, but that didn't seem to make much difference to him. He just said for me to make sure you got the message that he wanted to see you."

Without realizing it, I'd lapsed into a baffled silence. It was one of those infrequent moments we all have when the world tilts crazily. You need time to readjust, only I wasn't quite ready yet. I wasn't through reeling.

Dad said hesitantly, "Jack...?"
I sighed. "I guess I'm coming home."
"When?" asked Dad.
"Right now," I told him.

EIGHT

I HAVE A COUSIN who lives in Sacramento and works as a psychiatric counselor for a state-run mental health facility. Her specialty is suicide prevention. One evening while I was visiting her a few years ago, we stopped for drinks at a tavern near the capitol, where we chanced upon a discussion of unique methods of suicide. She asked me what I thought might be the messiest but most painless way of killing yourself, something that wouldn't hurt too much but would require a lot of time and effort to clean up afterward. Without asking her how someone might come to possess that particular combination of motives, I indicated several options. My favorite was a leap off the top of some extremely tall building, like the Sears Tower in Chicago. She disagreed. What she suggested instead was taking a hypodermic needle and, after anesthetizing the skin area, jabbing it into a vein and simply withdrawing the plunger. You would literally siphon yourself to death. You'd pass out from loss of blood, then fall into a coma, then die. It was no more excruciating than falling asleep, she claimed, but whoever found you would have to mop up the pool of four or five pints of blood in which your shrunken, shriveled body lay.

My cousin told me this because she knew I was capable of conjuring up the image of what it would look like if somebody actually tried that. She also perceived—correctly—that I'd find the idea macabre but amusing. I didn't think it was nearly so humorous when

I found out it was the manner in which Perry Cole's death had been engineered.

I DECIDED IT would be all right for me to hang the expense and get home as quickly as possible. After paying for a full night's lodging, I checked out of the La Valencia, got into the Taurus, and drove to Lindbergh Field, San Diego's airport. I dropped the car off at a branch of the same rental agency I'd gotten it from, then hopped aboard their complimentary shuttle tram. I went from terminal to terminal, searching for the airline offering the soonest available flight to where I wanted to go.

By 9:30 p.m. I was in a cab, heading from the Santa Barbara airport to the Amtrak station where my Cherokee was parked. An hour later, I was pulling up to a police barricade that blocked off the parking lot of the Costa del Sol old folks' home. As my headlights struck the youthful-looking deputy sheriff who manned the barricade, he held up a hand to stop me. I eased on the brakes. The deputy moved to the driver's window, motioning for me to roll it down. "There's an emergency situation here," he said tersely. "No visitors allowed till further notice. I'm afraid you'll have to go back."

"Somebody's expecting me," I said. "Lieutenant Fitch."

The deputy's eyes narrowed. He was asking himself who I was. Clearly, I wasn't a cop and I didn't look like a reporter. At last he said warily. "You sure about that?"

I pointed to the walkie-talkie attached to his Sam Browne belt. "Tell him Jack Donne is here."

It took him a few seconds to make up his mind. Then he unhitched the walkie-talkie, switched it on, and asked for Lieutenant Fitch. After Fitch's voice crackled at him, he announced my presence. Fitch's voice crackled again. The deputy switched off the walkie-talkie, stepped back, pulled aside the barricade, and waved me through.

I parked the Cherokee and climbed out. Minutes later I was striding through the open door of Bungalow Twelve. In the living room was an evidence technician, part of a team checking the place for fingerprints, hair follicles, blood smears, clothing fibers, and whatever other detritus might prove helpful in identifying the perpetrator of the crime that had brought them here. The tech wore surgical-type gloves, and he was kneeling between the sofa and the club chair, scrutinizing the floor. His back was to me. "Ahem," I coughed loudly. It startled him. He swung his head around to peer at me over his shoulder. It didn't matter that he didn't know who I was. He just didn't like being interrupted.

"Lieutenant Fitch?" I inquired.

The evidence tech jerked his head toward the rear, then went back to his task. I made my way down the short hallway that ended at the open door of the bungalow's single bedroom. Well before I reached the door I could smell blood. The aroma was thick and cloying and metallic—so strong that I knew a great deal of blood must have been let. When I paused in the bedroom doorway, I was stunned to see just how much it was.

It wasn't a large room. The furniture—a dresser, chest of drawers, double bed, night table beside the bed, twenty-one-inch Sony Trinitron on a stand near the foot—occupied almost all of the space. Most of the furniture barely registered on me, more of the same pseudo-Spanish motif.

What did register was the bed. It was rumpled and unmade, and one entire side—the left-hand side of someone lying on it on his back—was drenched with blood. A puddle had formed in an indentation made by the backside of the bed's recent occupant. The bedclothes and mattress were soaked with red. The bluish-colored material that upholstered the portion of box spring I could see was stained purple. On the floor next to the bed was a drying pool created by a steady drip from above. The blood was still fresh. It hadn't yet coagulated, hadn't begun to turn fetid and awful-smelling. Small consolation, since imagining what had happened to cause what I saw was nauseating enough.

Three people were there, two of them evidence techs. One of the techs, another man, was working in the bathroom attached to the bedroom. Another technician, this one female, was examining the dresser, gingerly picking up various objets de toilette—a hairbrush, comb, eyeglasses. She placed the objects in plastic bags, which she then carefully labeled.

The third person in the room was a Caucasian male a few inches shorter and twenty pounds lighter than me. He was dressed in polyester-blend slacks and a sport jacket of an obnoxious color and pattern favored by TV play-by-play announcers. I guessed he'd had the jacket for a few years, since it appeared to be a little snug, as if he'd put on weight since he'd bought it. He had on a shirt and tie combination that was no more stylish than the rest of his ensemble. His complexion was pock-marked with acne scars. His skin looked pale in the light of the ceiling fixture that illuminated the room, as if he didn't get enough sun. He had a narrow nose, brown eyes, a receding hairline, and a sparse mustache the same mahogany color as his brush-cut hair. He was

standing near the bloodied bed and studying the pages
of a pocket notebook. Seeming to sense my presence,
he looked up from the notebook and regarded me with
a pleasurable expression. "Long time no see, Jack," he
said.

I shook the hand he offered. "Do we know each
other, Lieutenant Fitch?"

The question seemed to hurt his feelings. "You don't
remember me?" I spread my hands apologetically.
"San Tomas High School?" he prompted. "The San
Tomas Conquistadors? The baseball team?"

"Yeah…?"

"Bradley Fitch? Brad Fitch? Third base and outfield?"

Dismayed, I shook my head. His wounded expression
deepened. "I know I was two years behind you in
school, and I rode the bench most of the time, but I
never thought you wouldn't remember me…"

I frowned for a moment, then slapped my head, a
gesture of How stupid can I be? "Jesus, of course!
Bradley Fitch! My god, it *is* you!" I took his hand again
and pumped it enthusiastically. "When my dad said
somebody named Lieutenant Fitch wanted to see me, I
never made the association with the Brad Fitch I used
to know in high school! I feel like such a boob!"

He grinned forgivingly, clapped a hand on my shoulder, and steered me toward the bedroom door. "Let's
go talk in the other room and let these people work,"
he said.

I nodded, then let him guide me away from the
bloody bed. I still hadn't the faintest notion who he was,
but, fortunately, there are rare occasions when I manage
to process quickly and react almost as fast. Like now,
when it struck me as a good idea to have a cop think

of me as an old buddy. Especially when that cop was a homicide detective investigating a killing in which I had a more than passing interest.

IT TOOK A WHILE to get Lieutenant Fitch onto the subject of Perry Cole's murder. After he dismissed the evidence tech in the living room, sending him to the bedroom to help out back there, he motioned me to a seat on the sofa while he took the chair. He spent the next fifteen minutes reminiscing about the lone season he and I had spent as teammates at San Tomas Senior High School, when I was in the twelfth grade and he in the tenth. It was my senior year and I was one of the team's star players, on my way to an athletic scholarship at San Diego State University. Fitch was a sophomore and a scrubini, which was why I didn't know him from Adam. I discovered that to him, apparently, I was some kind of idol. He knew all about my baseball career coming to an end before it really got started. He also knew about my hitch in the air force, my subsequent recruitment by the Treasury Department, my tenure as a private investigator, and my current position as co-owner of Donne Vineyards. Fitch had chosen to emulate my law enforcement experience by joining the Santa Ynez Sheriff's Department upon his graduation from junior college. He'd made sergeant at age thirty, and lieutenant a little over a year ago. I congratulated him.

At last he came to the details of Perry's death, what he knew for certain and what he'd concluded to be likely. The body had been discovered by a nurse named Battles a little after 4:00 p.m. Nurse Battles had dropped by to check on Perry and administer via injection his afternoon medication. Ordinarily that duty would have fallen to Zeke Carlin, but today was Carlin's day off.

He'd been seen leaving his bungalow—number thirteen—a little before noon, on his way to the parking lot. Nobody knew where he was now or when he might return, but Fitch had a man waiting for him in the living room of Bungalow Thirteen. As soon as Carlin returned, he would be brought directly to Fitch for questioning.

"You talked to Carlin yourself yesterday, didn't you?" Fitch asked me.

"How'd you know about that?"

He smiled a knowing smile and motioned toward the swinging doors. "Somebody wrote your number on a pad by the phone in the kitchen. I also talked to a receptionist named Costanza Aguilar. She didn't know your name, but she gave a good description of you."

I found myself having to upgrade my initial assessment of him. "I did talk to Carlin," I said. "And I also talked to Perry. Sort of."

"What do you mean 'sort of'?"

"You've seen Perry's doctor, haven't you? I'm sure he'd have told you."

Fitch shook his head. "The only ones I've talked to so far are the receptionist, some high mucky-muck of an administrator, and the nurse who found the body. The old man's doctor's on my list, but I haven't had a chance to get to him yet."

"So you don't know about Perry's having Alzheimer's disease?"

"This is the first I heard of it," said Fitch.

"That's what I meant when I said 'sort of.' Up till yesterday I hadn't seen Perry in years. I had no idea how bad off he'd gotten. I only talked to him for a couple of minutes, which was long enough to find out he was pretty far gone. Carlin had to put him to bed."

Fitch had flipped open his notebook and was scribbling in it with a black Flair pen he'd taken from a pocket inside his jacket. "So what did you and Carlin talk about?"

I couldn't think of a reason to withhold the information. "Perry's son Ozzie came by my place to see me a couple of days ago. He wanted to hire me."

Fitch looked at me curiously. "For what?"

"He had a problem he wanted me to look into."

The lieutenant's eyebrows drew together. "I thought you were out of the private eye business."

"So did I."

Fitch looked more puzzled. "You mean you're actually working on a case for Ozzie Cole?"

I nodded. "At first I turned him down and told him to go see you guys at the sheriff's department. Then that night I got a phone call from Zeke Carlin, who said Perry wanted to see me. That's why I was out here yesterday. Carlin told me that Perry was anxious for me to take Ozzie's case. I suppose you could say I got talked into it."

Fitch tapped his mustache with his pen. "Can I ask what you're working on, or is that privileged?"

I waved my hand, a gesture of It's no big deal. "Ozzie thinks somebody's counterfeiting his wine."

Fitch's eyes widened. "No shit?"

"No shit. I was just down in La Jolla checking out a lead he gave me and trying to find out if somebody really is ripping him off. And if so, who?"

"*Is* somebody ripping him off?"

"It's a better-than-even possibility. But I don't know enough to say positively one way or the other just yet."

Fitch was tapping his pen against his upper lip once more. It seemed to help him sift through what I'd disclosed. He asked, "When was the last time you saw him? Ozzie, I mean?"

"Last night. I went over to his place and took him a contract to sign. He gave me a retainer."

"And before that?"

"Yesterday afternoon. I bumped into him right there." I pointed toward the bungalow's front entrance. "He was on his way out as I was coming in."

"Ozzie was here?"

I nodded. "We didn't bother to chat, because he wasn't in a very good mood." Fitch looked up from the notebook again, his expression questioning me. "I walked in on the tail end of an argument between Ozzie and his father," I explained.

I'd piqued Fitch's attention. "You don't happen to know what they were arguing about, do you?"

"Carlin said it had something to do with Perry's doctor wanting to admit him to the hospital, and that he didn't want to go. Whether that's really what they were fighting about, I'm afraid you're going to have to squeeze out of Carlin. Or Ozzie. I'm assuming you're planning to talk to him, too, sooner or later."

"Oh yeah," said Fitch. "But I can't till after he's been booked and he's got his lawyer with him."

Like a lot of police types, I have a personal alarm system wired somewhere in my cerebral cortex. More than once it has served to warn me that something is serious amiss. A few times it has even saved me from grievous injury.

My alarm was jangling right now. I looked at Fitch narrowly. "What do you mean, 'till after he's booked'?"

The lieutenant seemed confused. "Didn't I mention that we arrested Ozzie Cole?"

"For what?"

"I thought I mentioned it." He shrugged. "We're holding him on suspicion of first-degree murder."

My mouth dropped open.

Fitch said, "I'm sorry, Jack. I was sure I told you."

"No," I said darkly. "You didn't tell me."

"Then I guess I'm telling you now," he said.

NINE

I LEFT COSTA DEL SOL around midnight and drove home in a sour mood engendered by the news that Ozzie Cole was being held on suspicion of killing his father. It wasn't that Brad Fitch's explanation as to why Ozzie had been taken into custody lacked merit, though to my thinking what the cops had so far was mostly speculative or, at best, circumstantial.

Connie Aguilar, the receptionist, had seen Ozzie pull into the parking lot a little after one that afternoon, as she was returning to the ad building from lunch. Presumably he was on his way to visit Perry. Connie also happened to see Ozzie leaving not fifteen minutes later, his truck heading down the driveway in the direction of Highway 154. This information, along with a preliminary report from the coroner placing Perry's time of death between 11:00 a.m. and 2:00 p.m., put Ozzie in the wrong place at the wrong time. Fifteen minutes would be all anybody needed to administer a sedative to the old man and then jab a needle into the juncture of his left medial veins.

According to Fitch, Ozzie admitted knowing that Zeke Carlin had Wednesdays off. He also admitted dropping by his father's bungalow, but no one had answered his knock. Assuming Perry might be somewhere on the grounds in the company of a nurse or an orderly, Ozzie considered searching for his father. Then he changed his mind, decided what the fuck, and departed.

Fitch didn't think much of Ozzie's alibi, and I

couldn't blame him. Nonetheless, I played devil's advocate, suggesting that any number of people could have called on Perry between eleven and two. The lieutenant granted my point. I'd then asked if there was any indication as to whether whoever killed Perry possessed a high degree of skill in manipulating a hypodermic syringe. Fitch said that Perry had been poked deftly and neatly, as if by a trained professional. Then wouldn't it make sense, I wondered aloud, to look for Perry's killer among the medical staff here? That's when Fitch told me something about Ozzie I didn't know. Ozzie had joined the National Guard in the early 1970s—his way of avoiding the draft and being shipped to Southeast Asia—and the Guard had trained him to be a medic.

Strike two. Ozzie had the opportunity, and he had the necessary skill to commit the crime. He also admitted having been near the scene around the time his father was being bled to death. Barring the discovery of an eyewitness—which seemed about as likely as Perry's sitting up on his slab in the county morgue and announcing his killer's identity—all that was missing to build a rock-solid case was a motive. That's why, said Lieutenant Fitch, Ozzie was being held on *suspicion* of murder. Which meant he could be locked up for only forty-eight hours, then he had to either be formally charged with the crime or set free.

Then Fitch mentioned something I already knew, that three-quarters of all murders are solved within a couple of days of their occurrence. He seemed certain that before forty-eight hours had passed he'd dig up a proper motive and perhaps a piece or two of corroborating evidence. As long as Ozzie was in the jug, insisted Fitch, he couldn't be out covering his tracks.

That I wasn't convinced of Ozzie's guilt—and that

my old high school "buddy" appeared to be unswayed by my point of view—put me in a bad humor. It didn't help that I couldn't articulate why I didn't believe Ozzie had killed his father. It was strictly a hunch. I didn't appreciate Fitch's telling me that my hunch and a dollar could get me a cup of coffee at most any diner of my choice.

My black mood was exacerbated by fatigue. While driving home, I could feel a dull pain throbbing in my left temple. It was only when I pulled into the gravel lot in front of my house that I remembered I'd been up since six that morning and on the go since seven. Over that time I'd traveled close to five hundred miles by air, rail, and road. I'd earned the right to be grumpy.

That was why I snapped at my dad, who was waiting up for me. For the second time in three nights he was up past his bedtime on account of something that concerned me more than it did him. When I told him how I didn't care for his missing so much sleep due to his inability to keep his nose out of my business, he snapped right back—in just as cross and soreheaded and weary a tone of voice as my own. Then he hobbled to his room, muttering ugly things about me under his breath, and slammed his door.

I trudged to my bed, pissed off at myself for barking at Dad, feeling guilty about it, and hearing in my head Grandma Donne's homily about the apple and the tree. And telling myself: Fuck it. I'll apologize in the morning. And trying to ignore the little voice in the back of my mind that cautioned me about going to bed without having made up after a fight with somebody you cared for, because you never knew what awful things might happen while you were asleep.

MY HEAD WAS STILL throbbing when I awoke at six-thirty the next morning. My back and neck and shoulders and legs ached, as well. It occurred to me that what I needed was something I'd unintentionally avoided for the past few days because I'd gotten so wrapped up in all the hugger-mugger surrounding the Cole family. I hadn't had any real exercise since the day before Ozzie Cole dropped by to give me a taste of his bogus pinot. Today my body was letting me know how displeased it was with my inattention. No wonder I felt so crappy.

I climbed out of bed, dressed myself in sweat clothes and flip-flop sandals, and packed a small gym bag with my gear—Speedo trunks, athletic supporter, goggles, towel. Coming out of my bedroom, I noticed that the house was dim and quiet. The door to my father's bedroom was closed. I paused outside his room for a moment, pressing an ear to the door and listening carefully. He was still asleep, his breathing deep and regular.

I crept out of the house, got into my Cherokee, and drove away as quietly as I could. My destination was my alma mater, San Tomas Senior High School.

San Tomas's athletic director, Mr. Vogelsmeier, is an old friend of the family. He's been at the school forever—he was AD even before I became a student there—and he has a warm spot in his heart for a lot of his ex-jocks. I exploited my relationship with him by getting him to allow me nearly unrestricted access to the school's Olympic-sized pool. Mr. Vogelsmeier saw to it that I had my own key to the field house that the pool occupied. I could use the facility any time, regardless of whether the school itself was open, just so long as none of the PE classes wanted it or there was no swim team event scheduled, like a practice session or a meet.

I try to use the pool three times a week. Like many athletes—or, I should say, *former* athletes—I'm something of a workout junkie. I got into swimming as part of my therapy after the first time I wracked up my knee, when I caught my spikes while climbing a chain-link fence in a futile attempt to pull down an opponent's home run. During my rehab, I discovered that I enjoyed swimming more than any other aerobic exercise I'd attempted over the years. Even after I got my knee back into good enough shape to tolerate the strain of hard running, I kept on swimming. After my knee was traumatized a second time—by a .22-caliber bullet instead of an outfield fence—there was no question that I'd have to abandon serious running for good. Fortunately, my knee healed to the point where most of the time I can walk without limping. I can even jog for a quarter mile or so before the pain really starts in on me.

I arrived at the field house at seven. As I'd hoped, the place was deserted. I went into the locker room and put on my swimming togs, then came out, stepped onto a starting platform, dove into the water, and began a measured, steady Australian crawl. Within minutes my body was moving of its own volition. I allowed my mind to float free, focusing on nothing in particular, letting whatever might bubble up from my unconscious do so without coercion or interference.

Forty-five minutes later I was back in the locker room, toweling myself off. I was feeling frustrated because my unconscious hadn't come up with anything memorable. But I was also pleased that the aches and pains of inactivity had been supplanted by the more gratifying soreness that accompanies a serious, prolonged, systematic taxing of the muscles. My body was no longer peeved at me. I felt sharp and alert. I was also hungry. It had been nearly fifteen hours since I'd had anything to eat.

Dad was up and dressed by the time I returned home. He was in the kitchen preparing breakfast—scrambled eggs, toast, fresh-squeezed orange juice, coffee. As I came in he regarded me coolly, until I apologized for the way I'd talked to him the night before. He smiled, apology accepted, and asked me if I'd like to join him for breakfast.

While we ate, I summarized what had occurred since I'd spoken to him from La Jolla. Like me, Dad found it all but impossible to believe that Ozzie Cole had killed his father. "What's with this Lieutenant Fitch, anyway?" Dad asked. "Is he just goofy or what?"

I shrugged. "I don't think he's any goofier than the average local cop. In fact, he struck me as having a little more on the ball than a lot of 'em I've known. Notwithstanding this hero-worship thing he seems to have for me."

"That's what I was talking about," said Dad. "Isn't that a little odd?"

"Being odd doesn't necessarily make him a bad investigator." I took a sip of my coffee. "I keep trying to look at this through Fitch's eyes. If I didn't know the Coles personally, I might think Ozzie did it, too."

Dad's reply was interrupted by the ringing of the phone on the wall near the refrigerator. "I got it," I said. I crossed the kitchen and picked up the phone. "Donne Vineyards."

"Jack Donne, please."

I recognized Fitch's voice. Clapping a hand over the mouthpiece, I whispered to my dad, "Speak of the devil." He showed me a puzzled look, until he heard me say, "Hello, Lieutenant. What can I do for you?"

"I just thought you'd like to know that I talked to Zeke Carlin," said Fitch. "He came home a little after one in the morning. He'd spent the day at the beach in Gaviota, then he went in to Santa Barbara to have dinner and see a movie."

"How'd he react to the news that Perry was dead?" I asked.

"He was pretty broken up about it. If I had to guess, I'd say that he and the old man were a lot closer than your typical employer and employee."

"That was my take, too," I said. "You didn't happen to ask him if he had an alibi, did you?"

"He said he was with some 'lady friend' from Lompoc. She works at Vandenberg Air Force Base. He wasn't anxious to be more specific, but I finally got a name out of him."

"Did you check her out?"

"That may not be necessary," said Fitch.

"How come?"

"That has to do with the other reason I'm calling. Ozzie Cole asked me to ask you to come pick him up."

"Pick him up where?"

"At the sheriff's station in Solvang. That's where I am right now. I'm using one of the desks in the detectives' bull pen."

"Whoa, whoa, back up a little," I said. "You're letting Ozzie go?"

"I have to," said Fitch. "He's made bond."

I said, "This is the first time I ever heard of somebody having to make bond on a charge of suspicion of something."

"That's because the charge got changed," Fitch said.

"To what?"

He hesitated briefly before saying, "First-degree murder."

I could tell that Fitch was trying to keep from gloating, but he wasn't managing very well. "I told you I'd find a motive before my forty-eight hours were up," he went on. "It didn't take anywhere near that long."

"You found a motive?"

"The exact same one I expected to find."

The sense of disorientation I'd felt the night before, when Dad first told me that Perry Cole had been killed, came back to me. "Wait a minute, wait a minute. What motive were you expecting to find?"

"What else?" said Fitch. "Money."

TEN

THE DETECTIVES' bull pen at the sheriff's substation in Solvang is smaller than that of a big city precinct's. Only a few investigators are assigned to the bureau operating out of Solvang, and none of them specialize. Instead they handle whatever comes along—robbery, homicide, arson, bunco, you name it. If a specialist is needed, for example, a homicide investigator like Brad Fitch, he gets sent up from headquarters in Santa Barbara. Given a crime such as this one, involving the murder of one of the county's wealthier and more renowned citizens, the specialist from headquarters is generally allowed all the time and manpower he requires to break the case.

As I was pulling my Cherokee into a parking spot near the intersection of Pine Street and Old Mission Drive, across the street from the sheriff's station, I thought about something I hadn't realized until after my retirement from the Treasury Department. The investigators' bull pens in all law enforcement agencies tend to be depressing as hell. Much of that has to do with the physical environment. Most bull pens have about half the floor space of a junior high school auditorium, give or take a few square feet, and they are furnished as cheaply as possible. The detectives' desks are arranged either in some more or less orderly fashion in the middle of the open space, or else they're separated into individual carrels by dividers—when the organization can afford such a luxury—which provide the illusion of privacy. The ventilation and lighting are invariably bad. The walls are painted one of three colors: institutional green, institutional beige, or institutional yellow. The floors are always grimy. The air usually reeks of body odor, stale tobacco smoke, rancid coffee.

The other factor contributing to the dreary atmosphere has to do with the nature of the business conducted there. You have one of only four reasons for visiting a police station. If you don't work there, then you've either been the victim of a crime, the witness to a crime, or the perpetrator of a crime. It follows that almost all of the emotional energy discharged in such a setting is negative. A certain amount of glum psychic residue—what back in the sixties and seventies used to be called "bad vibes"—can't help but build up over time. You sit in a room like that long enough, and the effluvium of misery and fear that's accrued over the years becomes palpable.

Climbing out of my Jeep, I noticed a knot of minivans parked haphazardly in front of the sheriff's station. Each van had a massive antenna mounted on its roof, and each bore the call letters of a TV or radio station. Most of the vans appeared to have come from Santa Barbara or Santa Maria, although I saw one that was all the way up from Los Angeles. As I made my way toward the station entrance, I was thinking that Perry Cole's murder was a bigger media event than I'd imagined. I suppose I shouldn't have been surprised, but I was anyway.

I stopped at the front desk and got directions to the bull pen from a surly, swarthy-skinned sergeant with a Frito Bandito mustache. He jabbed a thumb in the direction of a short corridor off to one side of his desk. I thanked him courteously. He acknowledged me with a grunt, then went back to reading the newspaper I'd pulled his attention from.

Passing through a set of double doors, I approached the steel-case desk behind which Lieutenant Fitch was sitting. There was only one other detective in the room, seated behind a desk in a far corner, chatting amiably on the phone. Fitch looked up at me from the file he was reading, nodded a greeting, and motioned with the open folder in his hand to an empty chair beside the desk. "How'd you like to hear what the pathologist had to say about Perry Cole?" he asked as I settled myself.

I nodded: Go ahead.

He peered at the report in the folder and said without looking at me, "The cause of death was a massive loss of blood."

"What a surprise."

My sarcasm evaded him. "There were remnants in his stomach of the last meal he'd had," he continued. "Breakfast, apparently, not all the way digested. Cream of Wheat. What's more interesting are the traces of phenobarbital they found in his blood. According to the pathologist, it was probably prescribed as a soporific. You know, something that—"

"Something that puts you to sleep. I know what the word means."

"One of the evidence techs found a bottle of sleeping pills in the medicine cabinet above the bathroom sink," he said.

"I guess that clears up one mystery, anyway."

Fitch nodded absently, my sarcasm once again having eluded him. "Where the heparin in his system came from is something else altogether."

I shook my head. "Heparin?"

His look challenged me. "Don't tell me you know what that is, too?"

"As a matter of fact, I do." The startled expression on his face gave me a feeling of pleasure. "My dad was on heparin for a while, after he had his stroke. It's some kind of blood thinner."

Judging by Fitch's incredulous stare, I'd just demonstrated that I was some kind of ratiocinating genius. "I didn't know Perry had a problem with his circulation," I said.

"It wasn't that," said Fitch, still registering awe. "Heparin's an anticoagulant. Whoever gave it to him did it to keep his blood from clotting the needle, so he could keep right on bleeding till he was drained dry."

I grimaced, recalling the grisly image of Perry's blood-soaked bed. Pushing the recollection aside, I said, "I assume you're thinking that this is another piece of evidence against Ozzie."

Fitch showed me a smug smile. "You'd have to have a medical background to even know about such a thing."

"I don't have a medical background, and I know about it."

"You've got to admit, Jack, you're kind of a special case."

I shrugged, accepting the compliment. "Where do you suppose it came from?"

"They've got a pharmacy right there at the old folks' home," answered Fitch. "Two, in fact. One's part of the hospital, and one's in the administration building. The second one is where the patients go to get their prescriptions filled. I talked to the chief pharmacist. They don't even carry heparin in stock at the pharmacy the patients use."

"So it came from the hospital?"

"Probably," he answered. "Though it's possible it came from someplace else. According to the pharmacist, this stuff is used almost exclusively in hospital settings, because you have to administer it intravenously. It's not usually something you can pick up at the corner drugstore."

I rubbed my jaw thoughtfully. "Are they missing any heparin from the hospital?"

"They're taking inventory," said Fitch. "I should know by this afternoon."

I took a moment to digest the information, then said, "I imagine you've got a theory about how Ozzie managed to get hold of the stuff."

Fitch tossed the file onto his desk. He leaned back in his chair, rested his feet atop the file folder, crossed his ankles, and knotted his hands behind his head. Casual. "Not just yet. But it'll come, sooner or later. Hell, Ozzie might even decide to tell me himself how he did it and save me the trouble of having to figure it out."

I felt the same sour irritation I'd felt as I drove home from Costa del Sol the night before. I had to work at keeping an expression of annoyance off my face. "What about the alleged motive you mentioned on the phone?"

Fitch raised an eyebrow. " 'Alleged' motive? You sound like a fucking attorney."

"So what about it?"

I decided that "smug" was not Lieutenant Fitch's most appealing look. "Ozzie's lawyer came by to see me this morning. Some guy named Daniel Wikert. You know him?"

I shook my head.

"We must've talked for an hour," continued Fitch.

"He seemed like a decent enough guy, for a lawyer, but he wasn't more than marginally interested in getting me to let Ozzie go." The detective made a face. "I'll tell you one thing. I sure wouldn't want him handling a case for me."

"Because he wouldn't force you to release Ozzie?"

"That and something else."

"What?"

Fitch waved a hand in the air. "You'd've been amazed at how easy it was for me to get Ozzie's motive out of him. I wasn't even trying to trap him. *He's* the one who brought up the subject."

"What subject?"

"Probate," answered Fitch. "Wikert wanted to know how long it'd be before he could start executing Perry's will."

I frowned, confused. "Hold on. Ozzie's lawyer is also *Perry's* lawyer?"

Fitch nodded. "Wikert represents the whole family. The other brothers, too."

The idea of the same lawyer representing everyone in the Cole family—most of whom hated one another's guts—struck me as ridiculous, though by now I should have realized that "ridiculous" was an apt descriptive for a lot of the Coles' behavior. I asked Fitch, "How did Wikert give you a motive for Ozzie's wanting to kill his old man?"

"Simple," said Fitch. "He let slip what's in Perry's will."

"Which is what?"

"That the bulk of the old man's estate goes to Ozzie. Except for a few odds and ends, he's virtually the sole beneficiary. The other brothers don't get squat."

I was rocked by the information. "You're shitting me."

"Nope." Fitch grinned, displaying pleasure that he could show off a little for me. "Ozzie's set to inherit nearly everything, including a big piece of what his brothers have control of at the moment."

"Hang on a second," I said. "Isn't it the law in California that if you're convicted of murdering somebody, you're not entitled to any share of your victim's estate?"

Fitch nodded. "Except Ozzie didn't know that. I asked him if he was aware of the inheritance laws, and he said no." Fitch was grinning again. "Not that he'd ever get a chance to enjoy it. Hell, he'll be lucky if he doesn't end up in the gas chamber."

"Yeah," I muttered. I was trying to shake the feeling that someone had bopped me on the forehead with a ball-peen hammer. "He's lucky, all right."

I SAT ON an uncomfortable wooden bench across from the desk sergeant, waiting for Ozzie Cole to be brought out from his hold-over cell. Eventually he emerged from the hallway beside the front desk, accompanied by a turnkey. It didn't appear as if a night in jail had had much effect on Ozzie one way or another. He looked no happier or crankier than usual.

I joined him at the desk, where he accepted the envelope containing his valuables from the sergeant. After Ozzie checked to make sure everything was there and signed the release form attesting to that, I guided him toward a side exit. It probably wasn't a good idea to go out the front, I told him, on account of the media buzzards gathered there.

Minutes later we were in my Jeep, heading north on

Alamo Pintado Road, in the direction of San Tomas. As we were passing through Ballard, Ozzie turned to me. "So what did you find out in San Diego?"

I glanced at him, then returned my attention to the road. "Don't you have something a little more pressing to worry about?"

He snorted. "You mean this bullshit about me killing my father?"

"If I were you," I said, "I wouldn't just blow it off. There's a reasonably sharp homicide detective back there who's damn near positive you did it."

"You mean Fitch?" Ozzie snorted again, sounding like a sick horse. "That dickhead. He's as full of shit as the day is long. Him *and* that asshole attorney of mine." Another snort. "Wikert. Can you believe that son of a bitch is refusing to defend me?"

I could feel my alarm beginning to jangle. "Come again?"

"He told me he couldn't take the case on account of criminal law not being his area of expertise. He's afraid he might botch up my defense. He said he'd find somebody else he could recommend to me. I tried to tell him it wouldn't be too long before the cops found out it was all a crock anyway, and that as soon as they dropped the charges, we'd sue their asses for false arrest."

The explanation made enough sense to quiet my alarm system, though I couldn't help feeling that there was something not entirely kosher about Mr. Wikert. The thought nagged at me, like an itch you can't quite reach. I debated whether to mention Wikert's spilling the beans to Fitch to find out if Ozzie knew about his father's will and see what reaction it might squeeze out of him if he didn't.

Before I could make up my mind, though, he repeated

his earlier question. "So what'd you find out in San Diego?"

There wasn't any reason not to say, particularly since he was paying for the information. I recounted my visit to the Mission Bay Wine Company and my trips to the other wine stores in the area. I also related what I knew about Teddie Ortiz.

"You see?" Ozzie exclaimed self-righteously after I'd finished. "Didn't I tell you somebody was trying to fuck me over?"

"That's the way it looks," I said, foregoing any stronger apology.

We'd reached the turnoff to the narrow road leading to the O.C. Vineyards property. As I swung the Jeep onto the road, Ozzie asked, "So what's our next move?"

"'Our' next move?"

"You know what I mean."

"Look, Ozzie," I said, "don't you think maybe we ought to back-burner your counterfeiting problem till after this business about your father gets settled?"

"Hell, no. This is important to me. Besides, aren't you charging me a healthy chunk of change to find out who's ripping me off?"

I sighed. "If that's what you want."

"That's what I want," he said.

ELEVEN

AFTER DROPPING OZZIE OFF, I went straight home. I arrived too late to join Dad and Jesus for lunch; they'd already finished eating and were off in the vineyards checking our chardonnay buds. I made myself a sandwich from the leftover meat loaf Dad had prepared for dinner the night before, poured a glass of milk, then carried my lunch with me into my office.

While I ate, I thumbed through my Rolodex. I was looking for the names of retail wineshops between here and San Diego, trying to deduce which ones might be targeted by Teddie Ortiz. By the time I finished my lunch, I'd compiled a list of a dozen or so likely prospects. Most of them were in the Los Angeles area, although three were in Orange County—one in San Clemente, one in Newport Beach, and one in Irvine—and another two were in Santa Barbara.

I returned to the kitchen to put my dirty dishes in the dishwasher and refill my glass of milk, then went back to my office and reached for the telephone. My first call was to Alan Feinberg in Los Angeles. I caught him just as he was returning from lunch himself. He hadn't expected to hear from me again so soon, but he didn't sound disappointed about it. "What's up, boychik?" he asked.

"I'm coming down to L.A. tomorrow," I said, "and I wanted to make sure you're gonna be around."

"What time?"

"As early in the day as possible."

"I usually get in around nine or nine-thirty. I can arrange to come in before then, if you like."

"Nine-thirty is fine," I said. "That's about the earliest I can make it myself."

"This have anything to do with that business we discussed yesterday?"

"Yeah. In fact, there are one or two favors you can do for me, if you got the time."

"Name 'em."

"First off, I need a picture of Teddie Ortiz. Any kind of mug shot will do, just so it's fairly recent."

"No problem," said Alan. "I can get a printout directly from the computer. What else?"

"I know I said yesterday I didn't want you to try and track him down just yet, but it's gotten a little more imperative that I catch up with him ASAP. I was wondering if you could get a line on somebody who might know where he is."

"How come it's all of a sudden so imperative you find him?"

I gave Alan a brief account of what had happened to Perry Cole. When I'd finished, he let out a low whistle. "You really think Teddie's mixed up in a murder? As I recall, he wasn't exactly the killer type."

"Maybe he's changed," I said.

Alan chuckled. "Maybe while he was in the joint he grew some *cojones,* eh?"

"Maybe," I said. "That's why I'd like to find him. So I can ask."

We confirmed our plans to meet at Alan's office at nine-thirty, and I hung up. Immediately I made a second phone call, this one to Maggie McKenney at her office in Buellton. I'd found myself thinking of her often while I was traveling the day before. Coming back on the plane from San Diego, I'd realized that I hadn't even told her that, per her urging, I found myself back in the detective business.

She greeted me cheerfully. "Hey, stranger. I didn't think you could go a single day without hearing my voice, much less two. I was just about to give up on you for good."

"Sorry about that," I said. "I had to go out of town."

"Where'd you go?" she asked, a note of genuine surprise in her voice.

"La Jolla."

"Without me?" she asked, pretending to be petulant.

"It was strictly business, dear. Which, incidentally, is pretty much your fault."

"*My* fault?"

"Uh-huh. It's all on account of you that I decided to get myself mixed up with Ozzie Cole. Which I'm beginning to regret."

I gave her a brief synopsis of what had happened since Monday evening, and it struck me while I was speaking that it seemed a lot more than three days since Ozzie had paid me his unexpected visit. Too much activity compressed into a short space of time—combined with the fatigue I was suffering from not getting enough sleep—created the dreary impression that I'd been involved with the Coles much, much longer than I'd actually been. Too long, in fact.

When I came to the part about having been in the room where Perry's murder took place only a few hours postmortem, Maggie sucked in her breath sharply. "Good god, Jack," she said, her voice edged with consternation and horror. "You don't really think Ozzie

Cole could have done something that awful to his own *father*, do you?"

"*I* don't. But the cops don't particularly care about what I think. What matters is what *they* think. Unfortunately, I also can't seem to convince Ozzie of the danger in dismissing them outright, regardless of whether they're right or wrong." I exhaled a weary sigh.

"Poor baby." She paused momentarily, as if making up her mind about something. "Maybe you and I should get together tonight. You could probably stand to spend a little quality time with someone who's barely heard of the Cole family. I suppose I could be talked into barbecuing something at my place. And by the way, I videotaped *Murder My Sweet*, which I haven't gotten around to watching yet..."

I sighed again. "I've got an early appointment in L.A. tomorrow morning. I was hoping to get to bed at a reasonable hour."

She said in a sultry voice, "I think that can be arranged."

I EASED BACK in my chair, wondering about how dicey a hunch I might be playing. I knew that Teddie Ortiz could fold his con any time, long before I had a chance to bag him. He could have folded it already, although I doubted that. It was only a hunch, but Teddie was the kind of weasel who, so long as he was still scoring and wasn't sensing any heat bearing down on him, would push it as far as it would go.

Brad Fitch telephoned while I was still cogitating on the subject of Teddie Ortiz. The sheriff's department had received a report from the hospital pharmacy at Costa del Sol, and as Fitch suspected, they were missing a supply of heparin. He told me he was still working on a way for Ozzie to have copped the stuff. I told him to call back if he came up with a theory.

Dad returned from the vineyards around three-thirty. I called to him as he was heading down the hallway toward the kitchen. He poked his head into the office doorway, the look on his face inquiring as to what I wanted.

"How far did you and Jesus get today?" I asked.

"About a quarter of the way through the chardonnay." Having to use a cane to caterpillar his way along row after row of grapevines slows him considerably, but he refuses to tend the plants any less meticulously than he ever did. "I'm hoping we'll be through by the weekend."

"I apologize for neglecting my chores," I said. "We'd probably be done with the chard already if I'd been around to help."

Dad shrugged. "You've been busy. It's not like what you're doing isn't important. Besides, I'm one of the ones who talked you into it." He paused. "Speaking of which, how're things going?"

I spread my hands noncommittally. "About as well as can be expected. Ozzie made bond, and they released him without much of a fuss. He didn't have a whole lot to say, other than for me to let you know that Perry's funeral is Saturday. He'd appreciate it if we could be there."

I told Dad about my trip to L.A. the next morning. After I'd finished, he made a face and looked away for a moment. When he turned back to me, I could tell by his expression that he was ready to change the subject from matters concerning Ozzie Cole. "You having dinner at home tonight?" he asked.

I shook my head. "I'm going over to Maggie's."

He raised his eyebrows suggestively. "I thought you were tired."

"I promise I'll get a good night's sleep."

"See that you do." He started off toward the kitchen, stopped, then returned to the doorway. "I almost forgot. Uncle Gerry called while you were out. He wants you to call him back. He said he had some news he thought you might like to hear."

I thanked him, and he shuffled away. I pulled over the phone and punched up my uncle's private number at work. A deep, sexy, contralto voice answered. "Gerald Donne's office."

"Grace? It's Jack. Is my uncle around? I'm returning his call."

"One second, Jack. I'll get him."

I was put on hold for too brief a time to do what I often do when I call Uncle Gerry at his office, which is ruminate about the envy I feel over his having Grace Treadway in his employ. She came to him nine and a half years ago, shortly after the death of her husband from a horrible intestinal cancer that had eaten him alive, slowly. Hal Treadway had been Uncle Gerry's roommate in law school. Grace was forty-three years old at the time of Hal's death. The two of them were childless, she and he having formed the sort of bond that couples occasionally do, the kind of union that cannot be intruded upon, not even by children. She came to Gerry because Hal's estate was in a shambles, having been raided by his less than scrupulous partners in the investment firm he'd co-founded. Grace was all but destitute when she knocked on Gerry's door. The partners ended up being as slick and careful as they were unprincipled, and there wasn't much Gerry could recover for Grace. So he offered her a job instead.

She remains the same stunningly handsome woman she was at the time Gerry hired her. That she's undeniably attractive is one of the reasons my uncle has never regretted doing his late friend Hal a favor by giving his widow a job, Uncle Gerry being as much an aesthete as any Donne male. But the real reason he's had no regrets is because Grace is so good at what she does. Often I tease them about being romantically involved, and both she and Gerry assure me that their relationship is nothing more than platonic. I believe them. They are as fond of each other as two human beings can be, but Grace will never love another man the way she loved her husband, and Uncle Gerry's one and only mistress is his work. Consequently, they make for a terrific pair. They look out for each other, which to my thinking is one of the best relationships you could have with another individual.

When my uncle came on the line, he said robustly, "Hey, Jack! Nice of you to get back to me so quick!"

"Any time I get a call from a lawyer, I return it promptly," I said. "What's up?"

"I just thought I'd pass on a little more gossip concerning June and Grant Cole."

"You heard about Perry, didn't you?" I asked.

His tone darkened. "I heard."

"The funeral's the day after tomorrow," I said. "Dad and I are planning to go. You want to come with us?"

"I'll check my schedule and let you know. By the way, I also heard about Ozzie being arrested."

"Is that asinine or what?" I said with irritation. "Ozzie had nothing to do with what happened to Perry."

"You sound awfully sure about that."

"I am sure."

"You have any proof?"

"So far it's just a feeling, but it's a strong one. I'm still looking into Ozzie's counterfeiting problem and hoping something'll turn up there. It strikes me there's a good chance of a connection someplace."

"You'd think there'd be, wouldn't you," said Gerry. "Anyway, speaking of the Coles, I did a little more digging on the q.t. I've been trying to confirm that story of Terry Elliott's one way or the other. It turns out he was right—June and Grant had a major deal in the works. Not with Trimbach, like I thought, but with somebody in that league. I hope you don't mind, but I promised my source I wouldn't tell who."

"No problem," I said. "Go on."

"The deal fell through," Gerry continued, "because the Cole brothers' balance sheet isn't looking so hot these days. They've been overextending themselves the last several years, investing in a lot of expensive new equipment, buying up land in Washington and Oregon and northern California, that sort of thing. Then boom, the recession hits, the dollar goes to hell in Europe and Japan, and the next thing you know, they're hemorrhaging money."

"How bad?" I asked.

"Very bad."

I thought for a moment. "You don't happen to know the Coles' attorney, do you? Some guy named Wikert?"

Gerry chuckled mirthlessly. "You're asking me do I know Daniel Gardner Wikert? 'Whiplash' Danny Wikert?"

"Beg your pardon?"

Gerry chuckled again. "That used to be his nickname when he was down in L.A. This was some years ago, you understand, before he moved to Santa Ynez. As he's gotten older, he's become more respectable. Not much, but a little. I presume I don't have to spell out to you why he used to be called Whiplash.''

"I think I can guess," I said.

"Then to answer your question, yeah, I know him. Why do you ask?''

"Something occurred to me while you were talking about Grant's and June's financial situation. Wikert was in Solvang this morning making arrangements to get Ozzie out of jail, and he happened to let slip what was in Perry's will to the detective in charge of the investigation.''

My uncle sounded puzzled. "What do you mean, he let slip what was in Perry's will?''

"Just what I said. The guy running the investigation used to play ball with me in high school, and we've gotten pretty chummy these last couple of days. He said Wikert told him what was in Perry's will without any prompting at all.''

I could picture the dubious expression on my uncle's face. "That doesn't make sense," he said. "No lawyer I've ever known would be dumb enough to let anything 'slip' to anybody, especially a cop. Not even Danny Wikert.''

"That's what I thought, too. Why I mention it is because what's in the will is what made the cops decide to charge Ozzie with first-degree murder. According to Perry's will, Ozzie gets damn near everything," I said. "And June and Grant get nothing.''

Gerry murmured, "Holy shit...''

"Ozzie also told me that Wikert's refusing to defend him. According to Wikert, criminal law isn't his forte. He's going to set Ozzie up with somebody else.''

"That's probably the only good idea the son of a bitch has had," Gerry said grudgingly. "He already represents every member of the family, which is silly as hell considering how poorly they get along. He probably would've been thrown off the case anyway for conflict of interest."

"That's why I asked if you knew him," I said. "I was thinking, since Wikert *does* represent everybody in the family, what if he's got more loyalty to one faction than he does to the others? What if he told June and Grant what was in their father's will, just like he told the cops? If the will is supposed to've given Ozzie a motive, what about his brothers—?"

"Slow down, son. If you're implying what it seems like you're implying, why would June and Grant kill their father if they've been cut out of his will? Where's the profit in that?"

"You're not thinking it through far enough," I said. "What if they killed Perry in such a way that it looks like *Ozzie* did it? You see what I'm saying? If Ozzie's the killer, he can't inherit a dime. In that case, maybe everything would fall back to June and Grant."

Another mirthless chuckle. "That's rather Byzantine, isn't it? It'd make for a helluva conspiracy, even if I thought June and Grant were clever enough to think up a scheme like that, much less had the balls to pull it off."

I scowled, chiding myself. "I suppose it does sound a little nutty at that."

"'Nutty' isn't the word for it." Gerry paused for a moment, then said, "This information about Wikert's blabbing to the cops about what was in Perry's will is damned interesting. Why don't I snoop around some more? I might be able to use this inheritance stuff as leverage to get a few people to open up for me. In the process I might also end up scrounging some dirt on Danny Wikert, which would give me a certain amount of personal satisfaction. I'll call you back if I find out anything." He paused again. "Something smells here, Jack. Something stinks to high heaven."

"Tell me about it," I said.

TWELVE

THANKFULLY, MY EVENING with Maggie at her place off Ballard Canyon Road outside Buellton couldn't have been more pleasant. For dinner we grilled a couple of thresher shark steaks, which she'd found time to marinate in a mustard and tarragon sauce of her own invention. The fish and the steamed asparagus tips and the boiled new potatoes and the fresh sourdough bread she'd bought from a bakery near her office went well with the sauvignon blanc I'd brought with me. We had avocado pie and coffee for dessert, after which we retired to the sofa in the living room with snifters of Calvados. She snuggled beside me, her legs folded beneath her. I rested my arm on the back of the sofa behind her, the two of us watching *Murder My Sweet,* the only light in the room coming from the TV set.

It was still early when the movie ended, not quite ten o'clock, but I felt so serene and drowsy that I was more than ready for sleep. Any thoughts I might have had of Ozzie Cole and his family had floated away, as wispy and insubstantial as fog. As Maggie got up to switch off the television and VCR, I stretched and yawned and smacked my lips like a fat, lazy tomcat. Maggie turned away from the TV, regarding my indolent leer. Then she took me by the hand and led me to her bedroom.

I woke up alone at six o'clock, more refreshed than I'd felt in days. I could hear the shower running in the bathroom attached to the bedroom. I threw back the covers and climbed naked from the bed, crossing to the chair onto which I'd tossed my clothes the night before. Slipping on my trousers and undershirt, I padded barefoot into Maggie's kitchen, intending to surprise her by fixing breakfast. She surprised me instead by having beaten me to the punch. The coffee was already made, and places had been set at the small dinette table in the breakfast nook. A basket of warmed blueberry muffins lay in the middle of the table, covered by a cloth napkin. All that was left for me to do was to squeeze a couple of glasses' worth of fresh orange juice and pour coffee into the cups she'd set on the table.

Maggie came into the kitchen as I was replacing the coffee urn on its warmer. She was dressed in a long silk kimono tied around her waist. Her wet hair was wrapped in a bath towel. The fresh fragrance, the contours of her body outlined beneath the silk robe, the memory of the fine, taut flesh now so tantalizingly hidden—all conspired to cause a stirring I found hard to resist.

We ate breakfast, then I showered while she dressed for work. She looked wonderful, and I told her so. She knows that I admire her appearance, and not merely on the level of sexual aesthetics, although that's certainly part of it. Maggie is one of those people who possess not only a distinct sense of how to present themselves to others, but have superlative taste as well. It isn't something you can learn, like why it's not a good idea to serve red wine with baked cod, nor is it something that begins and ends with an awareness of your physical attributes or the style in which you dress. It has to do with your very demeanor. The lucky few—like Maggie—seem to be born with it. The rest of us will never be anything but uncouth slobs.

During breakfast I'd asked her if she wanted to come

with my father and me to Perry Cole's funeral the next day. She turned me down, not because she thought there was anything creepy about the event but because she didn't really know the family. She then remarked that never before in her life had anyone asked her to go on a date to a funeral. This, she said, was yet another example of why she enjoyed going out with me, because of my unique opinion of what sorts of places women liked to be taken to by men who hoped to show them a good time. That's me, I said. When it comes to the ladies, I like to knock 'em dead. She groaned and threw her napkin at me. For a time, she let me believe my pun was so bad that she wouldn't go out with me ever again, before finally agreeing to have dinner with me Saturday night.

MAGGIE AND I left the house together at seven o'clock, she on her way to her office, me somewhat reluctantly making the drive to Los Angeles I'd evaded on Wednesday.

Ordinarily—if the freeway traffic is moving at a reasonable pace—I can make it from Santa Ynez to L.A. in two hours. Knowing that I was likely to catch a good portion of the morning commuter rush, and also knowing that my destination was all the way downtown, I was allowing myself an extra thirty minutes' worth of driving time to ensure that I'd be at Alan Feinberg's office by nine-thirty. I started the Cherokee, belted myself in, popped in the Van Morrison *Greatest Hits* disc I'd been listening to a lot lately, backed out of Maggie's driveway, and headed south.

The extra half hour turned out not to be enough. Congestion on the 101 started up just the other side of Thousand Oaks. By the time I reached Encino, it was stop and go. By nine-thirty, when I was at last reaching the juncture where the Ventura and Hollywood freeways split, I found out what the problem was. The driver of a Honda Civic had decided too late that he was too many lanes over to make the exchange between freeways, but had gone ahead and attempted it anyway. In the process, he'd sideswiped a brand-new Lexus sedan. The two cars had been pulled off to the shoulder, but that didn't prevent the rubberneckers from slowing down to gawk. As I rolled past the pair of crumpled cars, I saw a beleaguered-looking CHP officer standing between the owners—a young Korean man and a well-tailored, middle-aged businesswoman—holding them at arm's length, trying to keep them from tearing out one another's throats. Another shitty day in paradise, I thought. One more reason to be glad I didn't reside in this town anymore.

I turned down the volume on the CD player and reached for the cellular phone mounted beneath the stereo. The phone was a Christmas gift from my dad, one which I'd accepted a little unwillingly. I have an aversion to phones in general and car phones in particular. To me, the telephone is another of modern life's necessary evils. I realize that there are important reasons for contacting your fellow human beings on short notice, and for that purpose a telephone is indispensable. But I've never been one for casual phone schmoozing, having always preferred to deal with people face-to-face. And I feel a special dislike for car phones because I can't help being fearful of sooner or later finding myself slammed into by some asshole who's got only one hand on his steering wheel and is too busy yakking to pay attention to what he really should be paying attention to.

There are times, however, when—as my father and my uncle told me on Christmas morning—the car phone might come in handy. Like now, when I was able to call Alan at his office and inform him that I was running late.

It was ten minutes to ten when I finally arrived downtown. The Bureau had recently moved. In my day, the ATF's Field Office was in the Federal Building on Los Angeles Street, within spitting distance of L.A.'s city hall. Currently the Bureau was posted in the World Trade Center on Figueroa Street, near Third, not far from where I exited from the freeway. By 9:55 I was parking my Jeep, and by 10:00 I was striding into my ex-partner's eighth-floor cubbyhole.

As I entered, Alan greeted me with a grin. He rose from behind a stack of paperwork that littered his desk, looking much the way he had the last time I'd seen him, nearly a year ago—a bit thicker around the waist and thinner at the hairline, maybe, but otherwise the same. Though he's an inch or so taller than I am, to many people we appear to be the same height. It's because Alan's posture is rather vulturelike: Standing or sitting, he tends to hunch forward, stoop-shouldered, thrusting his head and neck ahead of the rest of his body. I supposed the vulture image served him well in his current capacity. I knew from experience that young agents often regarded the assistant special agent in charge as a hatchet man around the office, someone who executed a lot of the Bureau's dirty work, handling many of the disciplinary matters and such. Some guys enjoy the job of ASIC because they're pricks—though knowing Alan, I was sure he was a prick only when it was truly unavoidable. He'd spent too many years on the street and had too much awareness of what it was like out there to lose empathy for the grunts.

We shook hands, and I started for the chair on the opposite side of his desk. He motioned for me to stay on my feet. Then he was reaching for the sport coat draped over the back of his own chair and slipping it on.

"Are we going someplace?" I asked.

Alan paused to gulp down the remainder of a cup of coffee. I winced, having a vivid recollection of just how bad Bureau coffee tasted. Setting down the cup, he reached into the top drawer of his desk and pulled out his gun and holster. He attached the gun to his belt, above his right hip. "Terminal Island," he said.

"Terminal Island?"

Alan nodded, heading for the door. I stood there, looking puzzled. Halfway out of the office he paused and turned back to me. "You coming or what?"

Shrugging, I said, "I guess so," and followed him out.

THIRTEEN

I ACCOMPANIED MY ex-partner to the motor pool, where he checked out an ugly, late-model Chevrolet. The car wasn't very old, but it had already been used on enough stakeouts that its interior had acquired the permanent aroma of a detectives' bull pen, just like the one back in Solvang.

I rode shotgun as Alan drove us along the Harbor Freeway, toward the ocean. As he guided the Chevy to the freeway's inside lane, I asked, "What's at Terminal Island?"

"Not 'what,'" Alan said. "Who."

"Okay. Who?"

He reached into the side pocket of his sport coat and pulled out a couple of folded sheets of paper, which he handed to me. I unfolded the sheets and read the name at the top. "Marcello M. Martinez. AKA 'Buddy.'" I looked over at Alan. "Who's Buddy Martinez?"

"The Secret Service popped him two years ago for passing counterfeit welfare checks in east L.A. For his trouble, he drew a ten-year stretch in TI. From what I hear, he's very unhappy about having gotten such a stiff sentence."

I glanced over the pages and said sarcastically, "You mean he was surprised? For Christ's sake, he's got priors that go all the way back to when he was a kid. He's lucky they didn't throw away the key."

"Tell me about it. But you know how these assholes like to piss and moan." Alan started to whine in an exaggerated vato accent, "'I had a deal with the focking *prosecutor,* man! Check it out! I rolled over, you moth-erfockers! You can't *do* this to me, give me ten years! I wanna see my *lawyer!*'"

I chuckled knowingly, then held up the sheets. "What's Buddy got to do with me?"

Alan showed me a thin smile. "Guess who was his lone cellmate all of last year."

I was puzzled for a moment, thinking, then suddenly broke into a smile of my own. "No shit?"

Alan nodded. "No shit."

As WE CROSSED the Vincent-Thomas Bridge spanning the L.A. harbor's main channel, I was thinking about something that I often thought about when I visited what's euphemistically known as a "correctional facil-ity." What I was thinking about was recidivism.

I have never understood the mind-set of repeat of-fenders. Why I don't understand it is because of *jail.* There is no worse condition a human being can suffer than incarceration. Why you would do anything that might land you in jail—especially if you've already done time and know what it's like—baffles me. The only explanation I've ever come up with is that you don't usually become a criminal because you're smart. To go to jail more than once must mean that you're among the dumbest individuals to walk the earth. For that reason alone, the rest of us are probably much bet-ter off that you're there.

That thought was still running through my mind as we rolled off the Seaside Avenue exit in east San Pedro. A green and white sign at the bottom of the exit directed us toward Terminal Island Federal Prison, and within a few minutes we were pulling to a stop in the parking lot of the prison's dingy, mud-colored administration building. We got out of the car, and I followed Alan to the ad building. It had been several years since my last visit, but TI was just as dreary as I remembered: the entire grim compound surrounded by a high fence wrapped in razor wire; the gun tower and spotlight to the left of the ad building; at the back of the facility the chilly, gray ocean, constantly roaring just beyond piles of sharp, jutting rocks; a stench of diesel oil and rotting fish that permeated everything. I could scarcely image a more awful place, and I had to shake myself to force away the funk that had begun to settle over me.

Inside the ad building's reception area, Alan showed his badge and ID to a guard sitting behind a steel-case desk. Then he introduced me and explained who it was we'd come to see. The guard flipped through a bound folder of several sheets' worth of computer printouts, then nodded okay. He had Alan sign a logbook and turn over his gun, then he indicated a metal door and started to inform us as to which way we should go. Alan stopped him in mid-speech and told him to save his breath. We'd been to TI before, more times than either of us would care to count.

Presently we found ourselves in a small room with a single steel door and no windows. The room held a battered wooden table and three chairs, two on one side of the table, one on the other. In the middle of the table was a Styrofoam cup filled with cigarette butts.

Alan and I sat side by side, waiting. The steel door was opposite us, behind the third chair. A few minutes after we sat down, the door opened, and an overweight guard ushered in Buddy Martinez. He was dressed in penitentiary denims with a number stenciled over the pocket of his shirt. The guard gave a terse nod to Alan and me, then pulled the door closed.

Buddy stood next to the door, sullenly eyeing us with smoldering hostility. I knew from having looked at his sheet that he was thirty years old, though he could have passed for ten years younger. He was of average height, five feet eight or nine. The jailhouse costume didn't disguise his wide shoulders and broad chest and narrow waist—clearly he spent much of his yard time pumping iron. He had chiseled features and a dark complexion, more Indian than European blood in his genetic mix. He had straight black hair tied in a ponytail that hung almost to the middle of his back, accentuating his features: a handsome, twentieth-century Cochise. You could tell by his posture that he knew how good he looked.

Alan gestured to the empty chair and said in a friendly tone of voice, "Have a seat, Buddy."

There was no wasted energy as he settled himself in the chair. "I'm Special Agent Feinberg," continued Alan. "I'm with the Bureau of Alcohol, Tobacco and Firearms." He nodded to me. "This is Jack Donne. We'd like to ask you some questions, if that's all right."

It registered on me that Alan hadn't said anything about my being an agent, too, though by his tone when he'd introduced me he'd implied that I was someone of equal authority—which is what both of us wanted Buddy to think. That way, if, some time later, Alan or I found ourselves on a witness stand, we could state truthfully that neither of us had ever said that I was a law-enforcement officer of any stripe. Regardless of what Buddy Martinez might swear.

For the time being, though, Buddy was silent. Alan reached into the pocket of his shirt and pulled out a pack of Marlboros. He offered the pack to Buddy, who shook his head. "I don't smoke," he said. "It ain't good for you."

Alan shrugged and replaced the pack of cigarettes in his pocket. "We wanted to talk to you about a friend of yours," he said to Buddy. "Teddie Ortiz."

"Yeah?" Buddy grunted. He shook his head. "Never heard of him."

Alan raised an eyebrow. "Really? You spend thirteen months in the same cell with a guy, and you don't even know his name?"

Buddy shrugged.

I looked at Alan. "May I?" He waved a hand: Go ahead. I turned to Buddy. "We want you to understand something. This doesn't have anything to do with any ongoing investigation or anything like that. We're not asking you to be a snitch. All we want to know is, if when you last talked to Teddie, he might've mentioned what he's been doing lately."

"Man," said Buddy, "I ain't seen the dude in..." He paused to think about it. "Five months. Not since he got out."

"Is that so?" said Alan. He reached into the inside pocket of his sport coat, pulled out a small spiral notebook, and flipped it open. "According to the visitors' log, Teddie's dropped by to see you six times since his release. The last time just a week and a half ago."

"Can I see that?" Buddy asked. Alan handed over the notebook. Buddy nonchalantly scanned the page, then passed the notebook back to Alan. "I guess I forgot."

I thought bleakly: This is futile. "So what did you and Teddie talk about?"

Buddy's feigned indifference hardened. "Tell me

something, okay? Why should I say a word to you motherfuckers about anything? What the fuck good is it gonna do me, huh? You gonna talk to the judge, get my fuckin' sentence reduced? You can't! Hell, you ain't even the ones who put me here! You ain't Secret Service, you're fuckin' ATF!'' He sat back in the chair and folded his thick arms across his chest. Defiant. ''You want something from me, you put something on the table makes it worth my while to talk to you.''

Alan and I exchanged a look. Buddy's reaction wasn't something we hadn't anticipated—in fact, during the drive out we'd discussed the likelihood of his stone-walling us. Unfortunately, neither of us had come up with much of an idea of what to use for leverage.

Alan turned from me and looked across the table at the man opposite us, sighed, pushed back his chair, and got to his feet. ''Let's go, Jack,'' he said.

As Alan headed for the door, I stood up and started after him. He was just reaching for the knob when Buddy said, ''Hey, wait a minute...''

We paused. Buddy was looking us over, an expression of utter bewilderment on his face. ''What the fuck's goin' on here?''

''What do you mean?'' Alan asked.

''That's it?'' Buddy said with disbelief. ''You say, 'Let's talk,' and I say, 'No,' and you just up and leave?''

''You said it yourself,'' Alan told him. ''If we don't have anything to trade you in exchange for the information we want, you won't talk to us. I can respect that.''

Buddy frowned, regarding Alan and me with even deeper suspicion than he had before. Then the frown creased into an uneasy smile. "You're fuckin' with me, ain'tcha. You guys're fuckin with me."

"We don't know what you're talking about," Alan said.

"You two are fuckin' with me," said Buddy. He nodded. "That's what it is, ain't it."

"We're telling you the truth," I said to Buddy. "We came here hoping you'd want to do us a favor."

Buddy chuckled humorlessly. "Yeah, right."

"I'm serious," I said.

His bewildered expression returned. I looked to Alan and pointed to the door. Alan reached for the knob again.

"Hang on, hang on," said Buddy.

Alan and I paused once more. Buddy scratched his head. "You mean to say you go no kinda deal to offer me at all?"

Alan nodded. "I wish we did."

Buddy muttered, "I don't fuckin' believe this—"

Alan held up a hand to silence him. "If you did decide to tell us about Teddie, you'd earn a lot of... goodwill."

Buddy scowled. "Huh?"

"You never know when one of us might be in a position to do you a favor," said Alan. "Sometime in the future, maybe. All you'd have to do is ask."

Buddy looked as if it were hurting him to cogitate as hard as he was—a new experience for him. Alan and I waited for a few moments. Then we looked to one another, and I nodded toward the door: Let's go.

As Alan was reaching for the knob a third time, Buddy said quickly, "All right, all right."

We watched him coolly, neither of us betraying any expectation. Buddy peered at Alan. "Goodwill, huh?"

"Goodwill," Alan repeated.

Buddy took a deep breath and exhaled heavily. "Ah, well, what the fuck." He looked at Alan and me. "Last couple times he came out, Teddie told me he had a job workin' for some big-timer. A mob guy. He was real jazzed about it, you know? Said he was lookin' to make a lot of money."

"Did he mention the guy's name?" I asked.

Buddy nodded. "Setzer. Rudy Setzer."

A tiny electric charge raced up my spine. I turned to Alan. He'd turned to look at me, and I could tell by his expression that he'd felt the same charge I had.

Alan turned back to the man in the chair and said casually, "Thanks, Buddy. We appreciate it."

"Yeah, right." Buddy grunted sardonically. "In the future."

Alan pulled open the door. The guard was standing right outside. Alan nodded to him, and he came into the room to retrieve his prisoner.

As Buddy rose from his chair, I called to him, "Hey?" All three—Buddy, Alan, and the guard—looked at me. "How come Teddie keeps coming out here to see you?" I asked Buddy. "You'd figure once he was free he wouldn't come within two miles of this place."

Buddy smiled. It was a look that was totally down 'n' dirty, sexy and provocative and more than a little evil. "Man, you mean to tell me you can't guess?"

I shook my head.

The smile broadened. "Shit. Fuckin' Teddie, man, the dude's in *love* with my ass." Then he motioned to the guard to lead the way back to his cell.

IT WAS A LITTLE too early for lunch, so Alan and I stopped for coffee at a truck-stop diner on Seaside Avenue. We'd passed the diner on our way to the prison, just after we'd come off the freeway. The booth we sat in provided us with a panoramic view of a concrete overpass, and it occurred to me that in an area such as L.A. County, where architectural unattractiveness could achieve stunning proportions, San Pedro might be the lowest of the low.

Stirring his coffee, Alan said, "You think Buddy's bullshitting about Teddie and Rudy Setzer?"

"I don't know," I said. "What do you think?"

"I asked you first."

I sipped my coffee, which tasted better than I had any right to expect. "I can't come up with a reason why he'd lie to us."

"Neither can I," said Alan. "Unless he was just yanking our chains."

I shrugged. "I don't think he's that bright."

"I hear you," Alan chuckled. "Could you believe how it threw him when we started out the door? Jesus, I *never* expected that act to work." He sipped his coffee, then set it back down. "How much luck do you think I'd have if I tried to put in Buddy's name for Mensa membership?"

"Not much."

"Still," said Alan. "Even if he was telling us the truth, there's always the possibility that Teddie was bullshitting *him*. Just to impress him."

"It's possible," I agreed.

"I guess the only way you're going to find out is to catch up with Teddie and ask him yourself," Alan said. "If it does turn out that he's mixed up with Setzer, I'd appreciate it if you'd let me know."

"You can count on it," I said.

FOURTEEN

I PROBABLY SHOULDN'T have been surprised by the snarl of trucks and automobiles that snared us halfway between San Pedro and downtown L.A., but I was anyway. As a consequence of the second traffic jam I'd been in that morning, by the time we got back to Alan's office it *was* time for lunch. I took a rain check on his invitation to join him for a French-dip roast beef sandwich at Philippe's, on Alameda Street near Union Station. I still had many stops and many miles to cover before I could head back north, and the day was getting away from me.

Yesterday afternoon I'd mapped out an itinerary of what I supposed would be the likeliest targets for Teddie Ortiz that I could visit in a single day. Two of them were in Orange County, the others more or less clustered in west Los Angeles. The route I'd planned ran south to north, my first stop being Irvine, then Newport Beach, followed by Marina del Rey, Beverly Hills, Westwood, and Brentwood. Heading south on the Santa Ana Freeway, I deliberately focused my concentration on Teddie and tried not to think about what possible connection he might have with Rudy Setzer. I could think about Setzer later.

By the time I reached Anaheim, my stomach was growling like a jungle cat. With a sigh of resignation, I wheeled off the freeway, looking for a place to eat, trying to be as selective as time and hunger would permit, and found a Greek fast-food establishment tucked between a garish Mickey Mouse-themed McDonald's and a Kentucky Fried Chicken outlet. I wolfed down a pair of gyro sandwiches, chugged a large glass of spicy iced tea, and twenty-five minutes later was back on the road.

Tracking Teddie Ortiz wasn't too difficult. The routine varied little from wineshop to wineshop. Upon arrival, I sought out whoever ran the store. I introduced myself—if the manager or owner didn't already know me, as was the case in a couple of the establishments I went to. Then I showed them the mug shot of Teddie I'd gotten from Alan Feinberg and asked if the fellow in the picture had made an offer they couldn't refuse on O.C. pinot noir.

As I'd hoped, Teddie was moving north. On Monday—the same day I'd had my own taste of the bogus O.C. pinot he was peddling—he'd hit both places in Irvine and Newport. In L.A., I found out that he'd shown up at two of the other places just yesterday— The Wine Merchant in Beverly Hills and Briggs in Brentwood. Nobody at any of the shops had made him a definite offer, so he left his business card along with a promise to follow up with another call, either in person or on the phone, sometime the next week.

By 8:00 p.m., I'd finished my rounds and was heading home, exhausted from having spent so many hours behind the wheel of my Jeep, navigating L.A.'s convoluted freeway system. My neck and shoulders ached, my scalp itched, and I was dimly aware of the sour fragrance of my own body.

Still, I felt a sort of satisfaction at the way the day had gone. Ninety percent of police work is sheer drudgery—you spent most of your time knocking on doors, as I'd been doing today, or writing reports. Since I hadn't lost my knack for nuts 'n' bolts investigation, I knew a little more about Teddie Ortiz's recent movements than I had yesterday. All in all, a good, productive day.

I got home around a quarter to ten. Dad was in the family room watching an early news broadcast that he switched off as soon as I came in. As I was about to say good night and head for my bedroom, Dad asked if I wouldn't be interested in a few hands of cribbage before turning in. I started to shake my head, then I saw the expression of disappointment in his eyes. I smiled and nodded; sleep could wait.

We set up a card table in front of the fireplace and, hunched over the cribbage board, shared a portion of a bottle of '63 Dow's I'd decanted a few days before. We played for a penny a point, just as we've done for many years. By the time we quit, around midnight, I was glad he'd talked me into it. My good luck of the day was holding. I called him on a Muggins three different times, lurched him once, and ended up almost six bucks to the good—which lowered my cribbage debt to him to somewhere around seven hundred dollars. At that rate, I might actually break even in another decade or two.

WE'D JUST SAT DOWN to breakfast on Saturday morning when the telephone rang. It was Uncle Gerry, calling to let Dad and me know that he, too, was going to Perry Cole's funeral. I asked him if he wanted to ride with us. He declined. "I'll meet you at the church," he said.

Following breakfast, I went back to my bedroom and pulled the only suit I own from the closet, a charcoal-gray Armani with a barely discernible pinstripe. I'd bought it in Beverly Hills five years ago, while I was still with the Treasury Department, and had it cut in a style that was fashionably conservative then and will probably remain so. Since it was to be one of my costumes for an undercover gig, the government had let me expense it. They even let me keep it after I retired. I found a clean white dress shirt, a dark gray tie with a somber enough pattern, black socks, and the black Florsheim dress shoes I put on maybe twice a year, about as often as I wear my suit.

After dressing myself, I went into Dad's room and helped him knot his tie. We left the house at nine-thirty, in plenty of time to make it to the memorial service, which was scheduled to begin at ten.

We said little to each other on our way to the church. The reason I didn't have much to say was that I was thinking about the last time he and I had gone to a funeral together—my mother's, three years before, when she'd succumbed to a heart attack one sunny Saturday morning not unlike this one. I suspected Dad was quiet for the same reason.

The morning was bright and clear, the sky a cloudless cobalt blue, the air dry and warm. I wondered how uncomfortable it was going to be at the cemetery standing in the sun at high noon. I had to remind myself that you're not supposed to enjoy a funeral. There was only one time in my life when I did, and the enjoyment couldn't have been more fleeting. My grandfather died when I was five years old, and at his wake one of my older cousins demonstrated to me how the carpeting at the mortuary was perfect for a hilariously funny trick. If you scuffled your feet back and forth on the nap and then tapped somebody on the ear or the back of the hand with your finger, you could give them a little shock. I spent the next few minutes zapping some very sad-looking people, until my dad clutched me by the arm, drew me aside, and assured me in a menacing voice that if I didn't stop it, I'd get a spanking to remember for the rest of my days.

The drive to San Tomas Mission Church took less than fifteen minutes. We rolled past a gleaming gunmetal-colored hearse parked in front of the church, at the head of a line of three black limousines. I pulled the Cherokee into the parking lot that lay on the east side of the mission. The lot was designed to accommodate a hundred and fifty cars, give or take, and I was surprised that it was close to full. Either Perry was beloved by more people than I'd have guessed, was a bigger local celebrity than I'd assumed, or was more highly regarded by his business rivals than I'd supposed. Likely it was some combination of all three.

I helped Dad out and walked him to the front of the church. We climbed the steps and passed through the front door, entering the foyer. Gathered there was a circle of a half dozen men, speaking to each other sotto voce. One of the men was my uncle, who nodded hello to Dad and me. The rest were fellow winemakers from around the valley, all of them familiar faces. We joined the group, falling in beside Gerry, exchanged greetings, answered passing questions about our well-being, then joined in a conversation that had been going on before we'd been admitted to the circle.

The group separated a few minutes later. Gerry, Dad, and I went into the nave and took seats at the end of a pew close to the rear. The church was all but full, with only the first two rows nearest the chancel on the left-hand side of the center aisle appearing to be empty. Presumably the seats were reserved for members of the deceased's family, none of whom I'd spotted yet. A bier

had been set up just this side of the chancel rail, and
on the bier rested a sleek, torpedo-shaped casket of bur-
nished bronze. Sunlight streamed through the church's
stained glass windows, causing a bright rainbow to
dance along the casket's closed lid. The bier was surrounded by enough flowers for a Tournament of Roses
float.

The sight of all those lilies and roses and mums
brought to mind something I'd read one time about how
funerals provide two-thirds of all the business that flo-
rists do. I was thinking that Perry Cole's demise probably made the year for a lot of people in the Santa Ynez
Valley who sold flowers for a living, when Uncle Gerry
nudged me with an elbow. I turned, and he pointed his
chin in the direction of a man who was seated on the
aisle a couple of rows ahead of and across from us. I
glanced at the man's profile, then turned back to my
uncle.

"Danny Wikert," whispered Gerry.

I nodded, acknowledging I'd heard him, then looked
at Wikert again, this time closely. I couldn't tell exactly
how big a man he was, but judging by the width of his
shoulders and how much of him I could see above the
back of his pew, I guessed him to be around my own
height but somewhat heavier. He had straight, neatly
styled hair the color of pewter. He was clean shaven,
and his face was as tan as an America's Cup skipper's.
His features were patrician handsome—his eyes dark,
his nose narrow and sharp, his ears small and set close
to his head, his jaw firm and square, his jowls just fleshy
enough to tip off how old he actually was. If I'd encountered him on the street and didn't know him, I
might have thought him to be a middle-aged actor on

the verge of making the transition from leading man roles to character parts.

While I was studying Wikert, a pipe organ began playing an unfamiliar dirge. A priest in full High Mass regalia emerged from the vestry accompanied by a pair of altar boys, one of whom was swinging a censer filled with smoking incense. The priest took his place in front of the altar and turned to face the gathered congregation of mourners. As he raised his hands, I sensed activity going on behind me. I peered over my shoulder and saw the dead man's family entering the church from the foyer, where they had gathered. They'd arranged themselves in pairs and were coming down the center aisle two at a time, making their way to the pews closest to Perry's casket.

The few members of the family with whom I was acquainted marched at the front of the procession. June Cole, Perry's eldest son, was first in line, his wife, Regina, holding on to his arm. Behind them came their two children, both girls who looked to be around high school age. After the girls came Grant Cole, whose looks and build so closely resembled his older brother's that for years strangers had often mistaken them for twins. Grant held the hand of a boy about ten years old. Behind them walked Grant's wife, who was carrying a swaddled baby.

None of the other people in the procession—none of the cousins or aunts or uncles—was anyone I'd met before. As they were taking their seats, however, a conspicuous absence registered on me. The Cole family was all present and accounted for—save one.

I missed part of the memorial service because I was busy trying to spy Ozzie. My eyes are as good as anyone's, especially if that "anyone" happens to be in law enforcement and has been trained to pick specific individuals out of a crowd. I made a careful scrutiny of the entire congregation, then finally had to admit to myself the surprising realization that Perry Cole's youngest son hadn't bothered to show up for his father's funeral.

FIFTEEN

AFTER THE SERVICE ENDED, the congregation filed outside. There we waited for Perry's casket to be brought out and loaded into the hearse that would lead the parade of mourners to the cemetery. The dead man's pallbearers had been chosen from among the membership of the Santa Barbara County Vintners' Association, a group Perry himself had helped organize many years ago. Dad, Uncle Gerry, and I are members of the association in good standing, but we hadn't been approached to help deliver Perry Cole to his final resting place. None of us minded not having been asked.

While we were still inside the church, Gerry offered to drive Dad and me to the cemetery in his Cadillac Seville. There was no reason for us to take two cars, and he suggested we could pick up my Cherokee on the way back from the burial, after which he would follow us to our place and join us for lunch.

On our way out, I was handed a small placard by a whey-faced, black-suited young man wearing a well-practiced, hangdog look. The expression on the young man's face brought to mind an old joke about the definition of the word hypocrite being the mortician who tries to look sad at a $25,000 funeral. When the young man inquired as to whether I knew where to stick the card—on which was printed FUNERAL CORTEGE—I resisted an urge to say *How 'bout where the sun don't shine?* Instead I merely acknowledged him with a terse nod.

We emerged into bright daylight, and I had to shade my eyes in order to study a knot of people gathered near the limousines parked behind the hearse. At the center of the knot stood June and Grant Cole, their wives beside them. The brothers were dutifully shaking hands with sympathetic well-wishers. As my father and uncle made their way toward the parking lot, I stood at the bottom of the church steps, debating whether to follow them or get in the queue of people commiserating with the Coles. I didn't know if June and Grant were aware of my business relationship with their black-sheep brother. If they were, I would doubtless receive less than heartfelt gratitude for telling them how sorry I was about their father's passing.

I'd just decided to do the polite thing and fall in line anyway when I heard a rasping voice behind me. "How you doin', Mistah Jack?"

I turned around. Zeke Carlin was looking up at me with a wan, forced smile. He was dressed in a trim, well-fitted, dark brown suit, and appeared even more weary than he'd seemed four days ago in Perry's bungalow. His face was heavily lined and his eyes were bloodshot, as if he hadn't been sleeping. I held out my hand, and he shook it. "How's it going, Zeke?"

"Not too bad, considerin'."

I nodded, feeling restive because I had no idea what to say to him. The only soothing words I could think of were along the lines of *I imagine you'll miss Perry's not being around anymore* or *I suppose if you work for somebody for ten years, you get to feeling close to them.* I was relieved when Carlin broke the silence. "It's nice'a you 'n' yo' daddy and yo' uncle to come out," he said. "Mistah Perry would'a 'preciated it."

"It's the least we could do," I said lamely.

An uncomfortable silence descended. Carlin turned away from me to peer in the direction of the group gathered around June and Grant Cole. His eyes narrowed, and I thought I saw something ignite there, the flicker of an emotion stronger than mere resentment. The spark receded almost before I could convince myself that I'd seen it.

"It feels funny," he said in a faraway voice, speaking to himself as much as to me. "Mistah Perry bein' gone, I mean. He was awful good to me. He took care'a me as much as I took care'a him. Most people don' even know how generous a man he could be, when he wanted to. Them boys 'specially, they never showed him nowhere near the respect they should'a. 'Cept for Mistah Ozzie, sometimes."

"By the way," I said, "where is Ozzie?"

Carlin shook his head. "They wouldn't let him come."

"Who wouldn't?"

He pointed to Ozzie's brothers. "Mistah June called Mistah Ozzie personal and tol' him to stay away from Mistah Perry's funeral, or else they be trouble. What with Mistah Ozzie gettin' arrested and all…"

He bowed his head and frowned, deep in thought. Then he looked up at me with as resolute an expression as I've seen on the face of any man. "I wanted to ax you somethin', Mistah Jack."

"Go ahead."

He frowned again. "Is you tryin' to find out who really killed Mistah Perry, or no?"

"Everybody seems to be pretty sure it was Ozzie," I said.

"I ain't axin' you what ever'body else thinks. I'm axin' you what *you* think."

I hesitated before replying, trying to figure out what he was after. The shift in his manner, from sad to pugnacious, caught me off guard. At last I said, "It doesn't sound to me like you believe he did it."

Carlin's jaw tightened. "What I b'lieve don't matter."

It bothered me that I couldn't read what was going on behind his eyes. All of a sudden there was something cunning and impenetrable about him. He'd erected an emotional barricade for reasons I couldn't fathom, at least not at the moment.

"I don't think Ozzie killed his father," I said carefully. "But I don't know who did, either. I doubt right now I could even make a decent guess—"

I was interrupted by the young mortician, who had emerged from the church to clear a path for the pallbearers coming behind him. The people gathered in front of the church, including Carlin and me, stepped aside to give the pallbearers a wider berth.

We watched in silence as the driver of the hearse climbed out of the vehicle and went around to open its rear door. The pallbearers slid the casket into the hearse, then stepped back as the driver slammed the door shut. As if a signal had been given, those mourners who'd been straggling behind headed for their vehicles.

Before I could begin moving toward the parking lot where my dad and my uncle were waiting, Carlin said, "You ain't answered my question yet."

"Didn't I?"

"No."

He was challenging me again, and I still had no idea why. "I haven't quit working for Ozzie, but all I'm doing is trying to find out who's ripping him off. It's possible whoever's behind it had something to do with what happened to Perry, but I won't know for certain till I catch up with them. I'm not necessarily trying to find out who murdered him, though that may wind up happening anyway. Finding killers is a job for the cops, and I intend to stay out of their way as much as possible." I regarded him coolly. "Does that answer your question?" I said, making my tone of voice deliberately contentious.

He bristled. I tensed myself in anticipation of some aggressive move he might make in response. Then his expression began to soften, and he looked at me apologetically. "I'm sorry, Mistah Jack. I din't mean to sound like I was tryin' to pick a fight. You a good man, I know. You only mean to do what's right by Mistah Ozzie. It's jus' when I get to thinkin' 'bout what happened to Mistah Perry an' all…" He lowered his eyes as the words trailed away.

Way to go, Jack, I chided myself. "I'm the one who should be apologizing," I said.

Carlin brought up his head and showed me his pallid smile, letting me know we were friends again. "You mind if I ax you a favor?"

"Not at all."

"If you find out somethin' you think I maybe might want to know about, will you tell me? I'm s'posed to be movin' away from the old folks' home in a coupl'a weeks, but I can let you know how to get in touch wiff me after I go."

Until then it hadn't occurred to me that the person who'd provided him with room and board for the past decade was now gone. With Perry dead, I doubted any of the Cole brothers gave a damn about what happened to Zeke Carlin, if they thought of him at all. "Are you

all right?'' I asked. ''Do you need money or anything…?''

He shook his head. ''I already tol' you, Mistah Perry
done took good care'a me—''

Before he could finish what he was saying, an automobile horn bleated nearby. Carlin and I turned around.
I saw that most of the cars in the parking lot had departed and were trailing after the hearse and the limousines moving slowly east along Route 154, away
from the church. The horn belonged to my uncle
Gerry's Cadillac. He'd pulled the car to the edge of the
lot and was motioning to me. ''C'mon, Jack!'' he
shouted. ''Let's go!''

I waved to him. ''I'll be right there,'' I called back,
then returned my attention to Carlin. He was looking at
me expectantly. ''You'll let me know as soon as you
get settled someplace?'' I asked.

''I'll call you,'' he promised. Then we shook hands
once more, and I turned and walked away.

DAD SAID TO ME, ''That was an awfully serious conversation you were having.''

''Uh-huh.''

I was in the backseat. Gerry was behind the wheel,
Dad sitting beside him. The Cadillac's headlights were
on, as were the lights of every vehicle in the cortege.

We were near the end of the line, rolling south along
Alamo Pintado Road at a stately ten miles per hour.
Our destination was Oak Hill Memorial Cemetery, outside Ballard. We were still a mile away from the cemetery, having traveled four-fifths of the distance from
the church to the site of Perry Cole's interment.

Dad had turned around to look at me, resting his arm

on the back of his seat. "So what were you talking about?"

"Zeke wanted to know if I was still working for Ozzie," I said. "And also if I was trying to find out who killed Perry."

"What'd you tell him?"

"I said I was still looking for who was ripping off Ozzie, but that I wasn't actually looking for Perry's killer. I told him that was a job for the cops."

"Did he say why he was so interested?"

I shook my head. "But I'm starting to believe that he was a helluva lot closer to Perry than any of the kids were. Including Ozzie. Zeke's taking the old man's death pretty hard."

"Speaking of Ozzie," said Uncle Gerry, "I didn't see him at the church."

"Neither did I," said Dad.

"He wasn't there," I said. "Zeke told me June called Ozzie and told him not to come."

Dad said, "You're joking."

I shook my head.

Dad said sadly, "Can you believe that fucking family?"

My father isn't given to casual profanity, so it registered on me how much June's ordering Ozzie to stay away from their father's funeral—and Ozzie's compliance—had upset him.

"I'll be damned if I can figure 'em out," I said.

"It's the money," said Uncle Gerry. "That's what it always comes down to."

Dad and I regarded him with questioning looks. Gerry glanced at me in his rearview mirror, then turned to glance at Dad, noting our expressions. "If there's enough money at stake, you'd be astounded by how fast the closest families will turn on one another," he explained. "Even us."

"Do you really believe that?" I asked.

Uncle Gerry had returned his attention to his driving. "That we're capable of acting just like the Coles? Don't doubt it for one second, nephew."

"Good Christ, Gerry," said Dad. "What's made you so damned cynical all of a sudden?"

"Hell," I added, "we fight with each other all the time."

"Not like the Coles," Gerry said. "But we might, someday. I've seen it happen in the best of families. If ever we find ourselves at one another's throats, you can give odds a big chunk of money will be right at the heart of it."

"Isn't *this* a pleasant conversation," snorted Dad.

"I'm not saying it's bound to happen," said Gerry. "I'm just saying we may not be so high and mighty as we'd like to believe."

Dad grunted, then turned around in his seat to gaze out the front windshield at the passing scenery, a signal that, as far as he was concerned, the discussion was over. The three of us fell silent, and no one spoke a word for the rest of the ride.

As we were pulling into the Oak Hill cemetery, I wondered if he and Uncle Gerry were thinking about the same thing I was, asking themselves what circumstances might bring us to behave toward one another the way the Coles had. Then and there I made a vow that I would do everything in my power to prevent that from ever occurring. I couldn't imagine a more bleak situation than finding myself hating my father or my uncle or both—or them hating each other—on account of greed.

Fuck the money, I thought self-righteously, telling myself that if it ever came down to something like that, I'd rather be a pauper. And hoping that I wasn't lying.

SIXTEEN

PERRY COLE'S GRAVE SITE lay at the top of a gently sloping green hill that provided a splendid view of the cemetery grounds. By the time the cortege came to a stop along the concrete drive that wound around the base of the hill, the sun was almost directly overhead. As I ascended the slope on foot with the rest of the mourners, I noticed a canvas tarpaulin that had been erected on aluminum poles beside Perry's open grave. Beneath the tarpaulin were several rows of metal folding chairs. Upon our arrival at the grave site, I discovered that the only ones privileged to sit in the shade were members of the deceased's family.

My father, my uncle, and I found ourselves standing just to the right of the canvas overhang, not far from the first row of chairs. Seated in the first row were Grant and June Cole, their wives, and their children. All of us watched the pallbearers as they—assisted by a trio of workmen dressed in coveralls—placed Perry's casket atop a hoist that straddled the open grave. The workmen and the pallbearers moved aside, and the priest had just taken his place at the head of the casket when I heard a female voice stage-whispering poisonously, "Goddamn it, Junior, what the hell is he *doing* here? I thought you told him to stay away."

I turned in the direction of the voice—as Regina Cole had meant everyone to do. She was looking down the hill at a solitary figure standing near the parked hearse. It was Ozzie, his head bowed slightly, his hands folded in front of him. Seeing him, I knew that this was as close as he'd come to his father's burial place until the rest of us had gone away. But he couldn't not be here, couldn't not pay his respects, couldn't not say good-bye.

"That son of a *bitch*—"

Regina was shushed by the priest, who then cleared his throat sharply to bring our attention back to the business at hand. Out of the corner of my eye I watched Regina as she turned around. Her lips were compressed into a tight grimace, her nostrils flaring, her eyes nearly slits. It was the most rancorous look I had ever seen on the face of a woman, so hideous that I had to suppress a shudder. I told myself that I had absolutely no desire to spend time in the company of someone capable of such an expression of sheer enmity.

The rest of the service passed without incident. Just as I was beginning to swelter—and wondering if it were any pleasanter to be sitting beneath the tarpaulin—the priest, who looked as warm in his vestments as I felt, brought the ceremony to a conclusion. "May the Lord welcome our brother Perry to the table of God's children in heaven, and may he inherit the promise of eternal life," he said. He motioned to the people beneath the canvas overhang. They came to their feet, and one by one they walked up to place a rose atop Perry's casket. I could read the grief etched on their faces, and I decided that having a seat in the shade really didn't matter much to me after all.

As soon as the service ended, I gazed down the hill, searching for Ozzie. He'd already disappeared. It made sense to assume he'd be hiding someplace until the other mourners had departed, and he could be alone with his father. Just by showing up—against the express wishes of his brothers, and apparently, their spouses, too—Ozzie had raised my opinion of him substantially. He might still be a lousy human being, but he wasn't as lousy as some others I could think of. His oldest brother's wife, to name one.

The mourners began to file away, moving down the hill in clumps of two or three or four. As we'd worked out during our drive from the church, Uncle Gerry guided my father down the slope from the grave site while I hung back, looking for Daniel Wikert.

I spotted him as he was unlocking the driver's door of a silver Mercedes 450 SL parked a dozen vehicles ahead of where my uncle had left his Cadillac. It didn't appear that Wikert had brought anyone with him.

I trotted toward the Mercedes. "Mr. Wikert!" I called as he was climbing into the driver's seat. "Mr. Wikert, I need to talk to you!"

He was behind the wheel and about to pull the door closed when he heard me calling his name. He peered at me through the windshield, and a puzzled look crossed his face. He was asking himself how I knew who he was when he didn't have a clue about me. He watched me carefully as I crossed in front of his car, dark eyes following me as I approached.

I stood silently for a few seconds beside the open door, allowing him the opportunity to speak first and inquire as to who I was. Instead he looked at me, waiting for me to make the initial move. What was going on behind his eyes registered on me—they were the eyes of a shrewd, wary creature. Before we could exchange a word, I knew that whatever else he might be, he was neither an unintelligent individual nor someone who liked to be outfoxed.

"I'm Jack Donne," I said at last. "You know my

uncle Gerry. He pointed you out to me back at the church.''

Having given him my name, once again I allowed him some room to speak. But instead of asking me what I wanted, he simply waited, watching me, saying nothing. I'm impressed, I thought. Smartness and coolness are admirable qualities for any lawyer to possess, even an unscrupulous one.

I waited until a couple of mourners' cars had rolled past, then said, ''I'm a private investigator. I'm working for Ozzie Cole.''

His eyebrows narrowed so slightly that I wasn't even sure I'd seen it happen. ''So?''

It was a moral victory to have gotten him to speak at all. ''You're Ozzie's attorney, aren't you?''

''Who told you that?''

''Ozzie, for one. So did a homicide lieutenant named Fitch, who's an acquaintance of mine. He said you talked to him a couple of mornings ago, when you dropped by the sheriff's station in Solvang to take care of Ozzie's bond.''

Wikert mulled that over for a time, then said, ''I'm not defending Ozzie on that murder charge. I don't do criminal law. I only represent him on matters pertaining to his business. I'm surprised he didn't mention that.''

''He did.''

''Then why are you and I talking, Mr. Donne? We can't be of much help to one another if you're trying to prove Ozzie didn't kill his father and I'm not even handling the case—''

I held up a hand to quiet him. ''I didn't say I was trying to prove Ozzie didn't kill Perry.''

Wikert raised an eyebrow. ''Then what *are* you doing?''

Before I could answer, I heard the sound of approaching footsteps coming along the drive toward us. Wikert and I turned to look at my uncle Gerry. He was smiling pleasantly, first at me, then at the man in the Mercedes. "Long time no see, Dan. How've you been?"

Wikert nodded a perfunctory hello. "Gerry."

My uncle stood alongside me. "I see you've met my nephew, the private eye."

Wikert nodded again. "We were discussing a mutual friend."

"Don't let me interrupt," said Gerry. "I only came up to tell Jack that his dad and I are ready to go."

"I'm just about finished here," I said.

"I thought we *were* finished," said Wikert.

I shook my head. "Not quite. I still have something I wanted to ask you."

"What's that?"

"I was wondering if we couldn't get together privately sometime," I said. "Say, later today at your office? If you're available?"

"What for?"

I smiled. "Just to talk."

The muscles in his jaw tightened. He looked from me to Gerry, then back to me. Then he smiled a smile as feral and insincere as the one I'd shown him. "I don't think so," he said.

He reached for the handle of the door and was about to pull it shut when my uncle stepped up to grab the frame and hold it open. Wikert glared at Gerry, then gave the door another tug, a reflex move. Gerry held on tight, keeping the door open. Wikert relaxed his grip on the handle, peering up at my uncle as if to say, What the hell do you think you're doing?

Gerry turned to me. "Would you excuse us for a minute, Jack?"

I stepped away from the Mercedes, crossing to the other side of the drive. Several cars passed along, briefly blocking my view of his discussion with my uncle. Gerry was bent over, his posture relaxed, one hand resting on the door frame, the other on the roof of the car. I could see that he was doing most of the talking. Whatever he had to say wasn't going over well with the other man, though you'd almost have to be telepathic to know that, so subtly did Wikert's expression shift.

At last Gerry straightened, turned, and motioned for me to rejoin them. As I came up to him, Gerry said, "I'll go back and see how your dad's doing." He gave Wikert a little wave of farewell, then walked away.

As Gerry was moving off, Wikert slammed his door shut. He started the Mercedes's engine, then pressed a button that hissed down the side window. His face had reddened. He was reaching for the gearshift as he spoke. "I can't see you today," he snapped, biting off the words. "I don't want you coming by my office, in any case. I'll be at home tomorrow night. Eight o'clock." He rattled off the address, shifted the car into gear, depressed the accelerator, and shot away.

I watched the Mercedes recede into the distance, then heard the crunch of slow-rolling tires approaching me from behind. I turned around and saw Gerry wheeling toward me. He brought the car to a halt a few yards away. I walked up, opened the rear door, and slid into the backseat.

Gerry glanced at me in his rearview mirror. "Well?"

"Tomorrow night," I said. "Eight o'clock. At his house."

Uncle Gerry nodded, satisfied. "Good."

"Are you going to tell me what you said to get him to see me?"

Gerry's eyes were twinkling. He smiled evilly to show me how pleased he was with himself. "Let's have lunch first, all right?" he said as he brought his eyes down from the mirror and steered the Cadillac away.

"TWO WORDS," Uncle Gerry was saying a short time later. "That's all it took."

Gerry, Dad, and I were seated around the kitchen table. The three of us were in shirtsleeves, ties loosened around our necks. Spread over the table were the remnants of our lunch—an opened pack of Oscar Meyer pressed ham, jars of mayonnaise and Grey Poupon mustard and dill pickles, a plate of lettuce and sliced tomatoes, a half-empty bag of Ruffles potato chips, a loaf of rye bread, bottles of Amstel Light.

"What two words?" I asked, tipping a bottle of beer to my lips.

Gerry looked at me slyly. "A name. One I'd be surprised you haven't heard of."

"Who?" I asked.

"Rudy Setzer."

I paused in mid-sip and lowered my beer. Uncle Gerry was grinning at the look of stupefaction on my face. He raised his bottle of beer, gave me a brief salute, then took a long swallow.

Dad asked, "Who's Rudy Setzer?"

Gerry set his beer down and reached for what was left of his sandwich. "Tell him, Jack."

"You're the one who mentioned his name," I said.

"*Somebody* tell me," Dad said.

Gerry waved a hand at me, a gesture of Go for it.

"He's a hood," I said to my father, still trying to recover from the shock. "A big-time mobster from L.A."

"Long Beach, originally," Gerry cut in.

I nodded. "He got his start with the longshoremen's union or the Teamsters or somebody. Sometime in the late 1950s, if I'm not mistaken."

"You're not," said Gerry.

"From there he moved to Manhattan Beach or Marina del Rey, someplace like that," I went on. "He got into the usual mob crap—gambling, hookers, dope. Whatever. For a while, he was trying to worm his way into the movies. I've got a college buddy I talk to now and then who's an independent film producer. He told me one time, about ten years ago, that Setzer came sniffing around, supposedly looking to invest in some project my friend had in the works. It turned out that Setzer'd been feeling up a bunch of independent producers, trying to ingratiate himself in something legit, like a lot of organized crime guys are always looking to do." I smiled sardonically. "Or maybe he just wanted to be the new Bugsy Siegel."

Dad asked, "Where do you know him from?"

"I don't actually 'know' him. I just know of him. The government keeps tabs on all reputed mobsters, and anybody who's a federal law-enforcement officer is supposed to at least know the names of the local wise guys." I looked to my uncle. "Why I reacted the way I did when you mentioned Setzer's name is because it's the second time I've heard it brought up in connection with this damned Ozzie Cole business."

It was my uncle's turn to look stupefied. I took some time explaining to Dad and Gerry who Teddie Ortiz was and how I'd found myself on his trail. Then I recounted my trip with Alan Feinberg to Terminal Island prison the morning before, describing our interview with Buddy Martinez. My father and my uncle listened to me with rapt attention.

"What I want to know is," I concluded, "what is Rudy Setzer's connection with the Cole family's attorney?"

Gerry said, "As it happens, Wikert used to be Setzer's attorney, too."

My eyebrows went up. "You're kidding."

"Nope," said Gerry. "I happen to have a colleague who knows Danny Wikert very well. While he was still down in L.A., Wikert occasionally represented mobsters. Among them Rudy Setzer."

"I thought he didn't do criminal law," I said.

"He doesn't," said Gerry. "You just said yourself how these mob guys like to stick their fingers into legitimate pies. Wikert was just doing the same thing for Setzer and his pals that he's been doing ever since he moved up to Santa Ynez nine years ago—handling lawful business concerns. He cut loose his old clients after he moved up here. But a lot of his newer ones wouldn't much care for it if they knew what kind of people he used to deal with on a fairly regular basis."

I could tell by the look on Dad's face that he and I understood at the same moment just what my uncle had done. "You sneaky bastard," I said to Gerry, my voice tinged with admiration. "You blackmailed him into talking to me."

He faked a frown, mocking an expression of injury. "Jack," he said, shaking his head in disapproval. "What is it they say all the time in the movies? 'Blackmail is such an *ugly* term.' All I did—as a favor to my favorite nephew, mind you—was twist his arm a little."

"Then I guess I should be grateful."

Gerry turned to my father, who was scowling. "What's the matter with you, Ray?" my uncle asked.

"Lawyers," Dad grunted, uttering the word as if it left a foul taste in his mouth.

WILLIAM DELING ...-A- 147

Gerry turned to my uncle, who was scowling amid the spectacular sun... vi... The work ... red.

"Perhaps," he said, smiling the word as if it felt ....

SEVENTEEN

LATER THAT AFTERNOON, an hour or so after Uncle Gerry had left to return to Santa Barbara, I got a phone call from Maggie McKenney, canceling our dinner date for that evening. Her appointment of Friday morning turned out to be a client who'd come to her in a near panic because he'd put off taking care of his income taxes, and the fifteenth of April was imminent. The client was a million dollar a picture screenwriter who lived in an A-frame house on the southwest shore of Lake Cachuma. He'd arrived at Maggie's office bearing five shoe boxes stuffed with last year's receipts. Nothing had been sorted or organized. He simply dumped the stuff onto her desk, then pleaded with her to take care of everything and have the forms ready for him to sign by Monday. When she told him that she'd have to charge double her usual rate, since she'd be giving up her weekend, he didn't bat an eye. Teasing her, I suggested that the opportunity to make a lot of money didn't strike me as an acceptable excuse for blowing off our date. She proposed making it up to me by using part of her client's substantial fee to pay for dinner next week at the restaurant of my choice. I told her that sounded like a reasonable counteroffer.

After getting off the phone with Maggie, I made two calls of my own. I was playing a hunch that had occurred to me while I was driving back from L.A. the night before. The hunch didn't strike me as particularly dicey, since it was based on what seemed to me to be some fairly solid assumptions.

While it was still remotely possible that Teddie Ortiz might've folded his con, the fact that he'd hit both Briggs and The Wine Merchant just two days before was a good reason for believing he was still in operation. Another had to do with my awareness of how greedy he could be. Also, he appeared almost certainly to be heading north. Putting all of that together, I called Doug Beamish and Ed Janowitz, a pair of wineshop owners in Santa Barbara who maintained the type of upscale business that would fit Teddie's target profile. Besides being customers of Donne Vineyards, Doug and Ed are friends of mine. Both were in their shops when I called, but Teddie had yet to drop in on either of them. Both agreed to call me immediately when—or if—he showed up.

MAGGIE'S BREAKING our date left me free Saturday night, which is how I ended up taking my dad out to dinner. We drove up to Santa Maria and ate at the Landmark Restaurant downtown. After that we dropped into one of the local multiplex movie theaters and sat through 105 minutes' worth of Hollywood's latest *Basic Instinct* clone, which according to its credits was written, coincidentally enough, by Maggie McKenney's screenwriter client. The film's hero was supposed to be an investigator working for the San Francisco District Attorney's office. He was handsomer and more buffed-out than any cop I've ever known, nearly as gorgeous as the female serial murder suspect with whom he spent a quarter of the movie's running time engaged in grueling sexual gymnastics. The sex caused the audience, except for me, not to mind that he was the stupidest and most reckless detective imaginable. His flagrant disregard for his—and other people's—safety was nearly as infuriating as his inability to notice the most obvious evidence that his paramour was a hatchet-wielding nutcase.

Whenever I see a motion picture that takes great, wide turns away from the reality of law enforcement methodology—which occurs in damn near every cop movie I've ever been to—I get so annoyed that I swear I'll never pay good money to watch another one. I know doctors and lawyers who feel similarly about films that grossly misportray their own professions. We keep going anyway, probably because we're hoping against hope that sooner or later somebody will do it right.

Dad and I got home around 11:00 p.m. He went straight to bed, but I sat up for a while in the family room, sipping from a snifter of warmed brandy and watching a rerun of "Cheers" on one of our local television stations. I wasn't paying much attention to the show, because while driving back from Santa Maria I'd begun to ponder my meeting with Daniel Wikert the next night.

Several questions were buzzing around like irate hornets inside my skull. The first resulted from my impression that Wikert was no dummy. On the contrary, he'd struck me as a particularly cunning individual. My question, then, was this: How could a lawyer this smart "let slip" to Brad Fitch the contents of Perry Cole's will, thereby providing the police with a fundamental component of their case against Ozzie? I could see only two possible answers. Either Wikert wasn't as smart as I thought he was, or—and this seemed more likely— he'd done it on purpose.

Which raised another question. Assuming he'd

known what he was doing when he'd talked to Fitch, Wikert had to have had an idea of what the consequences would be. If so, why would he want to see Ozzie charged with Perry's murder? I spent a fair amount of time turning that over in my mind, but I couldn't come up with anything that made sense.

Eventually I moved on to my last few questions, each of which had to do with this: Assuming that what Uncle Gerry had told Dad and me was true—that while he was still in L.A. Wikert had occasionally worked for mobsters—as far as Gerry knew it was nearly a decade since the man had had a hoodlum for a client. Gerry had taken it for granted that Wikert would be so concerned for his reputation that he'd respond to the right leverage. Which was what had occurred.

Except that a big part of me refused to buy it. I asked myself what real harm Gerry could do by spreading the information that Wikert had worked for Rudy Setzer and other wise guys almost ten years ago, especially when what Wikert was doing for them didn't appear to involve any criminal activity on his part. Why should he care who knew?

It was possible that Wikert didn't want anyone dredging up his past because he feared the consequences for his business nowadays, however slight those consequences might be. Clients can get skittish about the least little thing, so lots of lawyers ardently protect their reputations as a matter of course. Wikert's reaction to my uncle Gerry's arm-twisting would seem to indicate that he fell into that category.

But the way he'd changed his mind about talking to me had happened a bit too fast. I couldn't help remembering what Gerry had said a few days before, how something about Wikert stank to high heaven. When I finally went to bed, I was wondering if by tomorrow night I'd be any closer to finding out what that "something" was.

EIGHTEEN

I'D HOPED TO spend my daylight hours on Sunday doing what I do on many weekend mornings and afternoons between April and October: settled into the most comfortable chair in the family room, eyes glued to the Mitsubishi thirty-five-inch big-screen television set, clutching the remote control and switching from baseball game to baseball game. That TV—as well as smaller ones in my bedroom and Dad's—are hooked up to a satellite dish I installed behind the house a couple of years ago. On a good day I can follow as many as nine ball games: the Dodgers, Giants, Padres, Angels, and A's from their local affiliates; the Chicago, New York, and Atlanta superstations; a network game of the week. Occasionally Dad will join me in front of the TV, but he loses interest after a while, unless it's league championships or World Series time. He can't seem to understand my consuming passion for the sport, and I've given up trying to explain it to him. It's like any other addiction—you have to have it yourself to understand somebody else who's got it, too. It really does take one to know one.

Shortly after lunch, however, in the top of the ninth inning of a tie game between the Braves and the Marlins, I heard the telephone ringing in the back of the house. A few minutes later Dad came into the family room. "It's for you," he said. "It's Uncle Gerry."

The Marlins had runners on first and third and only one out, and the Braves were bringing in their new closer, an off-season free agent pickup from Baltimore who'd cost Ted Turner many millions of dollars. Without looking up from the TV, I said to Dad, "Ask if I can call him back."

When my father didn't make a move to leave, I turned to him. He had a peculiar sort of frown on his face. His expression wasn't dire enough to cause my internal alarm to go off, but it was unsettling anyway. "What's the matter?" I asked.

More frown. "He says it's urgent. He sounded like he meant it."

Just like that I was out of my chair and heading to my office. My phone was off the hook, lying on my desk. "Uncle Gerry?"

"Jack? I'm sorry to bother you—"

I cut off. "No need to apologize. What's up?"

"Are you busy right now?"

"Not particularly."

"Can you come over?"

"Come over where?"

"I'm at home."

There was an odd, off-center quality to his voice. As a rule, Gerry is as calm and collected an individual you are likely to meet. Something had rattled him. "Are you all right?" I asked.

"I think so. I don't know. That's why I'd appreciate it if you could come over as soon as you can. If it's not convenient now, maybe later—"

"Don't even start with that stuff. I'm on my way."

MY UNCLE lives alone. He owns a town house condominium on the grounds of the La Cumbre Golf and Country Club, in an area of Santa Barbara called Hope Ranch. To describe the area as "exclusive" would be an understatement. There are probably more million-aires per acre in my uncle's neighborhood than there are in Palm Beach, Florida. If Hope Ranch isn't the most pricey piece of real estate situated on the Pacific Ocean, it's right up there.

The drive to Gerry's condo took about forty minutes. At the entrance to the country club is a guardhouse, where I was halted by a young man dressed in a crisply pressed security officer's uniform. He emerged from the guardhouse, smiled hello, and asked me to state my business. I gave him my name, and he went back into the guardhouse to check it against the list on a clipboard he had there. Uncle Gerry had called to let him know I was coming. The guard asked politely if I needed di-rections to my destination, and I told him I knew the way. He saluted, and I drove off.

My uncle's place is at the center of a cluster of units owned by club members, the units only a short walk from the clubhouse and the first tee. Most of the owners don't reside there—in fact, according to Gerry, better than half of them don't even live in Santa Barbara. As I was striding up the short flagstone walkway to my uncle's front door, I was thinking about just how large a personal fortune you'd have to have in order to afford such a luxury.

He must have been watching for me because he pulled the door open before I had a chance to ring his bell. He was dressed for golf—a short-sleeved Polo shirt, comfortable trousers. There were perspiration stains drying around his armpits and across his chest. He noticed me taking in his costume and said without preamble, ''I'd just gotten back from shooting nine holes and was on my way to take a shower. That's when I heard the phone.''

"Hold on," I said. "You're going too fast for me."

Gerry looked chagrined. "Sorry. I guess I'm more shook up than I thought."

He stepped aside to let me into the foyer and closed the front door behind me. His golf bag was resting against the closed door of the foyer closet. To the right of the closet was a sunken living room. Directly ahead of us was a short staircase leading to the second level, Gerry's dining area and, beyond that, his kitchen. An additional staircase on that level led to three bedrooms upstairs, one of which was Gerry's, the second a guest room. He'd converted the third bedroom into a study, a sort of scaled-down version of his office downtown.

I followed him up the two flights of stairs to the third floor. He went straight into the study. The lights were on, the shade pulled down over the room's only window.

He moved to sit down behind a partner's desk made of dark walnut and motioned me to a seat opposite him. Except for a short stack of manila file folders, the desk looked tidy. To Gerry's left rested a combined telephone and answering machine. He laid a hand on the machine, drumming his fingers there for a moment, lost in thought.

I prompted him. "You started to say something about the phone…?"

He nodded, coming out of his dark reverie. "I'd just come back from the clubhouse and was on my way to the john to get cleaned up. When I heard the phone I almost decided, what the hell, I'll let the machine answer it. I don't know what made me decide to go ahead and pick it up…" He paused, frowning at the phone.

"Go on," I said.

He continued. "I said hello, and this voice I'd never

heard before said, 'Is this Gerald Donne? Gerald Donne the attorney?'" He shook his head. "I don't know what it was…just some kind of spooky feeling. Something." He tapped the phone with a finger. "I can use this to tape conversations. I do that sometimes, when I want to make sure I get verbatim what's been said by me or whoever I'm talking to. There's a switch right here…"

He started to lift up the cover of the answering machine part of the phone, and I said, "I know how it works. Mine does the same thing."

He closed the lid. "You know that whenever you record a conversation with somebody, you're supposed to let 'em know they're being taped?"

I nodded. "Unless you've got a court order for a wiretap."

"Exactly. A lot of machines, when you're recording, they give off a little beep every few seconds. To remind you.

"You're not telling me anything I'm not already aware of."

The look of chagrin again. "Sorry." He took a deep breath. "Anyway, what I started to say was that I bought this machine because it doesn't beep. You can tape conversations without whoever you're talking to knowing about it. You're supposed to inform them when you do it…but I don't always." He looked a little shamefaced. "It's illegal, I know."

I grunted. "Like you're the first lawyer to cut a few corners once in a while."

He smiled for the first time since I'd arrived, but the smile didn't last long. "As soon as this guy started to talk, I said to myself: You'd better tape this. Like I told you, it was just this…creepy feeling…" He paused again, making up his mind. "I wanted you to listen to this, Jack," he said. "Tell me if I'm overreacting."

He opened the lid of the answering machine once more and pressed a switch. The machine clicked and whirred for a moment. Then my uncle's voice through a tinny-sounding speaker. "Who's calling, please?"

The caller was a man, and Gerry was absolutely right—there was something about the voice that was simply *creepy*. Nothing definable, nothing I could put my finger on about its pitch or timbre or volume. It was just cold.

"Is this Gerald Donne?" the voice said. When Gerry didn't immediately respond, the voice continued. "I have a piece of advice for you, Mr. Donne. You've been poking around in something that's none of your business. It'd be a good idea for you to stop doing that."

Gerry's voice: "I don't know what you're talking about."

The caller: "This business with the Coles."

Gerry: "I beg your pardon?"

Caller: "You've been asking questions about the Cole family. What goes on with them is none of your business. If you keep on trying to *make* it your business, you'll regret it. Believe me."

Gerry: "Who is this—?"

Caller: "Leave the Coles alone, all right? I won't warn you twice."

Gerry: "Are you threatening me—?"

There was a click from the caller's end, the line going dead. Then Gerry's voice once more: "Hello...? Hello...?"

He reached over to press a switch that stopped the tape, then looked at me. His expression questioned me seriously.

"You still want to know if I think you're overreacting?" I asked.

"Am I?"

"No," I said. "You're not."

"So you think it's a serious threat?"

"It'll do till another one comes along."

He ran a hand through his hair. "Jesus Christ."

"You honestly don't have any idea who that is?" I said, indicating the answer machine. "You never heard that voice before?"

"Never."

I paused thoughtfully. "I know you told me you weren't in a position to reveal your sources about the Coles."

"I really shouldn't. If it ever got back to them…"

"I understand that. But obviously, whoever gave you your information didn't feel any need to extend the same courtesy."

My uncle scowled thoughtfully.

"If you can't tell me, then you can't tell me."

It took him a while to answer. "It's a friend of mine, in L.A. Two friends, actually. Two different sources. You know one of them yourself."

Gerry mentioned a name, and he was right about my recognizing it. It was a friend of Gerry's and Dad's who published a monthly newsletter of insider information concerning the wine business. "He's the one who gave me the scoop about the Coles' European deal falling through. He didn't want me to spread it around because he wants to break the story himself."

"What about Wikert?" I asked. "How'd you find out about his mob connection?"

"Another acquaintance of mine," Gerry said. "Who used to be one of Danny Wikert's law partners."

I nodded, digesting the information. Then I said, "If I had to guess, I'd say it was probably the second guy who snitched on you."

Gerry opened his mouth to protest, then caught himself. A look of dawning realization crossed his face. "You're right," he said. "It'd *have* to be him." He scowled again. "That son of a bitch."

"We can worry about what to do with him later," I said. "We should take care of something else first."

"What's that?"

"You mind if I use your phone?"

"God, no," Gerry said. "Be my guest."

IT TOOK SOME TIME to track down Brad Fitch. When I called the sheriff's station in Solvang, I wasn't surprised to find out that today was his day off. Despite my entreaties, they wouldn't give me a number where he could be reached. The best they could do, they said, would be to page him. But if he wasn't carrying his beeper—even though he was supposed to have it with him when he was off duty—I was out of luck. All they could do in that case would be to give him the message in person, when he returned. Which wasn't due to happen till Monday morning.

Fortunately, as it turned out, Fitch was wearing his beeper. He returned my call from a pay phone at a park in Goleta, where he was watching his six-year-old son's T-ball team play their first game of the season. I couldn't remember if he'd mentioned to me that he was married, much less that he had a kid. Not that it was important, at the moment.

I told him where I was, then gave him a brief summary of the circumstances that had brought me here, which included telling him that my uncle had been poking around in the Cole family's business on my behalf. After I'd finished, Fitch was quiet for a time. Then he asked, "You really think your uncle's being threatened?"

"It *sounded* pretty damned real," I said.

"Is there any way you can play it back for me?"

"You mean right now?"

"Yeah."

I turned to Gerry. "Is there any way you can play back the tape so we can hear it over the phone?"

"I think so," he said. He leaned forward in his chair, opened up the answering machine, and peered at a set of operating instructions pasted to the inside of the lid. After a moment, he looked up to me and nodded. He pressed a button inside the machine. The tape whirred briefly, rewinding, then Gerry's recorded voice came over the phone: "Who's calling, please?"

I said to Fitch, "Can you hear—?"

He shushed me.

We listened through to the end of the tape. After it had clicked off, Fitch said in a low voice, "Jesus."

"Is that real enough for you?" I asked.

"I'd say so," Fitch replied. "But the question is, what did you want me to do about it?"

"What do you mean, what do I want you to do? It's a threat, for God's sake, isn't it?"

"So what?"

"So *what!*"

"Settle down, okay? First off, does you uncle know whose voice that is threatening him?"

"I told you already," I said sullenly.

"Has any attempt been made to harm him? Anybody try to run his car off the road or take a potshot at him or anything like that?"

"No."

"No," Fitch repeated. "So what am I supposed to do about this? I can understand how you're feeling, but be reasonable. You know how it is with this sort of thing. Even if it's a legitimate threat, there's not a damn thing I can do."

"Until something actually happens to my uncle," I said sourly. "Then you can help pick up the pieces."

He tried to sound conciliatory. "I know it sucks, but that's the way it goes. If you're that concerned, tell your uncle to hire a bodyguard or something. Or tell him to go out and get a gun. But giving him advice is about all I can do."

We hung up a few moments after that. I knew that Fitch was right, of course. There was nothing for the police to go on, no clue as to who had made the call. And the threat itself was vague enough that it barely qualified as one—unless you heard the voice and felt the same chilly certainty that Gerry and I did. And Brad Fitch, too, for that matter.

Gerry looked at me expectantly, waiting for me to relay Fitch's side of the conversation. I shook my head. "There's nothing he can do," I said. "Not now, anyway."

Gerry's expression became dismayed. "You should be okay," I went on. "Just stay put. The club's well enough protected that somebody trying to sneak on to the grounds would get rounded up pretty quickly."

I could tell he wasn't thrilled with the idea of being a sitting duck. "Look," I added. "It was a warning. As long as you do what they say, they'll leave you alone. I don't like it any more than you do, but we have to take it at face value. If only because we don't have any reason not to."

He said doubtfully, "I suppose."

"I'll stick around, if you like," I said. "I can always cancel my appointment with Wikert."

He managed a pallid smile. "And be my baby-sitter?" He shook his head. "I'm all right, Jack. I'll be fine."

I nodded. But he could probably tell by the look on my face that I didn't believe it any more than he did.

NINETEEN

I ATE DINNER with my father around six-thirty that evening. He'd slow-roasted a thick pork tenderloin in the Weber kettle we keep on the back patio. It seemed appropriate to open a bottle of O.C. '90 Pinot Special Reserve, which, while still a little young, went well with the roast pork. It was too bad I didn't have much of an appetite because I couldn't shake the feeling of concern I had for Uncle Gerry.

To give myself something to do after dinner to keep my mind off Gerry and kill the half hour I had before I left for my meeting with Wikert, I cleaned up the kitchen. By the time I was finished with my chores, it was seven-thirty. I went into my bedroom, put on a clean shirt, slipped into a camel's hair sport coat I'd bought in San Francisco during Maggie McKenney's birthday trip, and headed out to my Jeep.

It was dark when I got to Wikert's house, which lay on a street called Deer Trail Lane, near the eastern edge of the town of Santa Ynez. I'd come to an upscale neighborhood. Wikert's house, like those of his neighbors, rested on a good-sized piece of property—two-thirds of an acre by my estimate—and was set in the middle of what appeared to be wild woodlands. The house itself was good-sized, too; a long, two-story, Tudor-style structure with a three-car garage, the house and garage set some twenty yards back from the street. A concrete driveway led up from the street, ending in a wide, circular turnaround in front of the garage.

As I was braking the Cherokee to a stop at the top of the turnaround, I could see that a light was on behind a window in one of the rooms on the first floor. Also on was a porch light that hung above the front entrance. The rest of the rooms on the first floor and all the ones on the second were unlit. I hoped that the lights meant somebody was home, since there was no sign of Wikert's Mercedes. The garage doors were closed, so I presumed that the car had been put away for the night. It was something I might take care to do myself if I owned an automobile worth three times as much as the average American earns in a year.

I got out of my Jeep and walked up a narrow sidewalk to the front porch. I had to climb up a couple of steps to reach the front door, which was recessed slightly and surrounded by a fanlight and sidelight arrangement made of amber-colored glass. I pressed the doorbell, and a deep bonging sound echoed within the house. I stood on the porch for half a minute before Wikert came to open the door. He looked at me impassively, then gave me a brief nod. It was all the greeting I was going to get.

He was dressed casually: new Topsiders with no socks, ivory-colored twill trousers, a cashmere, V-necked sweater the same color as his shoes. He was shirtless beneath the sweater. Like a lot of white-collar types, he looked vaguely uncomfortable out of his usual uniform, as if unconsciously aware that he'd chosen too precisely an ensemble that was supposed to make him feel relaxed.

He opened the door wider and stood aside, allowing me to enter. The floor of the foyer and the hallway that led to the rear of the house was made of polished blonde oak. Ahead of me was a staircase leading to the dark-

ened second story. To my right, a pair of old-fashioned
oak pocket doors on a runner—the entrance to a formal
dining room—were slid halfway closed. To my left was
Wikert's living room. Near one of the windows in there,
beside a brass floor lamp that provided the illumination
I'd seen from outside, was an easy chair with a match-
ing ottoman. While waiting for me to arrive, my host
had been passing the time by catching up on his reading,
a hardcover John Grisham novel that lay open and face-
down on the seat of the chair.

Wikert shut the door behind me. "This way," he
said. He headed down the hallway. We went past a
closed door on the left-hand side, then came to a second
closed door before which Wikert paused. After glancing
over his shoulder to make sure I was still with him, he
pushed open the door.

He reached for a switch inside the door and flipped
it on. An overhead fixture filled the room—Wikert's
study—with brightness. It was an impressive room,
larger and more neatly kept than my office at home.
Three of the room's four walls were comprised, floor to
ceiling, of mahogany bookshelves. The shelves were
well-stocked, and I did Wikert the courtesy of assuming
that he didn't buy his books by the yard at rummage
sales. The remaining wall was painted the color of sand,
and in the center of the wall was a tall, double-hung
window that undoubtedly provided a splendid view of
the landscape along that side of the house. Claret-
colored drapes made of some heavy fabric hung on either side of the window frame, surrounding Venetian
blinds a few shades darker than the oak of the hallway
floor. I was certain that the blinds' slats had come from
real trees.

The drapes were the same color as the room's wall-to-wall carpeting. In one corner of the room was a large desk made of the same mahogany as the bookshelves and wainscoting. On top of the desk rested a green-shaded banker's lamp made of brass. Behind the desk was a thickly padded chair upholstered in calf's leather dyed the color of strong tea. In the center of the room—around and on top of a rectangular, three-by-five-foot dhurrie rug that complemented the study's color scheme—was a sort of conversation pit arrangement: a settee and two chairs, likewise upholstered in calf's leather, though of a paler shade of brown than the chair behind the desk. The settee and chairs encircled a brass and glass-topped coffee table. On the floor at one end of the settee stood an ashtray, also made of brass. A well-savored meerschaum pipe, a pipe tool, and a butane lighter lay in a bowl of the ashtray. The room smelled faintly of cherry-flavored tobacco smoke.

Wikert motioned me toward the settee. As I sat down, I said to him, "Do you live alone, Mr. Wikert?"

He'd settled himself in one of the chairs on the other side of the coffee table. "What makes you ask that?"

I shrugged. "It's as neat as a pin in here, but there's not a lot of what I'd call a 'feminine touch' to the way your house is decorated. I was just curious about whether you were married or not, that's all."

He showed me a humorless smile. "Not anymore."

"But you used to be?"

He nodded. "It wasn't exactly an amicable split." The bitter smile reappeared. "Learning that you're the kind of person who's better off living by himself can be a very expensive lesson. And I'm not just talking about what a good housekeeper costs."

I looked around the room. "You seem to have managed to save a little for yourself."

He snorted, which I took to imply that he didn't think much of my sarcasm. "Let's cut to the chase, all right? What exactly is it you want from me?"

Nothing like dispensing with the bullshit, I said to myself, cognizant that Wikert was also dispensing with any gestures of hospitality, such as offering me something to drink. "I told you yesterday at the cemetery that I was working for Ozzie Cole," I said. "You automatically assumed I was trying to prove he didn't kill his father, but I'm not. Not directly, anyway. What I'm doing is trying to find out who's counterfeiting his wine."

He said too quickly, "I don't know anything about that."

It was tough to keep from smiling slyly. "I didn't ask if you did."

He waved an impatient hand. "You want to get to what you *do* want to ask me?"

I let the smile peek through a little. "There are two things, actually. First off, I'd like to hear more about what sorts of things you do for the Coles, legally speaking. Not just for Ozzie, but the whole bunch of them. And second, since it appears you've been letting other people know what's in Perry's will, I was hoping you could clue me in, too."

He studied the bland, nonchalant look on my face, trying to gauge what I did or didn't already know. I could gather from his expression what was going on behind his eyes. He'd been cornered, and he was wondering whether he had some way out. He wasn't about to tell me the truth if he could help it, but he also didn't know at what point I'd recognize bogus information and start calling him on it.

He was good. "Perry's will has been filed with the

probate court, so it's a matter of public record. My telling you what's in it—or telling anybody else, for that matter—violates nobody's confidence.''

He was good, but so am I. "The question is," I said, "did you file the will before or after you talked to Lieutenant Fitch?"

Wikert regarded me with a cool look of challenge. "As far as I'm concerned, that's a moot point. As for what I do for the Coles, maybe you've heard of something called attorney-client privilege.''

"I've heard of it," I said.

"Then I imagine you know what it means. What I do for my clients is none of your goddamned business.''

I smiled once more. "I thought you might tell me anyway. If not as a favor to me, as a favor to my uncle—''

I was interrupted by the bonging of the doorbell. Wikert and I turned to look toward the front of the house. Then we looked at each other. His expression questioned me. The doorbell bonged again. "It's not my house," I said.

He got to his feet, still looking puzzled. The doorbell bonged a third time. "Excuse me," he said. I nodded, and he left the room.

I listened to his footsteps moving down the hallway toward the front door. I heard him pull the door open. I thought I could make out low voices, Wikert's and another man's, though I couldn't tell what they were saying to one another. One of the voices raised its volume in what seemed to be an expression of anger. It sounded like Wikert's, but I was too far away to tell for certain.

Then I heard a terrifying sound that literally raised the hairs on the back of my neck. It was a barely human howl of agony, as high-pitched as the shriek of a child. Except it wasn't a child. It was Wikert.

I was up instantly, running from the study into the hallway. The front door was open. Wikert was in the foyer, on his knees, clutching his face with both hands, violently jerking his head back and forth. The flesh beneath his fingers appeared to be steaming. "Oh god," he was wailing in the same high-pitched screech, the words seeming to gag him. "Oh god oh god oh god…"

I rushed up and knelt beside him. Before I could do anything, he pulled his hands away from his face and clutched me tightly. I could smell the odor of seared flesh at the same moment that I caught a glimpse of the hideous, raw mess that had been his mouth and nose and eyes. He pressed his ruined face against my chest and made mewling, choking sounds.

Somewhere outside a car door slammed, an engine roared, tires squealed. The roar of the engine diminished as the car raced down Wikert's driveway toward the street.

Somebody else might have decided it would be okay to leave behind the man I cradled in my arms for the short time it would take to get a look at the car that was speeding away, to note its make and model, perhaps even to read the numbers and letters of its license plate. Somebody else might have been able to leave Wikert alone, however briefly. But I couldn't.

TWENTY

ONE OF THE QUALITIES you must possess in order to do undercover work is an ability to react coolly and swiftly in an emergency. If you're hanging with a bunch of bad guys and pretending to be one of them, you have to possess a high degree of improvisational talent so as to handle whatever abrupt and unexpected curveballs are hurled your way. You have to know how to think on your feet, not just faster than an ordinary civilian is able to do, but faster than nine out of ten of your fellow police types. Otherwise, you end up dead.

I made the choice quickly, deciding it would be better for me to get Wikert to the hospital myself rather than call and wait for an ambulance. I hoisted him to his feet before the sound of his assailant's car had faded away. Assuming the kitchen to be somewhere in the back of the house, I slid my right arm under his shoulders, draping his arm around my neck. Clasping my hand onto his wrist, I guided him down the hallway. He wasn't much help. Barely conscious, he was having a difficult time staying on his feet. He'd stopped making intelligible sounds. All he could do was whimper.

We pushed through a door at the end of the hallway and entered the kitchen. Light bled in from the hallway through the open door, so I didn't have to pause to search for a switch. I lugged Wikert to a large double sink set in a counter across the room. I wasn't especially gentle about shoving his head beneath the faucet, but this wasn't the time for tenderness. I turned on the tap

and let cool water flush away as much as I could of
whatever had burned him. He struggled for a time, letting out little *eeks* of pain as the water flooded over his
raw flesh, but I held him tight. When I felt him go limp,
I turned off the water and let his body sag to the floor.

I found a stack of clean kitchen towels in a drawer
next to the sink. I draped a couple of towels around
Wikert's head, loosely covering his face from hairline
to chin. Then I crouched behind him, lifted him up, and
locked my arms across his chest in a fireman's carry.
As I dragged him out of the kitchen and down the hallway to the front door, I could feel the strain on the
muscles in my legs and back and shoulders. I'd spend
the next couple of days paying for the exertion.

I was scuttling backward out the front door, still dragging Wikert, when my heel bumped against something.
I craned my neck to look behind me at what I'd kicked
off the porch onto the lawn. A small glass bottle. The
residue of some clear liquid clung to its sides, glistening
to the light from the fixture above the porch.

I came back for the bottle after I got Wikert folded
into the passenger seat of my Cherokee. Knowing better
than to handle it with my bare hands, I stripped off my
coat, then bundled it around the bottle, putting several
layers of thick cloth between my skin and whatever it
was that had done such horrible damage to Wikert's
face. Then I went back to the Jeep, stuffed the bundle
underneath the driver's seat, climbed in behind the
wheel, started the engine, and sped away.

The distance from Wikert's house to the Santa Ynez
Valley Hospital in Solvang was a fraction under three
miles. The drive took less than ten minutes. I squealed
the Jeep to a halt in front of the entrance to the emer-

gency room. Wikert hadn't regained consciousness, so I let him stay in the Jeep while I hurried into the ER.

As I approached the desk, an overweight, ruddy-cheeked woman in her twenties peered up at me from a computer terminal into which she'd been entering data from a printed form clipped to a stand next to the computer's VDT. It was obvious that she'd dealt with enough distraught people to know the difference between somebody who was hysterical and somebody who had something seriously and genuinely wrong.

"There's an injured man outside in my car," I said gravely. "He's been badly burned."

The woman reacted instantaneously, reaching for a multiline telephone on her desk. She pressed a button on the telephone, then barked a terse command into her headset.

Within moments, three young men dressed in green scrubs seemed to materialize from nowhere, wheeling a gurney. They paused just long enough to look questioningly at the woman behind the desk. She aimed her chin at me. They turned. I nodded toward the entrance doors. "Out there in the Jeep," I said.

The men moved rapidly, with the precision of a close-order drill team. They rushed outside, lifted Wikert from the Cherokee, laid him on the gurney, and wheeled him back in. They disappeared through a set of double doors off to one side of the registration desk, leaving the woman and me behind.

THE WOMAN'S NAME—Claudette Wells—was printed on a photo ID badge pinned to her smock. She informed me that the doors through which Wikert had been taken led to the ER's assessment area, where the extent of his injuries would be determined. I nodded, acknowledging the information, and asked her where I could leave my vehicle. She gave me directions to the nearest visitors' parking area. I thanked her, then asked her to call the sheriff's station and request to speak to Lieutenant Bradley Fitch.

After parking the Cherokee, I took a seat in the waiting room, which lay on the opposite side of the desk from the treatment area. It was a slow night. Besides me, the only people waiting were a Mexican family, a mother and two small children. The mother looked to me to be a child herself, not yet out of her teens. They sat quietly, staring up at a television suspended from the ceiling. They were watching an Indiana Jones movie. All three were enthralled by what they saw on the screen.

I was wondering what it would be like to be a child raising children when a salt-and-pepper pair of uniformed deputy sheriffs arrived. Leaving their patrol car outside the entrance to the ER, they came in and strode purposefully to the registration desk. Claudette Wells pointed in my direction. I stood up as one of the deputies moved away from the desk and crossed to me. He was a black man who looked to be not much older than the woman watching TV with her kids. They were all young—the Mexican woman, the kids, both deputies, the woman behind the desk. Everybody was young but me.

The deputy, whose name was Grimes, didn't bother with any sort of greeting, friendly or otherwise. Stone-faced, he simply asked my name. I told him. He asked for identification. I took out my wallet and showed him my driver's license. He asked if I'd mind telling him what this was all about, he and his partner having come to the hospital in response to a call reporting an aggravated assault. I suggested we go someplace private where I could give him the whole story without upsetting anyone who might inadvertently overhear. He asked if their patrol car outside would be okay. I told him to lead the way.

We sat in the front seat, and I gave him a capsule version of what had happened, including a mostly truthful explanation as to who Wikert was and why I had happened to be visiting him. I'd come to the part where I was picking up the little bottle I'd found when Brad Fitch arrived. He jumped out of his car and was hustling toward the entrance to the ER when I rolled down the passenger window and called his name.

Fitch halted and turned around, a dozen feet from me. His eyes narrowed briefly, then widened with surprise as he recognized who had called to him. "Jack?" he said with amazement as he started toward the patrol car. "What are you doing here?"

"You and the lieutenant know each other?" Grimes asked.

"We go back a ways," I said.

Fitch came up to my side of the car and leaned casually against the door. "What in the hell's going on? I come back from Santa Barbara, and I'm lying on the bed in my motel, watching TV, when all of a sudden my beeper goes off for the second time today. I check in, and they give me the number of the Santa Ynez hospital's emergency room. I call the number, and this woman answers. 'Lieutenant Fitch,' she says, 'you need to get over here right away.' 'Who's dead?' I ask her. 'Nobody,' she says, 'but there's a man here who wanted me to get in touch with you and tell you to get over here.' 'What man?' I say. 'He didn't give me his name,' she says." Fitch grinned at me wryly. "I take it you're the man who wouldn't give his name."

I nodded.

"So what are you doing here?" he repeated. "Actually, the question should be what am *I* doing here?" His wry grin reappeared. "I'm gonna be miffed if you guys got me all the way over here without there being a nice juicy homicide for me to check out."

"I just brought Ozzie Cole's attorney to the emergency room," I said.

Fitch's cheerful expression transformed to one of bewilderment. "Wikert?"

I nodded again.

"What happened to him?"

"Somebody threw acid in his face."

Fitch looked as if somebody had slapped him very hard. "Who?"

"I don't know."

He regarded me doubtfully. "You were there, but you don't know who did it?"

"It's a long story." I gestured to the man in the driver's seat. "I just got through telling it to Deputy Grimes here."

"Fuck Grimes," said Fitch. "Tell *me*."

TWENTY MINUTES LATER Fitch and I were in the hospital's cafeteria, seated at a Formica-topped table and drinking coffee that had been fermenting in a large urn for several hours. Fitch hadn't wanted to join the deputy and me in the patrol car, so I'd accompanied him inside to the registration desk. This after I'd retrieved my bundled jacket from the Jeep and passed it on to Grimes and his partner. Fitch ordered them to drop the jacket off at the sheriff's substation so somebody there could begin an analysis of what was in the bottle I'd found and confirm that the stuff was what had been used to ruin Daniel Wikert's face. After that the deputies were to go to Wikert's house and secure the scene until the evidence technicians arrived.

Inside the ER, Fitch identified himself to Claudette Wells, showing her his badge. He asked her if there was someplace he and I could get a cup of coffee while we talked. She suggested the cafeteria and told us where it was. The lieutenant then asked her to have the doctor treating the man I'd brought in come find us when he had news of Wikert's condition. Fitch promised her we would remain in the cafeteria until the doctor showed up.

It was as slow a night for the cafeteria as it was for the emergency room. The only customers aside from Fitch and me were a trio of nurses on their dinner break. The nurses were sitting far enough away from us to be out of earshot as I told Fitch my story.

When I'd concluded, Fitch rubbed his chin, frowning thoughtfully. "You're sure that other voice you heard was a man's?"

"I'm positive," I said.

"But you couldn't make out what they were saying?"

I shook my head.

Fitch's hand was resting on the table, beside his cup of coffee. He drummed his fingers on the tabletop. "Too bad you didn't get a look at the vehicle."

"I told you why I didn't—"

He lifted his hand to silence me. "I'm not blaming you for anything. Hell, you couldn't just leave Wikert there on the floor screaming blue murder. I'd've done exactly the same thing. All I'm saying is it's too bad you didn't get a look at the car. Don't get so damned irritated.''

I grumbled, ''Yeah, yeah…''

''Anyway,'' Fitch went on, ''I appreciate your getting in touch with me like you did. I assume it's because you're thinking whoever attacked Wikert had something to do with old man Cole's murder?''

''Isn't that what you think, too?'' I asked.

He shrugged, showing me his thoughtful frown again. ''I suppose I should get hold of Ozzie Cole and ask him if he can account for his whereabouts this evening.''

''It wasn't Ozzie,'' I said.

Fitch looked at me condescendingly, shaking his head. ''After he got released the other day, didn't he seem to you to be rather pissed off at his attorney for refusing to defend him? I'd be mighty surprised if Wikert's name didn't come up in conversation while you were taking Ozzie home.''

''We talked about Wikert,'' I admitted. ''In fact, it was one of the reasons I went over to see him tonight.''

Fitch spread his hands, a gesture of *I rest my case*.

''But,'' I insisted, ''that doesn't change the fact that Ozzie Cole is not the kind of person who'd throw a bottle of acid in somebody's face. It's that simple.''

Fitch was shaking his head again. ''For Christ's sake, listen to yourself. You sound like one of those goofy civilians after they've just found out that the guy next door is an ax murderer. 'But officer, Mr. Smith was always such a *good* neighbor. Such a nice man, always polite and friendly and always taking such wonderful care of his property and all. I'd *never* have thought he'd be capable of chopping up a dozen people into teeny little pieces the way he did…'''

He paused to look past me, in the direction of the

entrance to the cafeteria. I turned around. Walking toward our table was an Oriental man in his early thirties.
He wore wire-rimmed spectacles, and he was dressed
in hospital scrubs similar to those of the men who'd
wheeled Wikert from my Jeep into the ER's treatment
area. The front of his shirt was spattered with purplish
specks of blood. The expression on his face was exhausted and disheartened. He came up to us and said,
"Is one of you Lieutenant Fitch?"

"That's me," Fitch replied.

"Philip Hong," the man said, introducing himself.
"I'm the ER resident on duty tonight."

Fitch motioned to me. "This is Jack Donne. He's a
private detective. He's the one who delivered your patient."

Dr. Hong greeted me with a brief nod, then sat in an
empty chair. He took a deep breath that he exhaled
slowly. "I never get used to this part of the job," he
said. He looked from Fitch to me. "I'm afraid Mr. Wikert didn't make it."

Fitch's flabbergasted expression mirrored mine. Before either of us could utter a word, though, Dr. Hong
was saying, "Even if he'd survived, he'd have been in
awful shape. Blind in both eyes. Severe disfigurement.
Plastic surgery wouldn't have helped him much, if it
could've been performed at all."

The doctor took off his glasses, rubbed his eyes with
a thumb and forefinger, then slipped the glasses back
on. "I'm guessing either sulfuric acid or nitric acid or
something just as corrosive. Whatever it was, it was
nasty. Whoever did it intended to hurt him. Bad." Hong
paused, shaking his head sadly. "He swallowed some
of the stuff. Probably not more than a few milliliters,
but that's all it'd take. Judging from how extensive the

tissue damage was, it looks to've been a pretty high concentration. His esophagus was eaten away so fast we didn't even get a chance to intubate him.''

The three of us were silent for a time. I turned to Fitch. ''Remember what you told me when you first got here?'' He regarded me with a sullen look of inquiry. ''You were bitching because I made you rush over here when there wasn't a nice homicide for you to play with.''

The doctor regarded Fitch with an expression that displayed his displeasure with the lieutenant's sense of humor. ''I guess that means you're happy now,'' Dr. Hong said, ''doesn't it?''

IT WAS NEARLY midnight by the time I left the hospital. Almost as soon as I'd settled myself behind the wheel I felt exhaustion wash over me like a wave. It was on account of the fatigue—plus the fact that I'd been preoccupied by other events for the past several hours— that the notion didn't occur to me till I was better than halfway home.

I pulled off the highway and left the Jeep idling while I picked up my car phone. I punched in my uncle's home number, then waited anxiously through a half dozen rings before he answered in a sleepy, tentative voice, ''Hello?''

''Uncle Gerry? It's Jack.''

''Jack?''

''Yeah. Are you okay?''

''I'm fine. Just drowsy, that's all. Only went to bed a while ago.'' He paused briefly, then asked, ''What time is it?''

''Around midnight,'' I said.

''Are you just checking in, or what? I haven't had

any more threatening calls, if that's what you wanted to know.''

"That's partly why I called," I said. "That and something else.''

"What?''

I hadn't worked out the best way to tell him about what had happened to Wikert, and I ended up more or less blurting it out in a rush. By the time I'd finished, Gerry was wide awake. "Good God," he whispered grimly.

I took a deep breath. "I don't want to alarm you, but the reason I called is because what happened to Wikert made me think about that call you got today.''

He wasn't able to keep the trepidation out of his voice. "You don't think whoever did that to him will come after me, do you?''

"I don't know," I said frankly.

"Well, for God's sake, what should I do?''

I'd expected that question and I was ready with an answer. "Do you have any business or anything that could get you out of town for a while?''

"How long a while?''

"A week, say? Maybe just a couple of days? Until the cops get a line on who killed Wikert.''

Silence from his end, then, "How far away do I have to go? San Francisco? The East Coast? Europe?''

"San Francisco's probably far enough. Just so as few people as possible know where you are.''

More silence, until, "I've got a client in the Bay Area who's been after me to come up and work with him face-to-face on something we've got going. He's Japanese. They're very big on personal contact, and so far I've only been dealing with him on the phone.''

"Will he be annoyed if you show up on his doorstep out of the blue?"

"I doubt it."

"How soon can you leave?"

"You mean tonight?"

"If it's possible."

"Jesus, Jack," he said. "You're serious, aren't you?"

"I'm dead serious."

He exhaled heavily. "Then I guess I'd better pack."

We made arrangements for him to contact Dad and me as soon as he arrived at his destination. After I hung up and steered back onto the highway, I felt somewhat better, at least as far as my uncle was concerned.

Though I had no proof, I felt certain that whoever had attacked Daniel Wikert had also been the person who had threatened my uncle. I intended to make sure that the son of a bitch would be nailed to a wall very, very soon. It had started off as a kind of lark, my little diversion with Ozzie Cole, but it wasn't anymore. Somebody had threatened a member of my family, which meant it was no longer a game to me. Now it was something personal.

TWENTY-ONE

I SPENT MOST OF Monday morning at the sheriff's sub-station in Solvang, arriving there a little after nine and not leaving until Brad Fitch and I went out for lunch around twelve-thirty. I was there to give an official statement concerning the incident in which I'd been involved the night before—namely, the murder of Daniel Wikert. I gave my statement, then waited around for it to be word processed so that I could read it over, attest to its accuracy, and sign it.

Wikert's autopsy report and the preliminary lab findings on the bottle I'd found in front of his house were delivered to Fitch right before we left for lunch. The lawyer's official cause of death was a massive internal hemorrhage, the consequence of his having ingested a powerful caustic substance that had been hurled into his face by person or persons unknown. The residue in the bottle turned out to be sulfuric acid—score one for Dr. Philip Hong. There was nothing unique about the stuff; it could be purchased anonymously at any chemical supply store. Nor was there anything special about the bottle itself, except that it yielded no fingerprints. Whoever attacked Wikert had worn gloves. Neither Fitch nor I registered much surprise over that bit of news.

We had lunch at the Belle Terrasse on Copenhagen Drive, a few blocks' walk from the sheriff's station. After we'd been seated, we placed our orders—linguine with clam sauce for two, along with a dry Erbaluce di Caluso I chose from the wine list, the lieutenant electing to disregard that he was technically on duty. He also mentioned that the County of Santa Barbara would be picking up the tab.

While the waiter was pouring our wine, Fitch asked me about my uncle. Gerry had telephoned from San Francisco that morning, while Dad and I were having coffee, to say that he'd tossed his briefcase and a suitcase full of clothes into the trunk of his car and driven all night. He'd just checked into the Mark Hopkins, and as soon as he got off the phone, he intended to sleep for about ten hours.

"So I guess he's okay?" Fitch said.

I nodded. Then I asked him if he'd had a chance to speak to Ozzie Cole that morning. He said that he had, then informed me, "Ozzie doesn't have an alibi for last night."

"Where'd he say he was?"

"Home," Fitch answered. "All by himself."

"How'd he take the news about Wikert?"

"Very matter-of-factly," said Fitch. "He didn't seem particularly surprised or upset, if that's what you're asking."

"Which doesn't prove a thing."

Fitch shrugged, conceding the point.

"What about a motive?" I went on. "You don't really believe what you said to me last night, do you?"

Fitch looked puzzled. "What did I say last night?"

"Some nonsense about Ozzie being pissed off at Wikert for not wanting to defend him."

He shook his head. "That was bullshit. I was just thinking out loud."

"So what's his motive?"

Fitch considered for a moment, tapping the bowl of his wineglass with a fingertip. Then he said, "First off,

I don't think he meant to kill Wikert.'' I opened my mouth to protest, and Fitch held up a hand to stifle me. '' 'He' not necessarily meaning Ozzie Cole. What I meant to say was, whoever did it probably didn't intend for Wikert to swallow the shit. The idea was to hurt him, not kill him.''

"If whoever did this to Wikert didn't mean to kill him, then they must've had some other reason for doing what they did.''

Fitch nodded.

"That brings me back to my earlier question. Where's the motive?''

"Why would somebody throw acid in Wikert's face?''

"Yeah.''

"Blind him, maim him, disfigure him? Why would somebody want to do that?''

"Yeah.''

Fitch showed me a mirthless, cynical smile. "Love.''

"Come again?''

He lifted his glass of wine, took a sip, and eased back in his chair. "I was talking to one of the old-timers at the station this morning,'' he said. "One of these guys who's been around forever. This old sergeant must be pushing sixty. Anyway, we were discussing Wikert, and he told me about a case he remembered down in L.A., ten or fifteen years ago. This young woman, very attractive girl—an actress or a model, something like that. She gets herself romantically involved with some sleazy, show-biz asshole who turns out to be a very jealous lover. After a while, she gets sick of his shit and she dumps him—only he's not the type to tolerate that very well. He goes and hires some scumbag to head over to her apartment, ring her doorbell, and when she answers, the son of a bitch throws battery acid in her face. The boyfriend figures if he can't have her, he's gonna make it so nobody else is gonna want her either. Only the same thing happens to her that happens to Wikert. She ends up swallowing the damn stuff, and a couple of days later it kills her.'' Fitch took another sip of wine. ''The L.A. cops popped both of 'em—the boyfriend *and* the guy who threw the acid. They're doing life in San Quentin, which is exactly where those two cocksuckers belong.''

While the lieutenant was speaking, our waiter appeared with our meals, served us, and went away again. As I listened to Fitch's anecdote, I was using my fork to twirl the pasta around on my plate, having lost interest in eating. After Fitch concluded his story, he awaited my reaction. I laid down my fork and reached for my glass of wine. ''Love, huh?'' I said, taking a drink.

Fitch had forked a bite of pasta from his plate. ''Love or money. Whenever somebody commits a murder, you can give odds they did it for either love or money. It's almost always one or the other.''

He might have been oversimplifying matters, but he wasn't wrong. ''You know,'' I said, ''last night Wikert mentioned that he was divorced. He didn't make it sound like the circumstances were too pleasant. Maybe you should check out his ex-wife's whereabouts and find out if she hated him enough to have this done to him.''

''I've already got some people working on that.''

I regarded him curiously. ''It sounds to me like you're thinking Ozzie Cole might not've had anything to do with Wikert. Maybe you're even thinking it's possible Wikert's murder and Perry's murder aren't related at all.''

Fitch eyed me with skepticism. "Do you think they're not related?"

I hesitated only a moment before saying, "No."

"Neither do I," said Fitch.

As I DROVE HOME, I replayed the conversation Fitch and I'd had over lunch. Love or money, I told myself sourly. Ninety-nine times out of a hundred, the reason one human being kills another human being is because of love or money.

In the case of Perry Cole, his death all but certainly was cash-motivated. While I couldn't put a precise dollar value on the net worth of Perry's estate, I could guess that the amount would be close to the GNP of a small country. More money than the vast majority of killers would need as a motive to commit murder. *Way* more.

Wikert, however, was another story. Assume that Perry's murder and Wikert's murder were linked. The two events were too coincidental to believe otherwise. Was money the connection here? It seemed more than possible—until you recalled that Wikert's murder wasn't intentional. Did that mean, then, that it *wasn't* money that motivated the attack on Wikert? Was there some other relationship between what happened to him and what happened to Perry? If so, what?

On one level, I could appreciate Fitch's single-minded pursuit of Ozzie Cole. Ozzie's being behind everything would make for a nice, neat package, all tied up with a pretty bow. Fitch's tracking down of Wikert's ex-wife was merely perfunctory. He'd already made up his mind that Ozzie was responsible for both murders. All he had to do was prove it.

I thought about driving over to Ozzie's and pinning down his alibi for the night before, but I was discouraged by a headache that had appeared midway through lunch. I decided that paying a visit to Ozzie Cole would only make the headache worse. I just wanted to be alone.

I AWOKE FROM my nap around three-thirty, feeling better. The Advil I'd taken before lying down had performed its magic. I got up from my bed ravenous, having left my meal at the Belle Terrasse virtually untouched.

Going into the kitchen, I rummaged in the pantry and found a large can of Campbell's Homestyle Chicken Noodle Soup. While the soup was heating, I made myself a cheese sandwich from two slices of whole wheat bread and a chunk of white cheddar I found in the refrigerator, from which I also pulled out a bottle of Anchor Steam. I dumped the hot soup into a bowl, then carried the bowl, the sandwich, and my beer to the kitchen table.

As I sat down to my meal, I began to run through various scenarios in which I rattled the cages of June and Grant Cole, who—it seemed to me—would be the ones to provide most of, if not all, the answers I was looking for. I'd just made up my mind to give them a call when the telephone rang.

"Jack Donne?" said a cheerful, vaguely familiar male voice.

"Speaking," I said. "Who's this?"

"Ed Janowitz. I'm at the store. You said you wanted

me to get in touch with you if that salesman you told me about dropped by to peddle some O.C. pinot.''

''I remember.''

''The guy was just here,'' said Janowitz. ''He left not ten minutes ago.''

''Teddie Ortiz?''

''Yeah,'' answered Janowitz. ''He gave me his card and a number in town where I can reach him.''

''He's still in Santa Barbara?''

''I guess so. It looks like a local number. Probably a motel or something.''

''He didn't say where he was staying?''

''Uh-uh. He just gave me his card and wrote the number on the back.''

''Read it to me, will you?''

As Janowitz recited, I reached for a pencil attached by a string to a little notepad stuck by a magnet to the side of the refrigerator. I scribbled Teddie Ortiz's number on the pad, then said to Janowitz, ''How late do you stay open tonight, Ed?''

''Till seven.''

''Can you wait until I get there before you close? I'll try to be there as quickly as I can.''

I could picture the rueful expression on his face. ''If I'm not home by eight o'clock on the dot,'' Janowitz said, ''my wife'll crucify me.''

''If I'm not at the store by seven-thirty,'' I told him, ''go on home.''

''It's a deal,'' he said.

TWENTY-TWO

I CAUGHT BRAD FITCH at his desk in the sheriff's station. "Hey, Jack," he chirped when my call was put through to him. "I was just about to give you a jingle. Probate faxed me a copy of old man Cole's will about an hour ago. I'm almost to the last page. I was thinking you might want to have a look at it."

"Maybe later," I said. "Right now I need a favor."

"What's the favor?"

"I need an address to go with a phone number somebody just gave me."

"Whose number is it?"

"I think it's a motel," I said.

"Where?"

"In Santa Barbara."

"That shouldn't be too tough," he said.

I read off the number Ed Janowitz had passed on to me. "Hang on," said Fitch. "I'll check it out." He put me on hold.

I'd called him assuming that somewhere around the station was a directory in which phone numbers were listed numerically rather than alphabetically by name. Even if the station didn't have one, all Fitch had to do was call an operator, explain who he was, and have the operator look up the name to go with the number. Having no legal authority, I'd be unable to get somebody to do that for me. Fitch could throw his weight around in a lot of places I couldn't.

He came back on the line only a couple of minutes

after putting me on hold. "The number you gave me is for the Holiday Inn, in Goleta."

How 'bout that, I thought, gratified. "Thanks, Brad. I appreciate it."

"You gonna tell me who's staying there?" he asked.

"It isn't anybody you know," I said. I considered for a moment, then added, "Though it might be a good idea for you to stick close to the phone for a while."

"How long a while?"

"The next couple of hours, at least. It'd make me feel better if I knew you were someplace you could be reached on short notice."

"Jack," he said distrustfully, "what's going on?"

"Maybe nothing," I said. "But maybe something."

"In the meantime I'm just supposed to sit tight and wait for you to call. Is that it?"

"That's it."

"I don't have to stay *here,* do I?" he asked, sounding peevish. I couldn't decide if he was being sarcastic or was genuinely miffed. "There's not a helluva lot to do, if I'm only gonna be killing time. If it's all right with you, I'd like to go back to my motel and get something to eat. If it'll make you happy, I'll stay in and order room service."

I told him not to put himself out on my account.

Twenty minutes after getting off the phone with Fitch, I was heading toward Santa Barbara on Route 154. Before leaving the house, I'd retrieved the pistol I keep in the top drawer of my desk. The gun is a 9-millimeter Browning automatic I've owned since my days with the Treasury Department. I clean and oil the gun regularly, and I keep it loaded. Its holster clips onto my belt, the whole rig fitting comfortably into the small of my back. After securing the gun, I slipped on one of my two remaining sport coats, the one I'd worn last night having been ruined after being wrapped around an unstoppered bottle of sulfuric acid. The tail of my jacket covered the gun, keeping it out of sight from anybody who might become nervous about seeing it.

IT WAS SIX O'CLOCK straight up when I pulled the Cherokee to the curb across the street from Janowitz Fine Wines & Spirits in downtown Santa Barbara. The shop is on Figueroa Street, near the corner of Figueroa and State, not far from the café where Dad and Uncle Gerry and I had met for breakfast. I was thinking about that as I got out of the Jeep, how it seemed impossible to have taken place such a short time ago, given all that had gone on since then. Six days. It seemed more like forever.

I crossed the street, entered the shop, and spotted Ed Janowitz building a display of Beringer White Zinfandel in front of his checkout counter. He stood up as I approached him, a burly man with kinky red hair and a bushy beard, looking like a displaced Viking. He grinned, glad to see me, and extended a meaty hand for me to shake. Then he reached into a pocket of his shirt and pulled out a business card. "This is the guy, isn't it?" he asked.

The card was identical to the one Jerry Wiedemeyer had shown me in La Jolla. Scribbled in blue ink on the back was the phone number of the Goleta Holiday Inn. "This is him," I said.

"So what's his story? He offered me as much O.C. '90 Pinot Reserve as I wanted at three hundred a case. It was damned tough to tell him I'd have to think about it instead of just having him send it on over."

Three hundred a case. The price had gone up, which

probably meant that Teddie was skimming money off the top for himself. "It's a scam," I told him. "Teddie Ortiz is a crook. By that I don't just mean you can't trust him because he's somebody who'll fuck you over in a deal. He's an honest-to-god professional con artist."

At first Janowitz looked startled, until his expression changed to an angry scowl. "Who's the son of a bitch trying to scam?" he asked. "Me?"

I shook my head. "Only indirectly. The wine's counterfeit. He's really scamming Ozzie Cole."

The startled expression reappeared. "Ozzie Cole?"

I nodded.

"Why's he scamming Ozzie Cole?"

"That's what I intend to ask him," I said. "You can help me out with that, if you don't mind getting a little more involved."

He regarded me dubiously. "What do you want me to do?"

"Just call up Teddie at his motel and make sure he's there," I said.

"Hell." Janowitz snorted. "That's easy."

"I was hoping you'd feel that way, Ed," I said.

MY CURRENT run of luck was still holding, Teddie Ortiz having just walked through the door to his room when Ed Janowitz's call was relayed from the motel's switchboard. Janowitz did just as I'd asked him to, informing Teddie that he'd made up his mind to go for the deal on the O.C. Pinot Reserve. Teddie was delighted with the news. Janowitz then told Teddie he'd be closing the shop in half an hour, and he was thinking he could stop by the motel on his way home so they could have a drink to celebrate. Teddie thought that sounded like a great idea. They made a date to meet at the bar in Teddie's motel at seven-thirty. That was perfect, Teddie said, since it would give him time to take a shower and put on fresh clothes.

At a quarter to seven I pulled into the parking lot of the Holiday Inn. I entered via the lobby, affecting an air of *I know where I'm going,* which makes for the best camouflage in a place such as this, where everyone— except for the employees—is a stranger to everyone else. It helped that I knew the number of Teddie's room, the switchboard operator having passed it along to Ed Janowitz so that the next time he called he could dial direct.

Moments later I was standing alone in the hallway outside the door to Teddie's room. Pressing an ear to the door, I could hear a television playing inside—a game show—then the sound of soft footfalls and a drawer being opened and closed. I straightened, pulled the Browning from its holster, and shifted the gun to my left hand. I knocked on the door—not too hard, not too soft. *Hey, Teddie, it's your old buddy Jack Donne, who thought since he was in the neighborhood he'd drop by and say howdy.*

A muffled voice came from the other side of the door. "Who is it?"

"Ed Janowitz," I called. There was no need to disguise how I sounded, since the door would muffle me the same way it had done him. Besides, it had been years since our last encounter, and I doubted he'd recognize my voice.

It wasn't hard to imagine what was going through his mind. *What the fuck is he doing here already? I thought his shop didn't close till seven? I thought we were sup-*

posed to meet in the bar? Annoyed, but only a little suspicious, if at all.

I heard the chain being unlatched, then the dead bolt being thrown. The door opened, and there stood Teddie Ortiz, a bath towel wrapped around his skinny waist. His black hair was damp, hanging limply from his skull, but the rest of him looked dry. He had the same mestizo complexion and Clark Gable mustache he'd had the last time I'd seen him. Behind him on the room's bed lay clean clothing—underwear, socks, a silk shirt, linen trousers.

He looked up at me, expecting to see somebody else, then was struck dumb when it registered that I wasn't Ed Janowitz. Then came the shock of recognition, his mouth opening to form a little "o" when he saw who I was. At the same instant I was bringing my right hand upward, twisting my hips to put some power into the blow, driving the heel of my hand into the center of his face.

Blood spurted from his crushed nose. He let out a squeal of pain, staggered, lost his balance, and fell heavily on his backside. Both hands flew up to protect his face from another blow. He peered at me with terror in his eyes. Wet redness seeped through his fingers. He looked as if he were about to start crying.

I came into the room and kicked the door shut. Transferring the Browning to my right hand, I stepped up and switched off the TV on the dresser opposite the bed, then dropped to one knee beside him. "Hello, Teddie," I cooed, grinning as I tweaked his earlobe with the barrel of the gun. "What's new?"

TWENTY-THREE

TEDDIE ORTIZ WAS whining, "You broke my fucking nose!" as he pressed a bloodied towel to the middle of his face. The distorted words came out sounding like "Yoo bwoke by puck-in nothe!" I'd gotten the towel myself from the bathroom, where I'd soaked it in cold water from the tap. He'd been holding it to his face for several minutes.

He was sitting on the edge of the bed. I'd pulled over a wing-backed chair that had been in the corner of the room near a window, and I sat in the chair, facing him. I'd put away the Browning. After having his nose smashed, he didn't need any more softening up.

"You're lucky I changed my mind and only hit you with my hand," I said.

"Man, the least you can do is take me to the fucking hospital! I'm in a lot of pain here!"

"There's something we need to discuss first," I said.

Purplish-yellow bruises had begun to form around his eyes. He looked like a hatchet-faced raccoon. He glared at me suspiciously. "What?"

"This wine scam you've been operating for the past month."

"I don't know what you're talking about."

"Don't fuck with me, Teddie. I'm not in the mood."

The suspicious look became sullen. Then something seemed to light up his eyes, as if a thought that he should have remembered earlier had occurred to him. "Didn't I hear you quit ATF?" he said, challenging me.

"Man, you aren't even a Fed anymore! Who the fuck do you think you are, busting me in the face like that? You're just a fucking citizen! I oughta call the cops myself and have you charged with assault and battery!"

I said nothing. I simply gave him a look I'd mastered during my time with the Treasury Department. The look said: If you don't stop giving me shit I'm going to squash you like a bug. It tended to work well on weasels like Teddie Ortiz.

He hadn't quite lost all his gumption yet. "Fuck you," he snapped. "I told you, I don't know what the fuck you're talking about. I don't know anything about any fucking scam."

I shook my head wearily. "That's not what Buddy Martinez says."

Bingo. Teddie's eyes widened with astonishment. Then he caught himself and turned away, scowling. When he turned back to me, I could read the defeat on his face. He made a final attempt at bravado. "How the fuck did you find me, anyway?"

"It wasn't hard," I said. "You leave a track like a goddamn snail."

Sullen again. The look of a loser.

"Tell me about the scam," I said.

"What do you want to know?" he asked.

A HALF HOUR LATER I was using the phone on the night-stand beside the bed to call Brad Fitch at his motel. I told him where I was and asked him if he wouldn't mind meeting me in Teddie's room as soon as he could get here.

Fitch arrived within an hour, having made close to record time on the drive from Solvang to Goleta. In the meantime Teddie had cleaned himself up and gotten dressed. He was back at his place on the side of the bed, holding a fresh towel to his nose, when Fitch knocked at the door. I got up to admit him, then re-locked the door behind him. He looked at Teddie, then at me. "What happened to him?" Fitch asked, pointing to the man on the bed.

"He banged his nose on the door when he was letting me in," I said.

"Hey, *fuck* you," Teddie snarled.

I ignored him. "Sorry there's no chair for you, Lieu-tenant. I'm afraid you'll have to stand."

Teddie's eyes widened. "'Lieutenant?'" He looked to me. "This guy's a cop?"

I made introductions. "Bradley Fitch, Teddie Ortiz. Teddie, this is Lieutenant Fitch of the Santa Barbara County Sheriff's Department. You're going to repeat to him what you just got through telling me."

Teddie shook his head. "I'm not saying one fucking word to him. Not without my lawyer here."

"What's the problem?" I said. "You're not under arrest." I turned to Fitch. "Teddie's not under arrest, is he, Lieutenant?"

"I don't even know what he's done," Fitch said.

"Fuck you, too," Teddie said to Fitch. "I want my lawyer."

"Ask him who his lawyer is," I said to Fitch.

"Who's your lawyer?" Fitch asked Teddie.

"Up here," Teddie said, "it's a guy named Wikert. Daniel G. Wikert."

Fitch looked at me. "Doesn't he know?"

I shrugged. "He must not read the papers."

"You didn't tell him?"

I shrugged again. "I didn't think it was my place to do that."

"Tell me what?" Teddie asked, his eyes narrowing.

"Wikert's dead," Fitch said to the man on the bed. "Somebody gave him an acid bath last night and killed him."

Teddie blanched.

"You wouldn't happen to know who might've done that, would you, Teddie?" Fitch asked.

Teddie lowered his towel. His nose was flattened and swollen, but the bleeding had stopped. He paled at the news about Wikert, and the bruises around his eyes and cheeks became more pronounced. The news had frightened him very badly.

I said to him, "Maybe now you should tell Lieutenant Fitch what you told me."

Fitch leaned against the dresser. "I'm listening," he said.

TEDDIE'S STORY WAS THIS:

Having been released from Terminal Island the week before Christmas, he'd spent the next month and a half hanging around L.A. Except for running an occasional short con and working as a part-time dealer for an illegal, high-stakes, floating poker game, he stayed away from trouble. Until the middle of February, when he was approached by a former jailhouse acquaintance who told him about an upscale wise guy looking to angle a big con. The wise guy wanted to bring in a freelance grifter, who, according to the job description, knew how to present himself with a little class. Teddie's name had come up. He agreed to a meeting with the mob guy, at which time the acquaintance revealed who was putting together the scam, asking Teddie if he'd ever heard of Rudy Setzer. Hell, Teddie said, who *hasn't* heard of Rudy Setzer?

The meeting took place on Presidents' Day at Setzer's home in Bel Air. Present were four men: Teddie, Setzer, Daniel Wikert, and Leo Lancaster, Setzer's jack-of-all-trades right-hand man. The game Setzer proposed was a simple one. He'd made arrangements to manufacture counterfeit bottles of an expensive wine—namely O.C. Vineyards 1990 Pinot Noir Special Reserve. The supply of bogus wine was virtually limitless. All Teddie had to do was go to the proper stores and present himself as a salesman offering the owners a sweet deal on the goods. Since the overhead was minimal, the profit potential was large. Teddie's cut would be 15 percent of the net. How much he made would depend on how much he was willing to hustle. According to Setzer, this initial scam was just a test to see if the con would even work. If things go the way we're planning, the mobster had said, this is only the beginning. He was letting Teddie in on the ground floor of an operation that could make millions. It wouldn't be long, Setzer had indicated, before they were ready to expand their counterfeiting operation to ripping off other winemakers as well.

Teddie spent the next several weeks giving himself a crash course in wine terminology, and by mid-March he was ready to hit the road. As Setzer had promised, the scam worked beautifully. The bogus wine all but sold itself. Everything had gone swimmingly—until I showed up on Teddie's doorstep.

Fitch asked him, "When was the last time you talked to Setzer?"

Teddie shook his head. "I only saw him that one time, when he gave me the spiel. The one I deal with is Leo."

"Leo Lancaster?" I said.

Teddie nodded, then said in a lowered voice, "I wouldn't be surprised if Leo's the one who did Wikert."

Fitch and I looked at each other. I could tell by his expression that he was having the same difficulty I was in disguising a reaction to Teddie's bombshell. He turned to Teddie and said carefully, "Why wouldn't you be surprised by that?"

"Man, that's Leo's style. He's an evil son of a bitch. The guy's a fucking sadist. He only does what Rudy tells him to do, but he really likes it when he gets to hurt people." Teddie made a face, recalling something unpleasant. "Last time we were together, he told me about this guy who'd fucked Rudy over on some deal, I don't even know what it was about or how much money was involved. It might've been just to make a point. Anyway, Leo sneaks into the guy's apartment one night and catches him and his girlfriend asleep. He ties 'em to the bed naked, then he goes into the bathroom and gets this hair-curling iron the girlfriend had there with the rest of her makeup and shit. He plugs the thing in, then he tells the guy, 'I'm not gonna do you. I'm gonna do *her*.'"

Fitch whispered, "Good Christ..."

"Nice, huh?" said Teddie. "That was Leo's way of warning me not to get out of line."

I was frowning. "Why would Setzer want Leo to do Wikert?"

"How the fuck should I know?" said Teddie. "Maybe Wikert pissed Rudy off."

Fitch asked him, "When was the last time you talked to Leo?"

Teddie thought for a moment, then said, "Five or six days ago. I met him for lunch at this place in Hollywood. That's where he told me the story about the curling iron.'' He shrugged. "We get together every other week or so to settle accounts.''

"When are you supposed to get in touch with him again?'' asked Fitch.

"As soon as I'm done up here. I have to let him know how much product I've sold so he can get the orders together and I can deliver 'em.''

It was then that something which had been nagging at me became clear in my mind. I looked pointedly at the man on the bed. "Teddie, if Leo's such a scary bastard, how come you're ratting him out to us? Aren't you worried about what he'd do to you if he found out?''

"Hell, yes, I'm worried,'' said Teddie. "But right now you're here and he's someplace else. You tell me who I should be more afraid of at the moment.'' He showed Fitch and me his bravado stare. "Besides, nothing I say here can be used against him *or* me. Even if you guys got me under oath, I'd deny every fucking thing I just said. You told me yourself I'm not even under arrest.''

I turned to Fitch just as he was opening his jacket and reaching for the pouch on his belt where he kept his handcuffs. "Maybe you weren't under arrest before, asshole, but you sure the hell are now.''

FOR THE SECOND evening in a row I was up late in the company of Brad Fitch. At midnight the two of us were sitting around an outdoor table at San Tomas's only Jack in the Box restaurant. Several hours had passed since Fitch had called the dispatcher from Teddie Ortiz's hotel room and requested a patrol car to come over, pick up Teddie, and transport him to the hospital, where somebody could treat his broken nose. Two deputies arrived at Teddie's room around nine-thirty. Fitch instructed them to wait at the hospital while Teddie was attended to, then bring him to the sheriff's station in Solvang, where Fitch would take care of bedding him down the for the night.

The deputies departed with Teddie, and I followed Fitch back to the sheriff's station. While he completed the paperwork necessary to charge Teddie with felony fraud and conspiracy to commit same, I used Fitch's phone to call the ATF office in Los Angeles. I left a message for Alan Feinberg to call Fitch as soon as he came into the office the next morning. That bootleg booze appeared to be central to Teddie's scam meant the Bureau would have to be involved. Alan and Fitch could negotiate about who had dibs on Teddie.

The deputies brought him in a little after eleven. Fitch had the paperwork ready, so all that needed to be done was have him photographed, fingerprinted, and tossed in the jug. Everything else could wait until morning, including a record check on Leo Lancaster. Fitch personally supervised Teddie's pictures and prints, turned him over to a jailer, then asked me if I felt like a cup of coffee.

The Jack in the Box was the closest place I could think of that would be open. We sat at a round metal table, across from one another. The coffee wasn't very good, but at the moment neither of us minded.

Fitch asked me, "You think Teddie's story about being in with Rudy Setzer is horseshit, or what?"

"Not really. My guess is he's telling the truth, mostly. He'll downplay his own involvement as much as possible. But I'd say that what he told us was basically straight."

Fitch said, "Even that stuff about this guy Lancaster being the one who did Wikert?"

I shook my head. "That I don't know. I never heard of him, but that doesn't mean anything. When you talk to Alan Feinberg you can ask him if he knows the guy. In any case, I can't think of a reason why Teddie would make him up."

"He sounds like the kind of shitbird who'd work for somebody like Rudy Setzer," Fitch said.

I nodded.

We fell into silence for a time, both of us sipping our coffee, both of us fatigued to the point of exhaustion. At last Fitch said, "I meant to bring along that copy of Perry Cole's will, but I left it in my motel room. You could've read through it while I was booking Teddie."

I'd finished my coffee and stood up, looking around for a trash can. "You can bring it along tomorrow when you pick me up on your way to see June and Grant."

Fitch's expression of surprise rang false, if only because he was too foxy not to have arrived at the same conclusion I had. The elements of the equation had been fitting themselves together in my head ever since we'd left Teddie Ortiz's room.

Rudy Setzer's decision to go after O.C. Vineyards wasn't a random choice. Ozzie was a deliberate target—which meant that whoever was *really* behind the con was somebody who had it in for him personally. Anybody who put the elements together would have to come up with the same answer. Take one scam engineered specifically to ruin Ozzie's business, factor in the late Daniel G. Wikert's personal involvement, and what have you got?

I said to Fitch, "I'm too tired to play games with you, Brad."

"Sorry," he said.

I sighed. "So what time are you picking me up"

"How's eleven o'clock sound?"

"It sounds fine," I said.

TWENTY-FOUR

To KEEP MYSELF occupied until Fitch showed up on Tuesday morning, I sat at my desk going over Donne Vineyards's accounts for the month. Not surprisingly, I had trouble concentrating on the lists of figures. But working on the books caused me to think of Maggie McKenney and something she'd said to me at Tito's, that it was possible June and Grant Cole were behind their brother's troubles. I'd pooh-poohed her notion out of hand. Now I was wondering how to go about owning up to her that she'd had it right all along without having my ego take too severe a whipping. By the time Fitch pulled up to the house at ten minutes to eleven, I'd decided to tell Maggie straight out and just take my lumps.

Fitch honked his horn, summoning me. I came out of the house, crossed to his idling Dodge, and nodded a greeting. "Morning," he said as I settled myself, slipped on my seat belt, and closed the door.

He passed over a manila "Evidence" envelope stuffed thick with sheaves of paper. As I was undoing the clasp, Fitch shifted into gear and headed toward the highway. He stayed quiet, not speaking while I skimmed the pages of the copy of Perry Cole's will.

The bulk of the estate—except for some money to be placed in trust for Perry's four grandchildren—went to Ozzie. He would probably have gotten an even bigger share if, like his brothers, he'd been a family man. But Ozzie had tended to avoid the company of women since his only marriage broke up a dozen years before. I gleaned from the will that he had no children, legitimate or otherwise. It would have surprised me if he had.

Not that I wasn't provided with a few surprises. It turned out that Ozzie's brothers weren't entirely disinherited by their father. What they got were the deeds to the houses in which they and their wives and kids already resided.

That June and Grant didn't own their homes was only the first surprise for me. I'd also assumed that when Perry passed his business on to his sons at least a portion of it was literally *theirs,* free and clear. This wasn't the case at all: Perry still owned everything. Though he'd "retired," the entire business had remained solely in his name. All these years his sons had been little more than caretakers, legally speaking.

I was also taken aback by the sheer size of the estate. I knew Perry was rich, but I didn't know he had anywhere near as much as the will seemed to indicate. One reason the document was so thick was because it included a detailed listing of Perry's holdings—stocks, bonds, real estate, and so on. There wasn't a precise dollar figure mentioned anywhere, but judging from the information that was there, it was a staggering sum. I was curious as to just how much of it June and Grant had managed to fritter away.

By the time I'd finished going through the will, Fitch had turned south onto Ballard Canyon Road. As I was sliding the pages back into the envelope, he said, "Well?"

"It's just like you told me," I said, laying the envelope in my lap. "Except for some crumbs, Ozzie gets damn near everything. I guess Perry must've had it in pretty bad for June and Grant."

"That's an understatement."

"It's a helluva lot of money," I admitted.

"It doesn't include a couple of life insurance policies the old man had. Nearly two hundred and fifty thousand more, right there."

"Ozzie gets that, too, I suppose," I said.

Fitch shook his head. "Zeke Carlin."

I'd forgotten all about Carlin. "He told me at the funeral Perry'd taken care of him. I guess that's what he was talking about."

The lieutenant nodded. "Still, a quarter of a million bucks, that's a drop in the bucket compared to the rest of it."

I caught what he was insinuating. "Like I've been saying all along, that still doesn't mean Ozzie murdered his father."

Fitch regarded me out of the corner of his eye. "I can tell you who *didn't* kill him."

"Who?"

"Leo Lancaster."

I looked at Fitch blankly. "When did I say I was thinking Leo did it?"

"You didn't *say* it," Fitch said, smiling. "But I'd be surprised if you hadn't been thinking it. I ran a record check on him this morning, and he's just as big an ass-hole as Teddie Ortiz says he is. Whether he did Wikert or not may be up for grabs, but he didn't do Perry Cole."

"How do you know?"

"I interrogated Teddie again. I got somebody from the Public Defender's office to hold his hand while I questioned him. He remembered what day it was he had lunch with Leo. Last Wednesday. At the exact same time somebody was siphoning old man Cole's blood out of him.''

''Are you sure Teddie's telling the truth?''

''Pretty sure,'' Fitch replied. ''When I was questioning him, I didn't lead him on at all. All I did was ask if he could remember specifically where and when he had lunch with Leo last week. 'Wednesday,' he said. According to Teddie, the place they ate at is fairly popular, and Leo's kind of a regular. Teddie's sure somebody'll remember seeing them there.''

''And you believe him?''

Fitch shrugged. ''It's like you said yourself last night. I can't think of a reason why he'd make something like that up.''

I frowned. Twenty-four hours ago I'd never heard of Leo Lancaster, but ever since Teddie Ortiz had dropped his name, I'd been hoping he'd turn into the prime suspect for Perry's murder. I was running out of excuses for Ozzie—not just for Fitch, but for me, too. ''What's Leo's record look like?'' I asked.

''Typical wise guy muscle,'' Fitch said with contempt. ''Caucasian male, thirty-six years old. One serious stretch in Raiford—seven years for an armed robbery he committed when he was nineteen. Back in Florida, which is where he's from. He's been charged with everything from loan-sharking to ADW. He's also been booked on suspicion of murder three or four times, but no convictions. All of this happened before he moved to California, two years ago. Since then he's kept his nose clean.''

''And you honestly think Teddie Ortiz is this guy's alibi?''

Fitch gave me another look. ''If I thought there was

a possibility Leo killed old man Cole, I'd drag his ass up here in a minute."

"What about Wikert?" I asked.

"I want to hear what Perry's kids have to say before I decide what to do about Wikert."

We were approaching the private road that was the access to the Coles' winery. Fitch eased on the brakes, slowing to make the turn onto the road. "While we're on the subject," he added, "I talked to Alan Feinberg this morning. He called me around nine o'clock. He recognized Leo Lancaster's name, and he also knew about him working for Rudy Setzer, but he's never had any dealings with either of them. He asked me to hold onto Teddie till he could arrange to pick him up and take him back to L.A. He seemed pretty excited about the possibility of getting something solid on a big-timer like Setzer."

"He would be," I said.

"He also told me to tell you to give him a call," said Fitch, flipping on his turn signal as he slowed the Dodge to a stop across from the Coles' private road. "After we get through with June and Grant."

"I assume they're expecting us," I said. "You called ahead to make sure they'd be here, didn't you?"

"You bet," said Fitch.

THE HEADQUARTERS OF the Cole Family Winery lies on the original three hundred acres of land purchased by Perry Cole when he arrived in the Santa Ynez Valley in the mid-1960s. Before Perry bought the land, it had been owned for generations by a family named Santiago. The Santiagos had been deeded the land by King Carlos IV of Spain two hundred years before Perry acquired it. When the Cole family took possession, all that existed on the property were some twenty or thirty acres of grapevines that hadn't been tended properly in close to fifty years and a vacant, two-story, tumbledown, stone and wood farmhouse built during the administration of President Roosevelt. Theodore, not Franklin.

Perry dramatically changed the look of "El Rancho Santiago," as it is occasionally referred to by a few longtime locals. During the first decade following his purchase he had the farmhouse restored and modernized, reconstructing the building to serve as both the family's living quarters and the winery's offices. He had the vineyards expanded, planting close to two hundred and fifty acres of grapes. He erected several large, quonsetlike structures made of corrugated aluminum and painted white. Inside the huts he installed state-of-the-art manufacturing and bottling equipment—a huge testing laboratory, massive fermentation tanks, presses, storage racks. The quonsets surrounded an asphalt-covered parking lot the size of a football field for the vehicles of the Coles's numerous full-time employees. Most striking were a dozen 25,000-gallon storage tanks that encircled the parking lot. If you were in a helicopter flying a thousand feet or so above the property, and you looked down, you'd think it was some kind of oil refinery.

As Perry prospered, he bought more and more acres of land throughout the valley, planted row upon row of grapes, bought thousands of pounds of fruit from other growers, and produced millions of gallons of wine. Eventually, as his sons grew old enough to leave home, only Perry—and Zeke Carlin—resided in the farmhouse. After Perry moved to Costa del Sol, nobody lived there anymore. El Rancho Santiago remained the winery's headquarters, and the business offices of the

Cole empire continued to be run out of the farmhouse. Over the years I've had occasion to wonder why they did that. Nostalgia, perhaps, though no members of the Cole family had ever struck me as the sentimental type.

They were, however, fanatical about privacy. That was another notion—along with their marketing and manufacturing strategies—that Perry had borrowed from the Gallos, whose Modesto headquarters up north were guarded only a little less securely than Fort Knox. The entire three hundred acres of El Rancho Santiago were surrounded by a twelve-foot-high Cyclone fence topped with spirals of concertina wire. All that was visible from outside the fence was row after row of grapes. The main road into the property was blocked by a high metal gate on which was mounted the sole indication as to whose property you were on: a small wooden sign with the name "COLE" burned onto it. Unlike most of the winemakers in the valley, the Coles discouraged visitors and the winery was closed to the public—another Gallo-ism. Before Perry arrived, the road itself belonged to the state and was freely accessible to anybody. It was only after Perry blocked it off, appropriating it for his own use, that our county supervisors voted a rubber-stamp approval of what he'd done. Another example of the sort of consideration that affluent and powerful folks like Perry Cole receive from politicians around the world, every day.

Fitch braked to a stop outside the main gate. On the driver's side was a grilled speaker box mounted on a cement pole. Fitch leaned out his window and pressed a button beneath the speaker. A few moments later a garbled voice crackled from the speaker, inquiring as to who had pressed the button. Fitch gave his name. There followed an electronic buzz that was as pleasant a sound as fingernails scraping on a chalkboard. The gate un-latched itself and swung inward, and we rolled on through. It closed behind us as we continued up the road, winding our way toward the complex of buildings that lay at the center of the property.

We pulled into an empty parking slot in the middle of the employees' lot. As I was getting out of the car, I noticed that there were fewer vehicles parked around us than I'd expected. It occurred to me that here was another piece of evidence that June and Grant were in the soup, financially speaking. The less than full lot might have been an indication that they'd had to lay off some employees, though I'd heard no confirmed reports or unsubstantiated rumors of that. Not yet, anyway.

We walked an eighth of a mile from the parking lot to the farmhouse, then climbed a short porch and went through the front door into a parlor that had been con-verted years before into a reception area. A young woman seated behind a low desk told us that June and Grant were waiting for us in the conference room, but Mrs. Cole was running late and hadn't yet arrived.

As we were about to start down the hallway the re-ceptionist had indicated, the front door opened and Re-gina Cole strode in. She beelined for the hallway, her head canted downward. Like the rest of the Coles, she was not an attractive human being, despite being un-related to them by blood. She also had her own curious sense of style, having dressed this morning in shades of green: green turtleneck pullover sweater, green Wran-gler stretch jeans, green socks, green shoes. The color of money, I thought. She resembled a mutated toad.

She failed to notice that Fitch and I were blocking her way until the receptionist blurted, "Mrs. Cole?"

Regina stopped short and looked up at us sharply. At

first she seemed startled, then she measured us with a spiteful gaze not far removed from the loathsome expression I'd seen at her father-in-law's grave site a few days before. She settled on me. "Jack?" she said, unsure whether to be puzzled, annoyed, or simply angry because I was there.

"Regina." I nodded toward the man with me. "This is Lieutenant Fitch, from the county sheriff's department."

She gave Fitch another glance, didn't seem impressed by what she saw, then turned back to me. "What are you doing here?" She nodded tersely toward Fitch. "How come you're with him?"

"I'm representing somebody else's interest."

Her eyes narrowed. "Whose interest is that?"

"Your brother-in-law's," I said. "Ozzie's."

AT ONE TIME, the conference room had been the formal dining chamber for the last generation of the Santiago family to reside at the farmhouse. Whatever Old California charm the room may once have possessed was absent now. Were it not for the windows that provided a view of the parking lot, the outbuildings, and the vineyards, we could have been inside any similarly functioned chamber in a glass-and-steel skyscraper in any big city on the planet. The room was blandly utilitarian. You held business meetings in here, and that's all you did.

A long, rectangular conference table took up most of the space. On one side of the table sat June, Grant, and Regina. The brothers were dressed for outside work—denim shirts, dungarees, heavy boots. Once our meeting was concluded, it was back to the fields for both of them.

After I'd introduced Fitch to June and Grant, the lieu-tenant and I took seats across the table from the Coles. As Fitch pulled his notebook and pen from the pocket of his suit jacket, he said to the people opposite us, "This isn't a formal interrogation. Nobody here is being charged with anything. I just have some questions I'd like to ask, that's all. If and when the time comes that I think somebody needs to be placed under arrest—and I'm not saying that's going to happen—then we'll go through the procedure of advising people of their rights and so on."

June Cole sat between his wife and brother. He looked from one to the other. Grant's and Regina's ex-pressions remained unchanged. June turned back to Fitch and nodded. "Okay."

"Good," Fitch said. "First of all—"

"First of all," Regina snapped, "what the hell is Jack Donne doing here?" She poked a finger in my direction. "And what the hell is he talking about, he's represent-ing Ozzie?"

"I could ask you the same question, Mrs. Cole," Fitch said calmly. "Not about your brother-in-law, I mean, but about what *you're* doing here. I told your husband on the phone I wanted to see him and his brother alone."

"Regina is co-executive vice-president of our com-pany," June said. "She and my brother have the same title. She's as intimately involved in the winery as we are."

Fitch nodded. "Then I guess she can stay. As for Mr. Donne, the reason he's with me is because Ozzie Cole is his client."

Grant said, puzzled, "His client?"

"Ozzie hired me as a private investigator," I said in as calm a voice as Fitch's.

"For what?" Regina asked.

"To find out why his brothers have been counterfeiting his wine and trying to put him out of business," Fitch said.

June blanched. Grant's mouth fell open. Only Regina was able to keep her face impassive. Their reactions reminded me of one of the differences between professional and amateur criminals. When you try to bombshell them, professionals have little difficulty maintaining a steely demeanor, because lying to the authorities—or anyone, for that matter—is second nature. Only the coolest amateurs, and the phrase "cool amateur" is almost a contradiction in terms, possess a similar level of self-control. Regina Cole, for example. If she and Fitch and I had been alone, she might have been able to convince us that he was blowing smoke. But both her husband and her brother-in-law had managed to give themselves away.

Grant stammered, "How...how did you—?"

"Shut *up*, Grant!" Regina said from between clenched teeth.

June barked at his wife, "No, *you* shut up!"

Startled by the outburst, Regina gaped at her husband. Watching them, seeing the expressions on their faces, I sensed that it had been a long time since June had had the temerity to speak to her in such a manner. The shock passed fairly quickly, but when Regina began to say something, June held up a hand to silence her. "Don't say a word, Regina," he warned. "Not one goddamned word." She closed her mouth.

June turned to face Fitch and me. "*Now* is somebody under arrest, Lieutenant?" June asked Fitch.

"I believe so, Mr. Cole," Fitch replied.

TWENTY-FIVE

FITCH ADVISED the three of them of their Miranda rights. After acknowledging that they understood what the lieutenant had said, June—speaking for the others— refused the offer to send for an attorney. "Our attorney's dead," he said hollowly. He sounded like a man who wasn't coping well with the recent fatalities of so many people close to him. It would be a relief to get everything out in the open.

"That's one of the things I'd like to talk about, Mr. Cole," said Fitch. "I'd like to find out what, if anything, you know about what happened to Daniel Wikert."

June nodded glumly. Neither his wife nor his brother made any response.

"Well?" asked Fitch.

"It was Dan's idea," said Regina. Her voice could cut glass. "The whole scheme. He's the one who came to June—"

"Regina, maybe you should let me tell it," interrupted June. "All right?"

She sat back in her chair and folded her arms across her chest, steamed. "Be my guest."

Such a charming woman, I said to myself.

"Dan called me in January," said June, "around the first of the year. He asked me to meet him at his office. It was something important, he said. When I got there, the first thing he did was show me the winery's balance sheet. He'd factored in our fourth-quarter profit and loss, and he wanted to let me know how the business was doing.''

June seemed to sag in his chair like a slowly deflating balloon. "It wasn't good. Last year was the fifth down year in a row for us. I asked Dan if he had any ideas about how we could turn things around. 'As a matter of fact, I do,' he said. That's when he told me about what was in my father's will, about Ozzie and the—''

Regina snorted. "The little bastard."

Grant leaned forward to glare past his brother at his sister-in-law. "Regina, do you mind?" She sat back, scowling.

"Go on with what you were saying, Mr. Cole," Fitch instructed June.

"Dan offered me a proposition. What if he could come up with a way to coerce Ozzie into rejoining Grant and me? You know, get him to merge O.C. Vineyards, which was solvent, with Cole, which wasn't. That way, whenever my father…passed away, Grant and I would still end up with equal-sized shares of the business. Since Dan was Ozzie's attorney, too, he could work out the details of the merger beforehand to make sure that we'd be full partners.''

June paused, his cheeks flushing with shame. He turned away for a moment, pressing a hand to his forehead.

Fitch prompted, "Mr. Cole?"

June straightened. "Sorry. Where was I?"

"Wikert's scheme," Fitch said. "To get Ozzie to merge with you and Grant."

June nodded. "It depended on two things. First, that Ozzie could be maneuvered into such a vulnerable position that he'd have to come to Grant and me for help.

And second, that my father wouldn't…that my father didn't have long to live…"

He read the look of reproach on my face. "I was desperate, Jack," he said defensively. "There was a damn good chance we might lose the whole winery. Things were that bad. They're *still* that bad."

"And that excuses what you did to your own brother?" I said angrily. "That makes it okay?"

"Jack," Fitch cautioned.

Disgusted, I waved a hand, dismissing them all. Fitch said to June, "Go on."

"After I left Dan's office, I came right back here. I called in Grant and Regina, and I told them just how bad things were. Then I told them about Dan's idea to get Ozzie to re-merge with us."

Fitch looked to June's wife and brother. "You two were in on this from the beginning?"

Neither of them said a word. They didn't have to. Fitch turned back to June and motioned for him to continue.

"Dan set up a meeting, at his house," June said. "Around the end of January. Grant and I both went. That's where we met Rudy Setzer and Leo Lancaster."

"Setzer and Lancaster were both there?" Fitch asked.

"Rudy never goes anywhere without Leo," Grant said.

"It was Dan's plan, basically," June said, "but Rudy and Leo both had a hand in working out the details. They also took care of producing the actual cases of bogus pinot. Grant and I supplied the wine, but they took care of the bottling and packaging and distribution. That first night we met them, Rudy said he already had somebody in mind to go out and hustle the store owners."

"Teddie Ortiz," I said.

June shook his head. "I don't know anything about that part of it. By that point, Grant and I didn't *want* to know any more. All we had to do was arrange to ship a couple thousand gallons of cheap pinot to some warehouse in L.A. After that, we were pretty much out of the loop. Dan and Rudy and Leo handled everything."

"What was Setzer's cut?" asked Fitch.

June took a deep breath. "Ten percent."

"Ten percent of what?" asked Fitch.

"Everything. The whole winery, after we re-merged with Ozzie. Rudy's been trying for a long time to get a toehold in the wine business, but he knew with his background and all that he'd encounter a lot of legal problems if he tried to go about it legitimately. He saw getting involved with us as a kind of silent partner as a way to get around having to screw with the federal government."

Fitch shook his head in disbelief. "Then what happened?" he asked June.

"Dan called me the day after Dad...after he was killed. 'This changes things,' he said. I had no idea what he was talking about...I guess I was still in shock and all...until he started saying how he wanted a bigger slice of the pie. 'What the hell are you talking about?' I asked him. 'Your father's getting murdered wasn't part of the deal,' he said. That's when it hit me, he was thinking Grant and I had something to do with killing Dad! Like we were trying to help things along! I couldn't believe it!"

Fitch frowned. "*Did* you have something to do with it?"

The brothers looked appalled. They began shouting at Fitch simultaneously, protesting their innocence.

Fitch had to raise his hands to quiet them. When they'd calmed down, he said to June, "Is this how you reacted when Wikert accused you of killing your father?"

"More or less," said June.

"But he didn't believe you?"

June shook his head. "All he did was keep going on and on about how murder wasn't part of the deal he'd bought into, and if we wanted to keep him on the team, he'd need a lot bigger share than what he was getting."

"What about Setzer?" Fitch asked.

"What about him?" June said.

"Where was he while all this was going on?"

"He wasn't involved," June said. "He didn't know anything about it until I called him."

"*You* called him?" Fitch asked.

Grant said quickly, "It was Regina's idea—"

She snapped, "Because *you* two clowns would have just sat around with your thumbs up your asses and let that bastard Wikert have whatever he wanted."

Fitch looked at her. "You suggested your husband should call Rudy Setzer?"

"That's right. *I* suggested it."

Fitch turned to June. "What happened when you called?"

June paled. "Rudy said not to worry about Wikert. He'd have Leo take care of him."

"Take care of Wikert?"

"That's what he said."

"His exact words?"

June nodded.

"By 'Leo,'" said Fitch, "you mean Leo Lancaster?"

June nodded again.

"What day was it you called him?" asked Fitch. "Setzer, I mean?"

"Last Friday," June said. "The day after Dan called me."

"And two days after that, Wikert was dead?"

June swallowed, then nodded again.

"Do you think Leo killed Wikert?" Fitch asked.

June hesitated before answering, "I don't know."

"Let's try another question," Fitch said. "Do you think he killed your father?"

June became exasperated. "I don't *know*—"

"Lieutenant?" I cut in. Fitch turned to me. "Can I talk to you outside for a minute?"

He gave me a quizzical look. I motioned toward the door to the conference room and got up from my chair. Fitch turned back to the Coles and said, "You three wait here, all right?" He rose and followed me out into the hallway.

We spoke outside for a few minutes, then came back into the conference room, re-closed the door behind us, and returned to our seats. After he'd settled himself, Fitch peered across the table at June. "What do you think are the chances of your getting hold of Setzer and convincing him that he needs to get up here right away?"

June shook his head. "That's impossible."

"Leo," I said to Fitch. "We'd settle for Leo."

Fitch nodded.

Grant said doubtfully, "You mean trick him into coming here?"

"Sort of," Fitch said.

"Like we're setting some kind of trap?" Grant said.

"Something like that," I said.

The color had drained from June's face once more. "I don't know if I can do that."

"June," Grant urged, "since he's already here—"

"Shut *up!*" June barked.

The room became silent until Fitch fixed June with a steely stare and said, "Leo's here?"

"Not *here* here," Grant said. "Not here at the winery. He's here in the valley."

"Where?" Fitch said.

More silence.

"Where?" Fitch insisted.

"He's at a motel," June said at last. "In Santa Ynez."

"Get him here," Fitch said. "*Here* here."

"What?" June said. "You mean now?"

"I think he means *right* now," I said.

TWENTY-SIX

WHILE GRANT, REGINA, and I stayed behind in the conference room, Fitch accompanied June to an office down the hall. From there, June was to telephone Leo Lancaster. Fitch went along to make sure June said the right things to Leo, including the magic words "Daniel Wikert," and impressed upon him the urgency of his presence at El Rancho Santiago.

They returned a few minutes after they'd left. For a time the five of us sat quietly, waiting for Leo to show up. No one spoke, not even Regina, until I pointed to the bulge on Fitch's hip and asked him in a low voice, "What kind of gun have you got there?"

He'd caught that I didn't want the Coles to overhear what we were saying. "Why do you want to know?" he asked, likewise keeping his voice low.

"I'm curious."

"A .357 Colt Python."

"You wouldn't happen to have another one, would you?"

"Why would I be carrying two guns?"

"I've known guys who do."

He made a face. "You think I'm some kind of cowboy?"

"I was just wondering if you had a spare gun, that's all."

"Why?"

"Because I didn't bring one," I said. "I thought if you had a spare, maybe I could borrow it."

He considered for a moment, then shrugged. "I got a short-barreled .32 in the trunk."

Not exactly a cannon, but it would have to do. "Would you mind getting it for me?" I asked. "I'll stay here and baby-sit."

"You really think you'll need it?"

"If I'd known we were going to be confronting Leo, I'd have brought my own."

Fitch let out a sigh of resignation, then got up and left. Moments later I saw him through a window, crossing the parking lot, making his way to the car. As I was watching him, Regina Cole said to me, "What happened to Dan wasn't our fault."

I regarded her frostily. "What do you mean, it wasn't your fault? Wasn't June the one who called Setzer?"

"So?"

"For Christ's sake, Regina, you must think I'm a total idiot. What's Leo doing in Santa Ynez if Setzer didn't send him up here? And if he's staying in a motel that means he either spent the night or is *going* to be spending the night. My guess is the former. I'm also guessing that he came up here yesterday to take care of Wikert, just like his boss promised he would, and now he's hanging around to find out what the cops are going to do about it."

Regina opened her mouth to speak, but I held up a hand to quiet her. "I wouldn't be surprised if Fitch decided to charge all three of you with accessory to murder."

That little piece of information stifled her for the moment. "While we're on the subject of murder," I went on, looking from Regina to June and Grant, "maybe you can tell me who it was that decided to arrange things so it looked like Ozzie killed your father."

Regina glowered. June and Grant exchanged looks of apprehensive indecision. I waited.

"That was Dan's idea, too," June said at last.

I frowned, bewildered. "Didn't you say before that he tried to put the screws to you because he thought *you'd* done it?"

Regina sneered. "Knowing Dan, he was probably playing both ends against the middle. Us *and* Ozzie."

I shook my head, not because I didn't believe it, but because I did. The more I learned about Daniel Wikert, the more he became one of those people who routinely worked every angle to their advantage, without regard for anyone or anything, including the law. *Especially* the law. Wikert had clearly been a master at the game of looking out for number one. Except that this time he'd rigged one angle too many, and it had blown up in his face. Literally.

I was about to ask how the Cole family could have become involved with a devious, avaricious shyster like Wikert in the first place when I noticed Fitch returning. I went out into the hall and closed the door. Fitch appeared presently and handed me the .32. It was a Colt, like his .357. "Sorry I don't have another holster," he said.

"No problem." The trousers I was wearing were baggy enough for me to fit the pistol comfortably into my pocket. Fitch watched me as I popped open the gun's cylinder. All six chambers were loaded.

By the time Leo arrived, a short time later, I was standing at the window of the conference room, watching the parking lot. He was driving a maroon, late-model Chrysler with rental agency plates. As he circled the lot, looking for a spot close to the farmhouse, I motioned to Fitch to join me at the window. The Coles

remained seated. As the Chrysler eased to a stop, Fitch
and I turned to one another. I wondered if I had the
same expression of foreboding in my eyes that I saw in
his.

We turned back to the window once more and saw
Leo on foot, striding in our direction. As he approached,
I was able to measure him against the portrait I'd con-
jured up in my mind. I found myself off by a ways. I'd
been imagining him as a large, hulking, bent-nose type,
like an extra from a *Godfather* movie. Instead he was
trim and compact—three or four inches under six feet
in height—with a build like a gymnast's. He wore expensive shoes and a custom-tailored gray suit over a
yellow, open-collared shirt. His head and torso were
inverted isosceles triangles, their "V's" pointing down.
His nose was pointy and sharp. He had sandy-colored
hair trimmed in the shape of a skullcap, as if whoever
had styled it had put a soup bowl on his head and
snipped away whatever fell beneath the rim. There was
something dangerous about the way he walked, all
coiled-spring energy with little wasted motion. As he
drew closer to the farmhouse, I could read an icy expression of displeasure that cinched his face. I suspected
that behind the mirrored sunglasses he was wearing his
eyes were black, like a shark's. Even from this far away,
I could tell he wasn't somebody I'd want coming after
me. Ever.

Heading for the entrance to the farmhouse, he disappeared from sight. Fitch muttered to me under his
breath, "Let's get ready."

We turned toward the door of the conference room,
standing behind the Coles. Like us, they were watching
the door. Approaching footsteps in the hallway outside

grew louder. The footsteps stopped, the door opened, and Leo Lancaster stood on the threshold.

He paused before entering, taking in the room. He'd slipped his sunglasses into a pocket, and as I'd guessed, he had predatory eyes. I watched his gaze flick from the Coles to Fitch and me. His eyes widened so slightly that if I hadn't been watching him closely I wouldn't have noticed. Looking at us, he registered something instantaneously. He'd been a criminal too long not to be able to smell cop, something Fitch or I should have realized. His eyes dropped back down to the Coles, and whatever he read on their faces—which I couldn't see— caused his lips to twist into a snarl.

Then he bolted.

Immediately galvanized, Fitch and I started after him. As we skirted the conference table, Fitch shouted to the Coles, "Call nine-one-one!"

I reached the hallway a pace or two ahead of Fitch and spotted Leo as he dashed through the reception area, heading outdoors. I chased him, Fitch on my heels. We burst through the front doors into bright afternoon sunshine, then halted, looking around. Assuming Leo would head straight for his car, I scanned the lot, trying to spot where he'd left it, until Fitch clapped a hand onto my forearm and cried out, "Over there!"

I turned. He was pointing in the opposite direction, toward one of the quonset structures at the other end of the parking lot. I glimpsed Leo just as he was passing through a metal door and disappearing inside.

Fitch took off after him, with me right behind. As we approached the quonset, I could see that it was larger than I'd assumed it to be when I'd first glanced at it while we were parking the car. The structure was a long half-cylinder resting on its flat, cut side atop a concrete slab. It was about twenty feet high at the apex of its curve and better than twice as wide at its base. I guesstimated the length to be a good 150 feet. I couldn't see through any of the high windows spaced along its side, so I had no idea what purpose the structure might serve.

All of this flashed through my mind on some subconscious level, since at the moment I was more concerned with the man we were pursuing. Fitch reached the door through which Leo had passed before I did. He grabbed the handle and pulled hard, but the door refused to budge. He turned to me, his expression soliciting my help.

Imitating him, I took the handle in both hands and pulled, just as a gunshot exploded from somewhere inside. A bullet *pinged* off the other side of the door, causing both of us to jump back reflexively. We stood, staring at the door, anticipating another shot. None came, but neither of us was about to try to open it again.

"There's probably another way in at the other end," I said. "I'll go check—"

"You stay here," Fitch said abruptly, cutting me off. He'd unholstered his Python. "I'd let you go if you were a cop, but you're not. Wait here in case he tries to come back out this way. And don't be afraid to shoot him if you have to."

"It'll be my pleasure," I said.

Fitch ran off, vanishing around the corner of the quonset. I reached into my pocket and pulled out the gun he'd given me. It felt very small in my hand and about as useful as a peashooter.

Just as I was wishing I had my Browning instead, I heard the sharp, echoing crack of a second gunshot from inside the structure. This time the shot wasn't aimed at me.

As I sprinted along the side of the quonset, careful
to keep my head below the windows, it occurred to me
that the second shot sounded different from the first—
much louder and deeper. Fitch's Python, I decided. His
gun was bigger than whatever Leo had. Not that it made
a difference. I had no doubt Leo was capable of making
you just as dead, regardless of the kind of gun he used.

Another shot—one of Leo's—came as I rounded the
corner at the other end of the quonset. The door I'd
expected to find was there, open. But unlike the door
at the other end, this one was taller and wider, and it
rolled up from the top via a chain and pulley arrangement, like the door to a commercial garage. A driveway
led away from the door and circled off to link up with
the other outbuildings.

Crouching, I approached the door cautiously, a step
at a time, one hand pressed against the quonset's wall
for balance, the other clutching Fitch's .32, my finger
on the trigger. I was less than a dozen feet from the
open door when a sudden whine of machinery re-
sounded from within. I paused, frowning uncertainly,
because I recognized the sound but couldn't quite convince myself that that was what I was hearing.

Inching to the doorway, I was able to peer inside.
Suspended from the ceiling was a line of fluorescent
light fixtures. The lights were turned off, so it took some
moments for my eyes to adjust to the gloom. At last I
saw the four massive grape crushers, two each on either
side of an aisle wide enough to accommodate a small
truck.

Crushers have big hoppers into which clusters of ripe,
just-picked grapes are dumped. The hoppers drop the
fruit into troughs made of stainless steel that's perfo-
rated along the bottom. As the fruit passes along the

trough, a set of large, whirling, stainless steel paddles—their edges as sharp as the blade of a meat cleaver—whack the berries from their stems and break open the skins. What we in the winemaking business call "must"—the mixture of juice and broken berries that comprise the basic stuff from which wine is created—oozes through the holes along the bottom of the trough and gets saved. The rest is lees, disposable sediment.

These particular crushers were huge enough to mash and de-stem several tons of fruit in a very short period of time—to be expected, given the Coles' mass-production of great quantities of generally not so great wine. The crushers were operated by switchboards that were accessed via twin catwalks suspended from the ceiling along either side of the curved walls and running along the entire length of the quonset. You reached the catwalks by using one of four ladders, one at each end. Waist-high handrails ran along the metal walkways, but the railings did little other than provide the illusion of safety to whoever would be operating the switches.

Both machines on my right-hand side were running, at a time when they shouldn't have been on at all. Winemakers run their crushers only once a year, following the fall harvest. The rest of the time, though the machines are regularly checked and maintained, they remain unused. It was the reason the quonset was deserted of any Cole employees.

I was puzzling over this when a voice coming from just inside the door hissed, "Jack!"

I whipped my head outside, ducking around the corner of the door. I barely heard the voice hissing once more, "Jack, it's me! Brad!" followed by a low moan of agony.

Easing my way back to the door, I scuttled inside in

the direction of Fitch's voice. I found him resting against the aluminum wall, hiding among shadows, using the farthest-away left-hand side crusher for cover. When my eyes readjusted to the dim interior light, I could see that his right shoulder and upper arm were soaked with a dark, spreading stain. The fingers of his right hand—also stained with blood—rested uselessly atop the gun in his lap.

I crouched beside him. He turned to look at me, the effort making him wince. Now that I was all the way inside, the reverberating whine and roar of the crushers on the opposite side of the quonset were almost deafening. I had to bring an ear close to Fitch's lips to hear what he was saying. "Only got off…one shot at him," he grunted. "Missed him…but it let him know where I was." He winced again. "It's not that bad, I don't think. Just my shoulder…"

He started to get up, and I pressed a firm hand against his chest to keep him still. "Where is he?"

He lifted a bloody finger and jabbed it toward the catwalk above the right-hand side crushers. "Up there. Heard him moving when I came in. That's when I . . . took a shot at him." Another wince.

"Is he still up there?"

Fitch scowled painfully. "I think so."

I gave him a comforting pat on his good shoulder. "Stay here," I ordered. "Don't try to move. I'll be right back."

I set the .32 on the floor beside him, then lifted the Python from his lap. He looked at me for a moment, then nodded weakly, giving me his okay.

Hefting the Python, I crab-walked away from Fitch toward the narrow space between the crusher's trough and the quonset's wall. I began making my way along the wall, gun ready, occasionally peering across the room toward the catwalk suspended above the keening machinery. As I edged along the wall, I couldn't help harboring a grudging respect for Leo Lancaster. I'd figured out why he'd turned on the machinery—in order to mask any sound he might make creeping along the metal catwalk.

I'd progressed some thirty feet or so along the wall when something moved directly opposite me. I saw the muzzle flash at the same moment I heard the shot—followed by the nearly simultaneous *chang* of a ricochet inches above my head. I ducked, then quickly straightened in time to spy the hunched-over figure hurrying along the catwalk in the direction of the door through which he'd entered.

It surprised me afterward to realize that I reacted almost instinctively, my years of experience still very much a part of me. Wrapping both hands around the Python, I sighted Leo. I didn't even have to remind myself to lower the gun slightly since I was aiming at a target moving above me, something for which many shooters fail to compensate, and, as a consequence, tend to fire high. I aimed, and I squeezed the trigger two times.

I'm not sure which shot hit him and which one missed. The one that caught him hit him in the thigh and spun him around. He stumbled against the railing of the catwalk, lost his balance, and tumbled into space. His arms flailed as he fell, but he didn't scream until he landed in the metal trough and the whirling blades began shredding him. His scream didn't last very long. It just seemed that way.

I DECIDED LATER—after the lookie-loo Cole employees had been shooed away and representatives from the coroner's office were scraping together whatever pieces of Leo Lancaster they could find—that he'd picked an especially messy way to die. It almost made me feel sorry for him.

Almost. But not quite.

TWENTY-SEVEN

BY SIX-THIRTY that evening the county sheriff's department had decided they'd had enough of me, and they let me leave El Rancho Santiago. There was no reason to charge me with anything, what with the ballistic evidence and a statement from Fitch backing up my assertion that Leo Lancaster had fired at me first. Besides, they already had their hands full trying to figure out what to do with June, Grant, and Regina Cole.

It was a little after sunset when I arrived at Santa Ynez Valley Hospital, the same place where two days before I'd brought Daniel Wikert. I stopped at an information desk in the main lobby and was told by a nice, blue-haired volunteer lady which room had been assigned to Bradley Fitch. He'd been taken to the hospital by ambulance several hours earlier. By the time I got there, he'd been assessed, prepped, operated on, awakened, wheeled to his room, and laid in bed. He'd been given a private room—not much bigger than a broom closet, but it was his alone.

He was awake when I pushed open the door to his room. He was propped against a stack of pillows, staring sleepily at a television set mounted high on the wall opposite his bed. He looked awful, his face the color of tapioca pudding, damp hair slicked to his skull. His injured shoulder was swathed in a thick bandage, his right forearm suspended in a Velcro and canvas sling adhered to his stomach. Attached to a pole on the left side of the bed, facing me, was some sort of monitor, the wires

from which disappeared beneath the gown he was wearing. On the right side of the bed was a pole from which
hung plastic bags filled with clear liquid. Feeder lines
from the bags converged into a single tube leading to
an intravenous needle stuck in his left wrist and held in
place by an elastic bandage.

My opening the door attracted his attention. He
turned from the TV, registered who I was, and smiled.
"Hey, Jack," he croaked as he lifted the remote control
in his free hand and switched off the TV. "Nice to see
you."

I found a chair in the corner of the room near the
door, pulled it to his bedside, and sat down. "I wish I
could tell you you're looking well."

He chuckled. "Actually, I feel pretty good."

"Probably because you're doped to the gills."

Another chuckle. "I used to wonder what the attrac-
tion was, how come people got into drugs. Hell, if I'd
known it felt like this, I'd've become a junkie years
ago."

"The charm wears off," I said. "Believe me."

He nodded. His chin started to sink to his chest and
his eyes closed, clues that I shouldn't stick around too
much longer. Then he brought up his head, shook himself, and focused on me again.

"So what's the diagnosis?" I asked.

"I got shot," he said.

"I'm aware of that."

He reached with his good hand to caress his bandaged
shoulder. "Goddamn slug shattered the ol' ball-and-
socket joint. They're pretty sure they're gonna have to
put in an artificial one."

"I guess this means you'll never play the outfield
again."

He chuckled once more. "I'll be back. If Bo Jackson can do it, I can..."

His voice trailed off, his chin sagged to his chest, and his eyelids fluttered. I was telling myself that it was time for me to leave when the door opened and a male nurse entered. His arrival perked Fitch up again. The nurse was a tall, thin black man in his twenties. He came in carrying a hypodermic needle on a small tray. He nodded hello to me, then said cheerfully, "Time for another shot, Mr. Fitch" in a voice colored by a Caribbean accent. "Somet'ing to put you to sleep."

I got up and drew aside my chair to give the nurse access to the IV equipment. I watched him take the needle from the tray, hold it up against a ceiling light and check for air bubbles, then insert the needle into a rubber valve attached to one of Fitch's tubes. I watched him depress the plunger, sending the stuff from the barrel of the syringe into the tube, and as I watched him it came to me.

"It can't be..." I was so stunned I didn't even realize I'd spoken out loud.

The nurse turned and said, "Excuse me?"

I shook my head, anxious to get out of there as quickly as I could. "Just talking to myself."

Groggy, Fitch smacked his lips as he peered up at me. "Jus' so you don't start *answerin'* yourself, Jack," he slurred. "Thass when you know...you're really losin' it..."

Then he sagged, his head dropping onto the pillow, his eyes closing. Within moments he was snoring softly. The nurse smiled at me, his expression seeming to say, *Isn't it wonderful how well this stuff works?*

I gave the nurse a brief, polite smile in return, then

said in a low voice, "If you're here when he wakes up, tell him I'll drop by to see him again tomorrow."

The nurse nodded, looking as if he were about to say something more to me. I didn't give him the chance, because by then I was already out the door.

IT TOOK ME twenty minutes to get to Costa del Sol. It was dark when I pulled the Cherokee to a stop in the all but deserted parking lot, a little after 8:00 p.m.

Presently I was standing at the door to Bungalow Thirteen. I listened for a moment to the sound of a TV speaker coming from inside. I didn't recognize the voice of the announcer calling an NBA game—the Lakers versus the Kings. I knocked. Waited. Saw the porch light go on. Heard the sound of a chain being unlatched. Watched the door being opened. Noted the look of surprise on Zeke Carlin's face when he saw me. "Mistah Jack? What you doin' here?"

"You mind if I come in?" I asked.

He was puzzled, but he held open the door. I moved past him into the living room. I looked around the room and saw it was decorated in the depressingly functional, bargain basement, nuevo hacienda style I'd come to expect from Costa del Sol. I sat down in a club chair that was a twin to the one in Perry Cole's bungalow. The chair was next to a floor lamp that provided the room's illumination, the lamp standing beside a roll-away table on which Carlin kept his portable television. I reached over to switch off the TV.

He returned to where he'd been sitting, on the sofa opposite the TV. He was dressed in jogging shorts, a T-shirt, and athletic socks. The shirt and shorts were stained with perspiration. His unlaced cross trainers lay on the floor in front of the sofa. He noticed me looking

at the shoes and said, ''I jus' come back from runnin'.
I do five miles a day, rain or shine.'' He shrugged.
''Roadwork. You know what they say 'bout ol' habits.
Sometimes they hard to break.''

I nodded. On the way up here I'd been trying to de-
vise a way to say to him what I wanted to say. I still
didn't have anything good, which is why I didn't say
anything at all until he prompted me. ''What you want
to see me 'bout, Mistah Jack?''

Let's get this over with, I urged myself.

''Mistah Jack?''

''You remember last Saturday at the funeral?'' I said.
''You asked me to tell you if I found out anything about
who killed Perry?''

He nodded. ''I remember.''

''That's how come I'm here,'' I said. ''I know who
did it.''

He showed me the same cunning, impenetrable look
he'd shown me on the steps of the church. ''Who?''

''You,'' I said.

His eyes narrowed.

''I just came from the hospital,'' I said. ''I was there
visiting Lieutenant Fitch, the guy who's been investigating Perry's murder. He talked to you that night, after
you got back from your date. Somebody shot him this
afternoon, a hood named Leo Lancaster who happened
to be mixed up with June and Grant in a scam to counterfeit Ozzie's wine. They were behind it all along.
They were trying to trick Ozzie into going back into
business with them again.''

Carlin watched me impassively, not speaking.

''Anyway,'' I went on, ''while I was at the hospital,
I watched one of the nurses giving Lieutenant Fitch a
shot. The nurse happened to be a black man, and while

I was watching him, all of a sudden something Fitch told me the day Perry was killed popped into my head. About the nurse who found Perry's body. She'd come in to give *him* a shot, because the person who was ordinarily responsible for that had taken the day off.''

"You mean me?''

I nodded. "That was part of the evidence against Ozzie, that whoever killed Perry knew how to use a hypodermic, which was something Ozzie'd learned to do when he was in the National Guard. When Fitch was telling me about the nurse, it didn't even register—on me *or* him—that you knew how to use one, too. Both of us were already assuming you didn't have anything to do with it.''

"I had to learn how to give shots,'' he said distantly, looking away from me. "Mistah Perry, he sent me to nursin' school, right before him an' me moved in here. I had to know how to take care o' things in case somethin' happened and there wasn't no nurse or doctor around to do it...''

He became quiet, his expression softening.

"It was you, wasn't it,'' I said.

He nodded, almost imperceptibly.

I went on. "While I was driving up here I thought about something else Fitch said to me a couple of days ago. About how people commit murder for only one of two reasons—love or money.''

I paused. Carlin was looking at me again, and his eyes had begun to glisten with tears. "I din't know nothin' 'bout him leavin' me that insurance money. You gotta b'lieve that.''

"I wasn't thinking you did it for the money.''

He wiped the tears from his eyes, then looked at me in such a way that I knew what he was about to say was the absolute truth. "Mistah Perry's doctor come in that mornin', the same day you come by, and he say, 'I'm sorry, Mistah Cole, but you got no choice. You cain't stay here by yo'self no more, even with Zeke here to he'p you out. You too sick to be any place but the hospital, where somebody can keep an eye on you, twen'y-fo' hours a day.' Then the doctor leave and Mistah Ozzie come over. Mistah Ozzie, he agree with the doctor. Only Mistah Perry don' wanna go, don' wanna be stuck in no hospital. Him and Mistah Ozzie have this big fight 'bout that, and right when Mistah Ozzie's leavin' is when you show up."

He swallowed and wiped away more tears. "After you lef', Mistah Perry wake up from his nap. He call me into his bedroom, an' he say, 'Zeke, you the only one I can trus' any more. Ozzie done turn agains' me, jus' like his brothers. You the only one be like a *real* son to me, all these years. You cain't let 'em put me in no hospital. You cain't...'"

He began to sob.

"What happened?" I asked gently.

Carlin sucked in a deep breath, composing himself. "He axed me to kill him."

"Perry *asked* you?"

He nodded. "He kep' tellin' me over an' over how he din't wanna go to no hospital and jus' be a veg'table, layin' in bed all day long. 'No dignity,' he say. 'No dignity.' Finally, they wasn't nothin' I could do but say okay..."

Another deep breath. "So I thinks 'bout it, an' I remember the times Mistah Perry say to me, 'You more of a son to me, Zeke, than my real kin. You really is. Them others, s'posed to be my blood, all they done is bleed me dry.' And thass when I says to myself, 'This is how you do it...'"

He paused again, pressing his face into his hands so I couldn't see him crying. I let him go on like that for a while, then said to him, "Zeke?"

He dropped his hands and looked at me.

"You need to come with me," I said.

He rubbed the tears from his cheeks. "You takin' me to the po-lice, Mistah Jack?"

I nodded.

He drew in another deep breath, turned away for a moment, then turned back to me. "You mind if I clean m'self up a little firs'?"

I couldn't think of a reason to say no. I wasn't worried about him trying to get away. Even if there were a back exit to the place, where would he go?

He rose from the sofa and padded down the hallway leading to the back of the bungalow. I sat in my chair for a time, feeling edgy and doubtful. I don't know what made me get up and open the front door and peer outside at the night. Maybe I was feeling a need for some fresh air. Maybe I wanted to look across the way at the dark, empty bungalow where Perry Cole had spent the final dark, empty years of his life. Maybe this, maybe that. Who knows?

Perhaps it was the sound of the shower running in the bathroom that kept me from hearing Carlin as he crept up behind me. Perhaps I wouldn't have heard him anyway. I didn't hear a thing. All I did was feel a sharp, powerful blow to my right kidney that caused a fiery, explosive jolt of agony. I twisted around, clutching at my side, and a second blow struck me in the belly. As I doubled over, the third and final blow came, a rabbit punch to the back of my neck. I collapsed like a puppet whose strings had been snipped. For a short time there were tiny lights dancing in front of my eyes, but soon the lights dimmed, turning gray and then, finally, black.

WHEN I CAME TO an hour later, I hurt badly in all three places he'd slugged me. I knew he hadn't hit me with anything but his hands. He didn't need to. There is a universe of difference in the kind of punch that can be thrown by someone who's done it for a living and the kind of punch thrown by even the most enraged or enthusiastic amateur. Professionals simply *know* how to hit people. To them it is as precise as surgery.

When I was finally able to bring myself to my feet, the stabbing pains in my side and stomach prevented me from standing erect. It took me fifteen minutes to stagger into the kitchenette, hunch over the sink, and splash cold water on my face. I resisted the urge to go into the bathroom and urinate because I wasn't ready to see the blood I suspected I'd be eliminating for the next several days.

It was nine-thirty by my watch before I was feeling pulled together enough to drive. As I climbed gingerly into my Jeep, I was hoping nobody at the sheriff's station would look at me closely enough to decide I could stand a trip to the hospital myself. I just wanted to walk in, see to it that somebody got after Zeke Carlin ASAP, and go home.

I was barely a mile from the old folks' home, heading south on Highway 154, when I saw the lights of the emergency vehicles ahead of me. There were four vehicles all together—two sheriff's department cruisers, a county ambulance, and a twenty-year-old, mint-condition, Pontiac Trans-Am convertible. The convertible was the reason for the presence of the other vehicles, its driver having sent the car head-on into a power pole while traveling at a high—likely illegal—rate of speed. The Trans-Am must have been traveling fast, because its front end was mangled and the power pole was knocked over, resting on the roof of the wreck. I recognized the car, of course. A short time ago it had been parked a few spaces away from my Cherokee, at Costa de Sol.

As I rolled past the site of the accident, I was telling myself it would be all right now for me to turn around and head for home. There wasn't a pressing reason for me to go to the sheriff's station. That could wait, at least till tomorrow, if not forever.

TWENTY-EIGHT

BY WEDNESDAY MORNING, most of the pain in my back and stomach and neck was gone. After dragging myself out of bed and into the bathroom, I was relieved to find my urine absolutely clear. I left the house as soon as I was dressed, drove into Solvang, and went directly to the county jail. On my way to the visitors' area, I did my best to avoid encountering anybody who might know Brad Fitch and mention to him that they'd seen me.

A deputy brought out Teddie Ortiz. He and I sat down at a low wooden table, on opposite sides of a wire-mesh screen. As Teddie settled himself, he was scowling. "What the fuck do *you* want?"

I looked around to make sure no one was within earshot, then said to Teddie in a low voice, "I want you to do me a favor."

He couldn't have been more surprised if somebody had just told him he'd been elected mayor. He shook his head, trying to convince himself he'd actually heard what I said. "Are you out of your mind, or what?"

"It's not that big a favor," I said. "And it'll be no skin off your ass to do it."

His eyes narrowed. "What?"

"When you talk to Alan Feinberg," I said, "I want you to tell him you lied to Lieutenant Fitch the other day when you told him what day you and Leo had lunch last week." I paused, thinking of something, then said,

"If you want, you don't even have to admit you were lying. You can just say you got the days mixed up."

"Who's Alan Feinberg?" Teddie asked.

"He's the ATF agent who's going to be taking you back to L.A. Rest assured he'll do everything he can to get you to testify in open court against Rudy Setzer."

"Fuck that shit—"

I cut him off quickly. "Listen to me, all right? You do this favor for me, and I'll do you one in return."

He sneered. "What the fuck can you do for me?"

"Alan's my ex-partner," I said. "If I ask him to be nice to you, he'll help you plea-bargain in exchange for your testimony against Setzer. He may not be able to get you off altogether, but he'll try real hard. *If* I ask him to."

Teddie frowned doubtfully.

"Alan also happens to be very tight with the guys in Justice who run the witness protection program," I went on. "If he was to say to them, 'Hey, I got a witness needs protecting, and maybe you can set him up in Hawaii or someplace nice like that,' they'd consider it very seriously."

Teddie's frown stayed in place. "And that's all I got to do? Say that Leo and me had lunch on some other day last week instead of Wednesday?"

"That and one other thing. Don't mention to Alan or Fitch that I came to see you."

Teddie turned away for a moment, letting the wheels spin around in his head. When he looked back at me, he was smiling.

"Is it a deal?" I asked.

"Hell," he said, "I wish *every* deal I made with you motherfuckers was this easy."

THAT EVENING, I went to visit Fitch at the hospital. He was feeling better and looked considerably more alert as I told him that I'd been in touch with my uncle, who'd said he'd be home again by the weekend.

Fitch told me that the case files on the murders of Perry Cole and Daniel Wikert had been closed—both cases marked "Solved," both crimes attributed to the late Leo Lancaster. He didn't say whether he believed Teddie Ortiz's admission that he'd got the days mixed up and, consequently, could no longer provide Leo with an alibi for Perry's murder. That Fitch would likely find himself praised by his superiors for so expediently clearing up the homicides of two of the valley's more prominent citizens may have had something to do with his deciding not to bother checking up on the restaurant in L.A. where Leo and Teddie had eaten.

There also wasn't any concrete proof that Leo had killed Wikert, only hearsay and circumstantial evidence provided by June, Grant, and Regina Cole. But Leo wasn't in any position to protest about what having the killings pinned on him might do to his reputation. Since nobody else was likely to stick up for him, either, he ended up taking both raps posthumously.

Over the next couple of weeks I was called to testify at three separate coroner's inquests. The first was Daniel Wikert's, whose death was officially determined to have been the responsibility of Leo Lancaster. This was later confirmed in a deposition given by Rudy Setzer to the U.S. Attorney in Los Angeles. Setzer had been angered by the phone call from the Coles concerning Wikert, and then further angered by a call from Wikert demanding that the mobster lean on Gerry Donne. Wikert had been informed by a former law partner that my uncle was sniffing around for information regarding the

Cole family's financial status. Following Setzer's orders, Leo had called Gerry and threatened him. Both Setzer and Leo presumed that would be enough to pressure a straight citizen like Gerry into backing off, and nothing more would need to be done about him.

Wikert, however, was another matter. Setzer assumed that Leo had gone to Wikert's the same night I happened to be there. Leo merely intended to scare the lawyer back into line, but Wikert had probably said or done something to piss him off, and in a pique of rage he brought out his bottle of acid.

The second inquest I attended was Leo's. The ruling was death by misadventure, my shooting him in self-defense having caused him to fall into a machine that chewed him into tiny pieces. I was exonerated of any wrongdoing in the matter.

The third inquest was Zeke Carlin's.

Under oath, I explained that the reason I'd gone to see him on the night of his death was because of a promise I'd made to keep him apprised of developments in the investigation of Perry Cole's homicide. I went to Zeke in person, because after leaving Santa Ynez Valley Hospital—where I'd been visiting Lieutenant Bradley Fitch, the officer in charge of the investigation into Perry's death—I'd decided that hearing his employer's murderer was dead was news Zeke would like to receive face-to-face. Did Mr. Carlin seem despondent when you spoke to him? No, he did not. Inebriated or under the influence of drugs? No. Do you realize you were likely the last person to see him alive? Yes, I do. Do you have any reason to think Mr. Carlin might have wanted to deliberately drive his vehicle into that pole? In other words, do you have any reason to suspect Mr. Carlin's death may have been suicide?

No, I don't.

Some time later, after the deputies and the paramedics and the pathologist had had their say, the ruling came down: accidental death, the result of an automobile crash caused by who knows what. It was the verdict I'd hoped for. But it still didn't make me feel any better.

I SPENT MOST of my time between testifying at inquests working in the vineyards I'd neglected while I was taking care of business for Ozzie Cole. I checked row after row of staked vines, examining the recently set buds of fruit, searching for evidence of bugs or disease or the ill effects of too much or too little sun. The last was a particular concern for Dad and me, since we'd had several near-freezing nights over the winter as late as mid-March. Fortunately, only a handful of the plants looked to be other than absolutely healthy. The bare bones of the vines were already covered with a fringe of pale green leaves. I noted a few weeds sprouting here and there along the rows of earth, an indication that Jesus and I should do some plowing to mulch them up.

We started plowing on the day after Zeke Carlin's inquest. By then the days were growing noticeably longer and sunnier. The rainy season was over, and soon tourists would be showing up at our door—on weekends, beginning in late May, when Dad and I opened up for public tastings. By then the clusters of fruit would be starting to swell and droop. Taking care of the weeds would have the vines and rows looking more presentable for company.

On the first Sunday in May, four days after Carlin's inquest, Maggie McKenney came out to our place to share some of my father's famous barbecued chicken with us. We were supposed to be celebrating. The day before I'd received a fat check from Ozzie Cole. He had remitted without a squawk every penny on the itemized bill I'd presented him, and he'd thrown in two cases of 1990 O.C. Pinot Reserve as a bonus. He could afford to be generous. Not only had he inherited the largest winemaking business in southern California, but it looked as if his despised siblings—and equally despised sister-in-law—were on their way to jail for a long time.

Ozzie wasn't the only one feeling cheerful. Upon his release from the hospital, Brad Fitch returned to Santa Barbara, where his boss put him up for two special commendations: one for breaking the Cole case, and one for having been wounded in the line of duty. My other buddy, Alan Feinberg, was in a merry mood himself, what with June and Grant Cole—as well as Teddie Ortiz—having agreed to testify against Rudy Setzer.

Everybody I knew was happy. Everybody but me.

While Dad and Maggie were getting the meal together, I took a walk in the vineyards, alone. It was late in the afternoon of a warm, dry, middle of spring day that couldn't have been more beautiful. I strolled, absently checking the plants, not really interested or disinterested in them, just giving myself something to do. The fruit seemed to be budding nicely. It still looked like we were in for a pretty good crop.

At that moment, I couldn't have given a damn less.

What the hell is the matter with you, Jack? I thought, fed up with myself. So what if I'd lied under oath? Hadn't I preserved the good name of a man who really did deserve that gift, at the expense of a sadistic, homicidal son of a bitch who didn't?

Except none of that changed the fact that a month ago there were four people alive who weren't alive today, and I was a big reason why. I felt shitty about that, because there's no such thing as a nice, neat package when what's being packaged is death. There's always a part of the mess that's never going to be cleaned up. And there's always going to be somebody who *knows* that, somebody who isn't ever going to forget. This time, that somebody was me.

It was at that moment that I heard my father calling, "Jack? Come on, son, it's time to eat!"

I turned toward the house. Dad and Maggie were on the patio, both of them waving to me, inviting me to join them. They were smiling. I returned the wave, thinking, What the hell, Jack. You've got all the time in the world to mope.

As I headed to the house I began to wonder how hard it would be for Dad and me to teach Maggie the rules of three-handed cribbage. Given her head for numbers, it probably wouldn't be too tough for her to pick up the game.

I was right. By eleven o'clock that night, when Dad finally gave up and decided it was past his bedtime, she'd taken us both to the cleaners.

RANSOM FOR A KILLING

FRED HUNTER

Eight years ago Ben Harvey was accused and convicted of raping Laura Shay, a high school classmate. Now, DNA tests prove he is innocent, and suddenly Harvey is free.

Then Laura Shay is murdered, and it's on Chicago police detective Jeremy Ransom's beat. The obvious suspect is Harvey. After all, who could blame him for wanting revenge? Not even Ransom's friend and unofficial partner, septuagenarian Emily Charters. But as Ransom is drawn into the case, he discovers the fine line of justice can be razor sharp....

Available December 1999 at your favorite retail outlet.

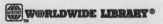

NEXT WEEK
— WILL BE —
BETTER

A CAT WILDE MYSTERY

JEAN RURYK

Spending the weekends rubbing shoulders in the summer heat with flea market hagglers isn't furniture restorer Cat Wilde's idea of fun. But she couldn't refuse her friend Rena, who needed someone to run her table at the flea market while she recuperated from surgery.

Luckily she has the space next to Old Sam, a true flea market diehard. But when Sam is murdered, Cat starts digging into the discordant world of flea market shopping, and discovers people will do anything for a bargain. Even kill.

Available December 1999 at your favorite retail outlet.

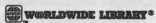

WORLDWIDE LIBRARY®

Visit us at www.worldwidemystery.com   WJR333

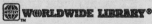

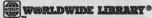

Denise Dietz

**AN ELLIE BERNSTEIN/
LIEUTENANT
PETER MILLER
MYSTERY**

Throw Darts at a Cheesecake

Fat Free Murder

At the weekly meeting of Weight Winners, losing is everything. Group leader Ellie Bernstein herself has shed fifty-five pounds, along with a cheating husband and an unfulfilling life. But she quickly discovers losing weight is not only murder, it's downright lethal.

One by one, the group's Big Losers are being murdered. Is some jealous member of the Friday meeting a secret killer? Motive aside, Ellie's got to watch her back as well as her calories before she finds herself on the most permanent diet of all...death.

Available December 1999 at your favorite retail outlet.

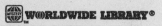

WORLDWIDE LIBRARY®

Visit us at www.worldwidemystery.com

WDD334